Praise for _____ ~~~ ~~~ Dealers

"Husom goes dark in this well-written, masterfully-plotted and page-turning tale of drugs, murder and revenge made even more compelling by its family dynamics." ~David Housewright, Edgar-Award winning author of _What Doesn't Kill Us_.

"Husom's _Death to the Dealers_ is a fast-paced ride. With likable protagonists in Sergeant Corky Aleckson and Elton "Smoke" Dawes to root for, you will be enthralled and entertained from beginning to end as the pair unravel the perplexing drug and homicide cases plaguing Winnebago County. I couldn't put it down!" ~Midge Bubany, author, the Cal Sheehan Mysteries.

"Christine Husom's firsthand knowledge of police procedures shines through in _Death To The Dealers_. This gripping thriller will keep you enthralled from beginning to end." ~Gary R. Bush, award-winning author of the Jamie Sharpe historical adventure series.

"In Husom's latest Winnebago County suspense, Sergeant Corky Aleckson, aided by her partner Smoke, is not only in hot pursuit of the person responsible for a rash of deaths among local drug dealers, but also trying to track down the source of illicit drugs in the local school. Her life keeps crisscrossing in unexpected and troubling ways with that of Dr. Watts, whose relentless quest to find justice for the death of his wife will put the doctor and Corky on a perilous collision course." ~Barbara Deese, author of the No Ordinary Women Mysteries.

"Sergeant Corky Aleckson is in a real mess this time! A vengeful serial killer has taken a personal interest in her just as a mysterious drug dealer's illicit activities get too close to home. When both threats collide in her face all bets are off in the exciting finale of *Death to the Dealers*." ~Michael Allan Mallory, co-author of the Snake Jones Mysteries.

"Drugs, revenge, and love intertwine in this gripping "Corky" Aleckson and "Smoke" Dawes adventure." ~Michael Stanley, author of the award-winning Detective Kubu series.

"Corinne Aleckson is a bright, together woman. She excels at her tasks whether patrolling in a deputy sheriff's uniform with a loaded pistol at her hip or sliding through the brush of a local park in an undercover role. And always in her mind, the risky activity of a teen-aged girl for whom she had some legal responsibility, in this finely written Winnebago County adventure." ~Carl Brookins, author, *Traces, Sins of Edom, Red Sky, Grand Lac,* and the Sean Sean Mysteries.

Also by Christine Husom

DEATH
TO
THE
DEALERS

Ninth in the Winnebago County Mystery Series

Christine Husom

The wRight Press

The wRight Press edition published November, 2021.

Cover photo by Ali Pazini
Cover design by Precision Prints, Buffalo, Minnesota.

The wRight Press
46 Aladdin Circle NW
Buffalo, Minnesota 55313

Printed in the United States of America

ISBN 978-1-948068-11-6

Dedication

To all the professionals who provide help and facilitate recovery for people with substance use disorders. Thank you. And to everyone who has been through treatment and recovery, congrats to you and your loved ones. This story follows a man whose deep grief sends him down a wrongful path to avenge his wife's death instead of enlisting help from law enforcement.

Acknowledgments

I am grateful to everyone who helped bring this book to fruition. Many thanks to Chief Deputy Matthew Treichler for sharing his knowledge and professional expertise, and to Kelly Zitzloff, for sharing her firsthand, eye-opening experiences. They gave me perspectives that helped craft this tale. My humble thanks to my faithful beta/proofreaders and editors who gave their time, careful reading, and sound advice: Catherine Anderson, Arlene Asfeld, Judy Bergquist, Cathlene Buchholz, Barbara DeVries, Rhonda Gilliland, Ken Hausladen, Diane Hopkins, Elizabeth Husom, Chad Mead, Timya Owen, and Edie Peterson. And to DJ Schuette at Critical Eye Editing & Publishing for formatting the manuscript. Also, thank you to all the respected authors who read the manuscript and wrote a review. I greatly appreciate each one of you and your talents.

And again, with deep gratitude to my husband and the rest of my family for their patience and understanding when I was stowed away for hours on end, researching and writing.

Thank you all from the bottom of my heart.

1

The corners of Blake's lips curled upward as he lifted a snack-size baggie to the dealer's level of vision. "Top grade icing. You got something to pour this on, piece of paper maybe? No offense, your table looks a little dusty."

"Oh." The dealer shrugged. "Yeah." He went into the kitchen, came back with an eight-by-ten-inch cardstock ad, and laid it on the coffee table.

"Hey man, steady yourself. You're gonna spill some." The dealer's pale, thin hands shook as he cautioned Blake. Then a muscle under his eye went into a series of twitches.

"Yeah. I get pumped before the sniff." Blake dug his elbow into his ribs to still his hand. It was critical that the powder not touch his skin or go airborne and land in his eyes, nose, or mouth. He poured the baggie's contents onto the cardstock.

"I get that. Top grade coke, huh. Where'd you say you got it?"

"Where the best stuff comes from. Colombia. By way of my supplier in Chicago." A credible lie, and one his witness wouldn't live long enough to call him out on.

The dealer pulled a couple of short straws from his t-shirt pocket and handed one to Blake.

"No time like the present, man," Blake told him.

The dealer did not protest or hesitate. He pushed the powder in a line with the straw, bent over, inserted it in a nostril, closed the other with his pointer finger and sniffed in deeply. As he straightened, his satisfied smile faded in a flash. He collapsed before he drew another breath. The dealer's upper body landed bent over on the table, one arm flung up, the other down. His knees pushed into the side of the table, his feet at odd angles on the floor.

Blake pocketed the unused straw, stared at the dealer, and counted to sixty. Carfentanil. No detectable taste or smell. A minuscule amount, less than a grain of salt, was enough to kill a human being. The perfect weapon to avenge the lives the dealer had stolen.

After not so much as a twitch from the body, Blake withdrew two pairs of vinyl gloves from his windbreaker's side pocket, pulled them on one at a time, then fished out a lint-free cloth from the other pocket. He picked up the baggie and wiped it clean, over and over. Careful not to step on the dealer's legs or disturb the evidence on the coffee table, Blake moved to the dealer's left hand. With practiced stealth, he held the baggie in his right hand and placed his left hand on the back of the dealer's, closed his fingers around the baggie's bottom edge, then let go.

Beads of sweat broke out from the pores on Blake's head and neck. *Damn.* He willed himself to calm down and finish the job right. He took a step back and wiped his head and neck with the arms of his jacket to catch any drops before they fell. As he did, it seemed that every pore on his body had opened to release more nasty fluid.

Move. He gathered the dealer's right fingerprints on the baggie's top half with the same two-step technique and laid it on the table near the deadly powder. He backed away and visually scanned the room for any sign he had been there. Blake had touched nothing in the room with his bare hands, save the baggie that now had only the dealer's prints on it, and the straw he had pocketed.

Blake left the same way he had entered; through the back door of the ground level condominium the dealer had opened for him. He slowly peeled off the outer pair of gloves, inside out, taking care not to touch the outsides. He reached into his pocket for a plastic bag, dropped them in, did the same with the second pair, and tied a knot that sealed the bag.

Blake's vehicle was parked on a residential side street two blocks away. A breeze stirred and blew some loosened autumn leaves around his legs and up to his chest. He pulled the hood of his windbreaker over his head and made his way like he was out for an evening walk in the dark.

2

My phone jingled and I wrestled it from the back pocket of my jeans. Oak Lea High School flashed on the display and my first thought was, is Rebecca okay? I had been her legal guardian the past four years. Long story.

"Corinne Aleckson—"

"Sergeant Corky." It was Rebecca herself. "They . . . umm . . . like, took me to the principal's office."

My protective instinct kicked in. "Who took you?"

"Officer Dey." The school resource officer contracted from the Oak Lea Police Department.

"Oh, Rebecca. Are you okay?"

Her voice quivered. "I guess. I mean, no. I'm in trouble. I like got suspended. Can you come and pick me up 'cause Mom and Dad are with their classrooms?"

Rebecca suspended?

"Be there shortly." She knew my work schedule. I was on the last of three days off and she had caught me at the grocery store. I put the two items I held back on the shelves then scooted outside to the parking lot. A good thing my red 1967

Pontiac GTO was easy to spot because I was focused on Rebecca and what in the world she had done for suspension. At the awkward age of fourteen, her teenage ways posed a challenge now and then. What I considered mild, normal, expected rebellion as she moved from childhood toward adulthood. Overall, she was a good kid. Serious, smart, resilient, respectful. Precious.

I had graduated from Oak Lea High School three years before a larger, better equipped one was built two miles east of town. In my years with the Winnebago County Sheriff's Office, I had responded there many times; when a student reported an abusive family situation, was assaulted, or was the victim of a crime that might result in gross misdemeanor or felony charges. On the flip side, it was also when a student got into trouble. And that included a long list of offenses. My heart was heavy as I contemplated the violation Rebecca may have committed.

I arrived at the Oak Lea High School complex, signed in at the front desk, and headed to Principal Lora Goldin's office. During my school years, I never gotten detention or suspension. But first as a deputy and later as a sergeant, I had been called into the former sheriff's office when he deemed it necessary. Thankfully, for nothing serious. I felt more anxious for Rebecca than the times I faced the sheriff myself. I rolled my shoulders and shook the tension from my hands.

The door to the inner office was open and I spotted Principal Goldin seated behind her desk, her deep-wrinkled face serious as all get-out when she waved me in. Officer Casey Dey stood next to Rebecca who was perched on a visitor chair. Rebecca swiveled it in my direction as I entered. Her tear-streaked face was blotchy red, and my whole body ached for her, for all the trauma she had been through in her early life, and for whatever trouble she was in now.

A snapshot of the time I met her four years before came to mind. A sickly little waif, paler than pale in her hospital bed as she clutched a stuffed animal, her security blanket. Each time that memory bubbled to the surface my emotional response was almost as strong as it had been then. I wanted to pull her into my arms and not let go until she was healed and happy.

I pushed back the thoughts and zeroed in on Officer Dey. A conspicuous frown creased his forehead. "Thanks for coming in, Sergeant."

I nodded. "Officer?"

"Rebecca was caught vaping in the girls' bathroom."

His news bomb caught my breath as though I had inhaled something myself. I searched Rebecca's eyes for a second until she cast them down to her lap. Guilty as charged. My leg muscles tightened to keep me upright as I closed the space between us and leaned in inches from her face. "You were *vaping?* Do you know what was in the cartridge, what you were inhaling?"

Her head dropped forward. "Umm, it was like mango-flavored mist."

"You mean a cigarette with a mango flavor."

Rebecca lifted her head and our eyes met at the same level. More tears sprung from their ducts. "I guess."

It was the first time in our relationship I felt angry at her and with sheer force of will stopped myself from shouting, "*You guess, you guess? Are you kidding me?*" I dug my thumbnail into my pointer finger to shift my internal pain to physical discomfort instead. Rebecca had a medical history of lung problems, and she risked her health by vaping? Fourteen-year-olds did not always have the best judgment, but that should have been a no-brainer for her.

"We'll talk about this later," I told her.

Principal Goldin pushed a clipboard and pen toward me. "As long as you were available, we decided it was best to wait until the end of the school day to contact Rebecca's parents." Dale and Jean Brenner were teachers, and they'd need substitutes to pull them from their classrooms. It may not be classified as an emergency, but it surely felt like one to me.

"You'll take Rebecca home with you, to your house?" Principal Goldin said.

I hadn't thought that far. "Ah, yes. I will."

She nodded at the clipboard and pen. "Sign to verify that you're the one responsible for Rebecca."

My hands shook as I accepted the items. This was uncharted territory, and nothing about it was familiar or comfortable. What Rebecca did should never have happened. Ever. I scribbled something that somewhat resembled my signature and handed it back to Goldin.

I knew the principal was a kind, compassionate person and recognized this was a time she needed to be resolute. The way her eyes locked on Rebecca even gave me the heebie jeebies. I resisted the urge to scratch at what felt like critters crawling on the back of my neck.

"Rebecca, Officer Dey and I will meet with you and your parents as soon as we can arrange it. Sergeant Aleckson, you should join us as well," she said.

I nodded. It would be a huge relief if Rebecca and I were magically beamed to my car to save on final comments. My voice had taken leave. I reached for Rebecca's arm. She picked up her backpack and slung it over one shoulder, then I guided her from the office and out the building. Neither of us said a word as we settled in my car, buckled our seatbelts, and drove away.

"Thanks for getting me," Rebecca offered about a mile down the road.

"You're welcome. I will always be here for you, as long as I'm able. You know that, right?"

I glanced over and caught her nod as she picked at a hangnail.

"That doesn't mean I can always get you out of trouble. Not if it's something that's against the law." I stole another quick look at her. "Like underage vaping." Technically, since she was a minor, vaping was a status offense.

"I don't think I really did. Inhale, I mean," she said.

Give me a break. The old "I didn't inhale" excuse? "You would know. The vapor would get in your lungs, probably make you cough, make you lightheaded," I said.

"Oh. I guess I did then. Um, the third time I took a puff."

I tried to picture Rebecca puffing away on a device. Who was she with, who had given her the device, convinced her to try it?

I had asked juvies tough questions over the years, but this put me in an awkward place with Rebecca. I was an officer of the law, but she wasn't my arrestee. I was her legal guardian, but she wasn't my daughter. She had adoptive parents who took care of her daily needs, who loved her like their other children. Given our relationship, the Brenners might not care if I questioned Rebecca in their absence, but I thought it was best to wait until they were brought into the loop.

"I'm not like my grandma."

Her words came out of left field and blindsided me. Was she trying to assure me she wasn't planning a life of crime? "Your grandma?"

"She was sick. Mentally. That's why she hurt people," Rebecca said.

"You're right, what you said. You're not like your grandma, and she was ill."

"When I got older, I noticed she was kinda different. Like she had no friends. Didn't talk to people much. Except me. And some to Uncle Henry when she took him stuff."

Henry was in a group home, on psychotropic meds to keep him stable. "Your grandma was good to her brother, Henry."

"And me."

"And you."

"But she didn't talk about all the bad things that went on in her family." Her voice strained.

Was that it? Her family's reprehensible history was rolling around in her head and she tried to escape it through vaping? I gave her forearm a gentle squeeze. "We talked about this before, that your grandma kept secrets to protect you when you were a child, too young to understand."

"I guess."

Her grandmother Alvie didn't want Rebecca to know sordid details of the past she hadn't been able to deal with herself. She needed professional help but had not sought it, and it led to further disaster. The year before, Rebecca begged me to tell her what I knew about her family, and I felt she deserved to know the information her grandmother had withheld. At least some. As much as a thirteen-year-old could process. That memory brought on a slight shiver. Someday Rebecca would get the whole truth.

"One thing we both know, no matter what your grandma did, she loved you very much," I said.

3

Blake

Blake drove his wife's small gray SUV west on the road that crossed the dealer's street. He spotted several Winnebago County Sheriff's cars, plus a black van with the Midwest Medical Examiner's logo on its door. A group of people, curious neighbors he presumed, gathered by a clump of trees across the street. Only one person glanced his way as he passed. The others were no doubt focused on the apparent reason authorities were inside the dealer's condo.

An unlikely combination, angst and relief, burned across his face then rushed through his innards. Blake continued on, took the next right, drove around the block, and pulled over to the curb, half a block from the dealer's street. He parked back far enough so he was away from the neighbors' views. Without craning his neck too far, Blake glanced at the few houses in his line of vision, and no one peered out the windows, from what he saw.

He lifted a notebook and pen from the seat, laid the pad on the steering wheel column, and kept the pen in his hand. His phone rested in the breast pocket of his quilted vest. He didn't expect to be questioned by the authorities, but if anyone looked at him, he would either grab his phone and pretend he was on it, or use the pad and pen, like he was reading or writing something. Whichever seemed like the best option at the time.

An hour passed. It was late morning and he wondered how long the crew had been in the condo and how much longer it would take. When his phone rang in his pocket, his heart pounded against it. It was difficult to distinguish the phone vibrations from his heartbeats. Dueling forces. Blake fished the phone from his pocket and looked at its face. His office. He sucked in a quick breath and cleared his throat. "Yes?"

"Hello Doctor, checking to see if you'll be back by one?" his receptionist asked.

"Um, yes, I plan to. Yes, and I'll let you know if I get delayed."

"Thank you. See you then."

They disconnected. Blake's heart rate slowed, and his breathing settled at a steady rate. He kept watch until a man and a woman dressed in coveralls emerged from the dealer's front door with a gurney. A bag with the body inside lay on its top. After a minute, with the help of a detective named Dawes, a man he could never forget, the dealer was loaded into the van. The male examiner closed the door.

Finally. He had been by the condominium more times than he dared count in the last two days, and they were among the longest forty some hours of his life. Had no one missed the dealer until this morning? He was not sure how he felt about that.

4

When we pulled into my driveway, Rebecca sat up straight, as much as her seatbelt allowed. "Detective Smoke is *here*?" My fiancé, Elton "Smoke" Dawes. He was Detective Smoke, and I was Sergeant Corky to her, no matter how many times I told her it was fine to call me Corky. Or Corinne if she preferred.

"Maybe he stopped by for lunch," I said.

"Yeah."

I hit the garage door opener, drove into the stall, then closed the overhead door behind us. Smoke must have freed my English Setter Queenie from her kennel, a large fenced-in area on the garage's back wall, equipped with a doggie door so she had outdoor access. We climbed out, me with my purse and Rebecca toting the name brand gray and plum backpack I had given her as a "first year in high school" gift.

Smoke opened the inside door for us, and Queenie poked her head around his thigh. He raised his eyebrows and smiled when he saw Rebecca. "That's why I heard two car doors slam. How are you doing, young lady? No school today?"

"I'm okay." Sadness was wrapped around her words.

"She's off for the day." And tomorrow and the next day.

Smoke stepped back to let us in, and Queenie pushed her snoot against Rebecca's hip to get her attention. "Hey, girl." Rebecca dropped her backpack and used both hands to rub the sides of Queenie's head.

I squeezed by them and touched Smoke's face in place of a kiss to save the teenager from embarrassment. He gave my waist a gentle pinch in return.

"What are you up to?" I asked.

"On a little break. I had a hankering for some of that leftover chili in the fridge."

"Ah, good idea." I turned to Rebecca. "My mother made it, and since Smoke made a special trip home for a bowl, you know it's good."

Smoke gave his hand a small wave. "Correction, it's the best."

"You heard the man. How about it, are you ready for a bowl of the best chili?" I asked Rebecca.

"Okay, I guess," she said.

"Good. Throw your backpack on the couch and I'll heat up lunch."

Rebecca headed into the living room with Queenie close behind her.

Smoke mouthed, "What's up?"

His sky-blue eyes, long dimples that creased his cheeks, and full lips did me in. I rose on tippy toes for a sweet nibble then whispered, "I'll tell you the whole story later."

Smoke lifted a shoulder in response. He retrieved the chili from the refrigerator while I got bowls from the cupboard and a ladle from the drawer. He scooped chili into them, and I covered one bowl, set it in the microwave, and selected two minutes.

"My day got off to a bad start. Not as bad as the guy they found, however," Smoke said, his voice at low volume.

"What?"

"Got called to a ten seventy-two." A deceased person. "Another overdose. Been dead two days, by the ME's estimate."

I shook my head then walked over and looked in the living room. Rebecca was on the couch, her phone held up close to her face in one hand as she scratched Queenie's head with the other.

I rejoined Smoke. "That's the second OD in what, a week?"

"Exactly a week, Sunday and Sunday."

"Who was it?"

"You know him. Tad Michels," he said.

"Oh no. Not Tad. Oh my gosh."

"You saved him from an overdose a few months back." Our deputies all carried naloxone, an antagonist that blocked and reversed opioid overdoses. We had saved nineteen lives that year alone.

"Tad said he was done with drugs after he woke from the naloxone spray, when it brought him back. Told me he had been scared straight. I guess not." After a person was given a second chance at life, I believed it was for a reason; someone needed them, or they had something more to contribute to the world.

"Nope. Sad to say he was a long-time addict. Court ordered to treatment at least once that I know of. In and out of jail the last few years. Small time dealer, big time user," he said.

"The self-destructive path a druggie takes can go downhill fast. Michels was alone, no one there to call for help when he stopped breathing?"

"We wondered if someone was with him when he went down, got spooked, and took off. But found no sign of that. Looked like a party for one. We collected the evidence, so we'll see what turns up."

"The team was properly suited up?" I asked.

"From head to toe, took all the necessary precautions. With all the dangerous drugs floating around out there we can't do it any other way, put our deputies at risk."

"For sure." The microwave dinged. I replaced that bowl with the next.

Smoke got out spoons and napkins and set them on the counter. "Reminds me, we got the autopsy results from the overdose we had last week. Cocaine and carfentanil."

"Carfentanil? No wonder he died. Isn't that usually mixed with heroin, to make it stronger, or make it go farther? It's cheaper than heroin," I said.

"That's a fact. And it's more likely cocaine would be laced with fentanyl, not carfentanil. A deadly enough combo. Remember the string of overdoses we had last year? Carfentanil was mixed in the heroin."

I nodded. "Like I could forget. Seems to run in streaks. Cocaine, heroin, meth. Or some combo of 'em."

"They pick their poison, cocaine and meth for a high, heroin for a low," he said.

None were good choices. "Who found Michels?"

"His on again, off again, girlfriend. Couldn't get a hold of him, so she went over to his place, used her key to get in. The scene wasn't a pretty one, not something she expected. His death threw her for a complete loop. She placed a frantic nine-one-one call when she realized what she was looking at was real, not a 'bad dream' as she put it. It might be the push she needs to get off drugs herself," he said.

"If it saves her life, it would be one positive thing that came from this."

"Yep. Trouble is, cause and effect aren't always forefront in an addict's mind. The convincing misbelief, 'It happened to Tad, but it won't happen to me.'"

"A sad truth, all right." The second bowl was heated, so I put in the third bowl and called for Rebecca to join us.

Despite the circumstances, the few hours spent with Rebecca were relaxed and pleasant, the best we had together in some time. We played board games and talked about her favorite subjects in school—English and history—her life with the Brenners after they adopted her. Her adjustment from an only child raised by her grandmother to a two-parent household with an older brother and a sister her age. Her adoptive sister Tina had been her best friend since kindergarten.

"My new family showed me what a regular family is like. I knew my grandma was kinda different, but not how much." Rebecca had told me that many times over the years.

"None of us really know what it's like to be in somebody else's life, do we?"

She shrugged.

Her grandmother had tried to kill my probation officer friend Sara, and me. After Alvie was caught, incarcerated, tried, and awaited sentencing, she asked to see me. I will never forget her steel-colored cold stare when I met with her in a small conference room inside the jail. Alvie knew she would spend her life—no one knew at the time how short that would be—in prison. She told me she trusted me more than anyone she knew and asked me to act as Rebecca's legal guardian, find her a good home. All things considered, it was the most ironic request I'd had in my life, before or since.

So that's how Rebecca and I ended up playing board games in my living room after she got suspended from school.

"Have you seen your great-grandmother lately?" I asked.

"Yeah, and I call her Gram."

"Like my Gram Brandt."

"That's why. It sounds like we're really family," she said.

I smiled. "As you are."

"She asked me something I didn't know, like something my grandma never told me."

"What was that?" I asked.

"She wondered who my grandpa was."

"Oh."

"Do you know?" Her eyebrows lifted.

"Yes."

Rebecca's eyes filled with tears. "You know and never *told me*?"

"I found out when your grandma was questioned by investigators, after her arrest. She had never told anyone before that," I said.

"Not even my dad?"

"I don't think so." Her father had been my classmate. He started a life of crime as a teen, spent most of his time in juvenile detention facilities until he was sent to prison as an adult where he took his life. His wife had not coped well with his death and left Rebecca with Alvie. She took off, never to be heard from again.

"Do you know where my grandpa is? Does he live around here?"

"When Alvie was in prison, she wrote a letter to you. What she called a 'confession letter' and sent it to me, said to make sure you got it when you were old enough to understand. She thought maybe when you were sixteen. She didn't tell me what was in the letter. It's still sealed so you'll be the first to read it," I said.

"I'll be fifteen next month."

"I know, and your parents should take that into consideration when they make a decision. In the meantime, it's locked away in a safe." *In my home office.* "I'll tell you what—how about we talk to your parents, see what they think?"

"Do they know who my grandpa is?" she said.

"I believe so."

"Everyone knows but *me*?"

Rebecca broke down into sobs. It was a comfort when she let me gather her in my arms and we cried together. She'd had unspeakable trauma in her life due to her father's and mother's and grandmother's actions. I believed Rebecca's grandmother's crimes were the direct result of her grandfather's abuse. And Rebecca didn't yet know who he was.

Principal Goldin called at three twenty-one and asked that Rebecca and I come back at four for *the* meeting with her, the Brenners, and Officer Dey.

I laid my hand on Rebecca's shoulder. "Sorry this turned into such an emotional day for you. Lots of stuff to deal with, huh?"

She nodded. "I kinda understand why nobody wanted to talk about who my grandpa is and why he wasn't around. Like my grandma shoulda told me, so I'm glad she wrote that letter."

"I agree. She is the best one to tell you. The rest of us may have an idea of some of the things that happened to her, but we didn't live it with her."

"I guess I sorta did. Part of it, anyway."

"You did." I gave her shoulder a squeeze. "Well, we've got some people ready to meet with us. And remember, each one of us cares very deeply about you."

We returned to the principal's office to face the music, otherwise known as an explanation session with Rebecca's parents. The lids around Jean's round brown eyes were red and puffy. Dale's blue eyes had darkened to a shade of navy. He blinked several times before settling his gaze on Rebecca. Jean shot me a look I read as, "*What is the best thing to say to her?*"

"How about we all have a seat?" Mrs. Goldin said and motioned to the circle of chairs.

Rebecca sat down first and the Brenners took a chair on either side of her. I settled in next to Jean. She leaned over toward me slightly. We'd both had experience working with troubled kids, but nothing in Rebecca's behavior had hinted she had issues.

Jean and Dale Brenner turned thirty-nine on the same day the previous month. It was a fun fact I learned when they invited me to their birthday dinner celebration after Rebecca joined their family.

Officer Dey pulled a memo pad and pen from a chest pocket and flipped it open. "Rebecca, you didn't have much to say when we talked earlier. Are you ready to tell us where you got the vaping device?"

"It was from my friend's boyfriend's friend."

It took me half a second to process that.

"And who would that be?" he said.

"Um, Kelvin."

"Kevin?" Dey said.

"Kelvin," Rebecca clarified.

"Last name?"

Rebecca shrugged. "I don't really know him. He like sat down with us at lunch yesterday. Him and Wyatt. And he handed this pen-like thing to Emmy and told her to try it. It was all ready to go. Emmy put it in her backpack for later. Between classes today we met in the bathroom. Emmy tried it and passed it to me and then she went into a stall to, you know, to go. I was the one Krissy saw when she came in the bathroom. I sort of hid it, but she must've seen it and busted me after she left." *Busted* her?

"Rebecca, it wasn't Krissy. We have vaping detectors in the restrooms. We waited for you to come out," Goldin said.

Officer Dey nodded. "And you admitted you had the device in your possession when I asked you. Thank you for your honesty."

"Like I didn't want to lie," she said.

"You told us who you were with, who gave you and Emmy the device. Are you talking about Emmy Nelson?" Goldin said.

Rebecca watched her fingers as they intertwined and nodded.

"Emmy Nelson. Is Wyatt Emmy's boyfriend?" Goldin asked.

"Yeah. Um, not that they really go out on dates or anything."

"We'll need his last name so we can talk to him," Dey said.

"I don't know it. But I guess he's a sophomore. Emmy hasn't known him that long," she said.

"And Kelvin? Is he a sophomore, too?" Dey asked.

Rebecca shook her head. "I don't know. He looks kinda old. Like even eighteen, a senior maybe."

Officer Dey closed his memo pad but held on to it. "Okay. Well, those are all the questions I have for you. For now. Principal Goldin, Mister and Missus Brenner, Sergeant Aleckson?" He looked around the circle at us.

Principal Goldin leaned forward and locked her eyes on Rebecca. "For your cooperation, I will reduce your suspension to one day. You may return to school tomorrow. I trust that you will not violate the rules here again."

Officer Dey nodded. "Keep in mind if you do, the consequences will be worse, and you could end up with a juvenile record."

Jean sucked in a loud "ah" sound. Rebecca leaned her upper body onto her thighs and wrapped her arms around her knees. I sat there like a bump on a log.

Dale stood then touched Rebecca's shoulder and held out his hand for her. When she took it, he gently pulled her from her chair and into his chest for a hug. I had witnessed unconditional acts of love Dale and Jean bestowed on Rebecca many times.

"Thank you, Missus Goldin, Officer Dey. We'll have a family discussion, and Rebecca will be back in school tomorrow." Dale gave Jean a slight "let's go" head jerk.

"I'll catch you later," I said, and the three shuffled off.

5

Blake pulled into his office parking lot after his last—hopefully—call of the day. He sat in his truck another minute and thanked his lucky stars he was able to help the Deans again. They raised American quarter horses that had an inborn propensity to buck and were sought out by top rodeos around the country. The Deans were among his top clients, and when they called, Blake dropped what he was doing and headed to their farm.

He got the frantic call late afternoon when their foaling mare's membranes ruptured, but she had not delivered in a timely manner. The Deans checked and saw the foal's head was turned to the side and blocked the birth canal.

Blake hightailed it out there and found the Deans with the mare in the sizeable barn stall they used for foaling. They had kept a close eye on their horse, monitored her progress, and watched for any problems that might occur. It happened with their mares during the birthing process from time to time. Like today. Blake successfully used a head snare to guide the foal into position and enabled the mare to deliver.

He remained in the barn for another hour and drank coffee with the Deans while they watched the mare and foal. When he was certain all was well with the horses, Blake bade them farewell and took his leave. When he was on the job, he kept his full attention focused on his clients' and patients' needs and attended to them well. It made him a top-rated veterinarian.

On the drive back Blake rode a natural high, thankful he had been the savior once again, had safely delivered another fine, healthy foal. As he sat outside his office, his thoughts and concentration switched from the Deans' foal to his newfound personal mission: to rid the world of dealers who supplied dangerous, illicit drugs that killed unsuspecting addicts.

A year ago, he couldn't have imagined where his wife's death would lead him. Two Winnebago County deputies had come to his office. They gave him their names, but he didn't hear what they said. The somber looks on their faces stirred panic in him. It tunneled his vision and caused his heart to quadruple its speed. The female deputy said, "Is it okay to talk here, or would you rather we go somewhere else?"

Blake had no idea why they were there. "Why do you ask?"

"We have some sad news about your wife," she said.

Dear God, not another car crash. "What is it?"

"I'm sorry to tell you she was found in her vehicle. Deceased."

He could not comprehend what she said, thought she had switched to a foreign language. "Can you repeat that?"

"Your wife was parked at the far west end of the Cub lot. Sadly, that's where she died. A shopper spotted her and called nine-one-one. We are deeply sorry."

"No, you don't understand, my wife is young, on her way to good health again after her car accident. She can't die," Blake argued.

"EMS responded and tried to revive her, but it was too late. They took her to the hospital. We can give you a ride there now," she offered.

Blake nodded because he had lost the ability to speak. He followed the deputies and heard the husky male tell the staff at the front desk that Doctor Watts would be out for the rest of the day and would be in touch. Blake couldn't make eye contact with his staff.

The male deputy opened the squad car's back door. Blake climbed in and in robot-like mode, buckled his seat belt. The deputies got in next, the auburn-haired female in the driver's seat. The male talked into his sheriff's radio about being ten-something with one passenger en route to Oak Lea Hospital.

Blake was numb inside and out. They were at the hospital in minutes. The female opened his door and offered her hand to help him out. He took it. She helped him escape the cramped space then released his hand when he was somewhat steady on his feet. They led him in through the emergency entrance of the building he had hoped he would never have reason to enter again.

The male deputy talked to the woman at the reception desk. She phoned someone then nodded and said, "They are expecting you." She pushed a button that clicked open a lock and allowed them access into the inner sanctum. The three walked down the hallway, past rooms with curtains pulled across the openings. Voices rose out from behind a couple of them. They stopped in front of an elevator.

"It's down one level," the male said.

Blake grabbed for the door when his toe caught. The male put his hand under Blake's arm to assist. That's when he noticed the deputy's name plate. V Weber. He looked at the female's plate. A Zubinski. His stomach knotted up in the less-than-smooth ride down and jumped into his throat when it stopped. The doors opened and they stepped into a large room Blake identified as a morgue by the four cold storage lockers against the back wall. Dear God, was his wife in one?

That was when the grandfatherly-looking doctor, dressed in white from head to toe interrupted his thoughts. "Doctor Watts, over here, please."

His wife was on a gurney on the opposite side of the room from the lockers. The sheet was pulled up to her chest. He heard a loud breath get sucked in, and then realized it was his own. The first thing that struck him was how serene she looked, like she was before the car crash changed her, filled her body with pain. A pinkish line ran across her forehead. He pointed to it and looked at the doctor. "From the steering wheel," he explained.

He laid his head on his wife's chest and tucked his hands under her arms. She was cool, but not yet cold. He wept like never before, in all his thirty-eight years. His beloved wife could not have left him. And why? What had caused her death? He had no idea how much time had passed when he slowly lifted himself from his wife's chest and zeroed in on the doctor. "What happened to her?"

The doctor handed him a stack of tissues. "We don't have the answer to that yet, but there is evidence she had sniffed a substance. A small baggie and a straw with powder residue was on her lap."

Blake swayed and grabbed onto the gurney for support. "*What*? You can't mean that. My wife does *not* do drugs."

The doctor held a congenial expression. "We'll know more after her autopsy."

Autopsy. The connotation, the actions encompassed in that word, sent Blake into more sobbing. His head throbbed and his abdominal muscles ached.

The doctor laid a hand on his shoulder. "Doctor Watts, this is a tremendous shock, and I'm truly sorry for how you must be feeling."

Blake dabbed the tissues at his face and shook his head. All feeling had floated away, deserted him.

"I have a form for you to sign, verifying your wife's identity. And your consent for her autopsy." The doctor handed him a pen and clipboard with the forms. An X indicated where his signature went. His shaky scribble was more illegible than usual, but he didn't care. He should not be here at all. His wife should be home, not in a hospital morgue. Nothing about this was real.

The doctor and deputies waited quietly as he said his final goodbye to his wife. It tore at his heart and soul, and he would never be whole again.

6

Officer Dey slid his memo pad into his pocket. "Over lunch, I turned the vape pen over to the evidence folks at the PD. They'll send it to the lab for tests." He shook his head. "Too many good kids playing with fire in this vaping craze. Most of them don't have a clue what they're inhaling."

"Like mango-flavored mist, right? You heard about the two kids from Emerald Lake High School who overdosed and were taken by ambulance to the hospital?" I asked.

Goldin nodded. "Awful."

"They got poisoned by the high level of THC in their vape cartridge. Like you said, Casey, no clue," I said.

"Scares me something like that will happen here," he said.

"Public health conducted a survey of our sophomores last spring. Forty percent of them admitted to vaping. *Forty percent.* Of our tenth graders," Goldin said.

"It seems it's getting worse all the time. Not just here. Around the state, across the nation. The Department of Health has gone all out on campaigns, but kids don't see the dangers and many parents don't know what their kids are up to," I said.

"It's an epidemic. Major issue, that's for sure. We've had our share of sick kids who have passed out, thrown up. Sorry to say, we administrators and teachers were a bit slow to catch on at first. Vapers smell like bubble gum or fruit, not tobacco. Kids were plugging their chargers into school outlets, and we thought they were for cell phones, not vape pens," Goldin said.

"When things seem to drop from nowhere, it often takes a while to catch on." I shook my head. "Back to Rebecca's situation. She told us where she and Emmy got their stuff. That gives us a place to start."

Goldin's eyebrows drew together. "We don't have a Kelvin in our school, and that concerns me. Nor is there a Wyatt in tenth grade, and I verified that in the student records." She sat down at her desk and concentrated on the monitor's screen as her fingers flew over a series of keys. "There is a Wyatt in twelfth grade and two in eleventh." She typed some more. "Again, no Kelvin on the student rosters in the four grades. I don't recall a student by that name in all my years here."

"Unless Kelvin is enrolled under a different name," I said.

"Goes by his middle name?" Dey shrugged.

"You've got video cameras in the cafeteria," I said.

"From every angle to cover the space, yes," Goldin said.

"It was a busy afternoon, so we haven't had a chance to look at the footage. Let's do that now, try to pin down who Wyatt and Kelvin are," Dey said.

"Do you mind if I stay, take a look with you?" I asked.

"Of course not, stay." Goldin clicked on more keys and brought up footage from the previous day. "Casey, you're more adept at this. Why don't you take over so when we spot the kids you can zoom in for a close-up and take a still shot."

"Sure."

Goldin slid her chair back. Dey wheeled his over then sat down. I didn't want to hover over his shoulder and hung out some feet back. Goldin's screen was huge, a fifty incher. When Dey zoomed in I could have identified the students' faces from thirty feet away. The cafeteria was equipped with round, square, and banquet tables. The teens had choices we didn't have back when.

"Rebecca and Emmy have second lunch hour and they always sit in the same spot, like most creatures of habit." Dey advanced the time on the video and found their table in a flash. They were the only ones at a square table and sat on either side of a corner, their elbows nearly touching, their faces toward the camera.

We watched them eat sloppy joes and apple slices for some minutes before the two young men in question joined them and took the other seats. One had a lunch tray, the other did not. Their backs were to the camera, so Dey switched the video view. But it didn't help much. The four conversed. At least Emmy and the boy I guessed was Wyatt did.

"The boy without a lunch, with his head low and stocking cap pulled down over his ears makes it about impossible to see his face. Do you recognize anything about him, otherwise?" I asked.

"I gotta say, he doesn't look familiar to me," Dey said.

"Nor to me," Goldin said.

"I'll zoom in." When Dey did that, their images were less distinct, fuzzier, grainier. The boy we presumed was Wyatt also kept his head down, but his mop of wavy, reddish-blond hair set him apart from other teens I'd seen at the school.

I pointed at his image on the screen. "How about that one? Wyatt. Do you know him?"

"Casey, will you pause and minimize the video? I'll bring up photos of the three boys named Wyatt so we can see which one is that boy," Goldin said.

Dey traded places with Goldin, and she navigated her way through student photos, printed one of each boy, and laid them out on her desk. We studied them a moment then Goldin nodded. "Wyatt Crocker. Sure. His hair is longer now. He's new; moved here last May. He's a junior this year. I don't know why Rebecca thought he was a sophomore."

"Some kind of mix-up," I said.

Goldin went on, "I had a pleasant chat with Wyatt last spring during his orientation. He was quiet, seemed a little shy. Not unusual with a transfer. I get around the school as much as I can, mingle with the students. But come to think of it, I haven't seen Wyatt more than once or twice since school started three weeks ago."

"Has he been attending classes?" I asked.

Goldin checked her computer. "Yes. Did miss one day." She stood up. "Casey, let's go back to the video. Rebecca said Kelvin gave the vaping device to the girls and I want to double check that."

It took six more minutes before that happened. The boy presumed to be Kelvin slid his cupped hand across the table to Emmy. Before she covered it with her own hand, we got a glimpse of the device. Then she dropped it in her backpack, as Rebecca had reported.

"We'll speak to Emmy Nelson and Wyatt Crocker tomorrow, get them to admit to what we witnessed, tell us who Kelvin is, why he provided the girls with the vaping device, and how he got into the school," Dey said.

I nodded. "Good. I need to find out if Emmy's boyfriend offered the girls the vape, or if she asked him for it. And whether Rebecca was in on it, or not. If Emmy is going down a bad path, I don't want Rebecca walking alongside her."

It was a relief to be home, as unsettled as I felt by the way things turned out with Rebecca and the poor decision she made. The pressure she had given into. I hoped I had passed my fear of illegal drugs on to her over the years. They frightened me. As did many legal prescription medications that met Food and Drug Administration guidelines.

I had friends in high school and college who smoked weed, and some dabbled in other drugs. I didn't want an unknown chemical in my body, especially one from dealers on the streets. My professional experience with people high on uppers or low on downers affirmed I wouldn't take that kind of risk myself.

My maternal grandmother, Gram Brandt, was prescribed an opioid for relief from her arthritic pain. She was elderly with no past addiction issues from other pain medications, no indication she was susceptible to addiction. But she got hooked on the opioid and increased her dosage beyond the prescribed amount. It was before more stringent regulations and tracking methods were in place. The pharmacist knew my mother was involved in her parents' care and phoned to tell her he was concerned because Gram had gotten a refill ten days into a thirty-day prescription. Gramps had not kept track. He didn't realize he needed to.

My mother took Gram's medication bottle to her own house and each morning brought over the two pills she was prescribed per day. Mother entrusted Gramps to dispense them morning and evening. They kept up that routine until Gram's death. Gram argued at least once a day she hadn't gotten her morning med, but Gramps assured her she had. Without intervention, had she continued to increase the number of pills she took, it would have killed her.

One of my high school classmates got into heavy amphetamine use and was later diagnosed with schizophrenia. The doctors said the drugs did not directly cause her schizophrenia but increased her risk to develop the illness. Semantics, as far as I was concerned. Cause and effect.

I had called for backup many times when I needed to take custody of someone under the influence. People high on phencyclidine—PCP—methamphetamine, and crack cocaine were the ones who had put up the toughest, most unpredictable fights.

Enough about drugs, I told myself. Between the day's events and memories called from the recesses of my mind on that subject, I felt exhausted. I stretched out on the couch to retreat and unwind. Queenie joined me and laid her head on my belly. It soothed me and I rested my hand on her back.

"Well, girl, I can now officially relate to parents of teenagers who get into things they should not touch with a ten-foot pole." She whined and moved her head to coax a scratch from me. I closed my eyes and obliged. The next thing I knew she barked and woke me up. She had heard my phone ping. I blinked a few times as I pulled the phone from my pocket. Jean Brenner. "Hi, Jean."

"Corky. I don't even know where to start. Where did we go wrong?"

I sat up. "Time out. I know you did nothing wrong. At all. You and Dale are topnotch parents. Teenagers don't always have the best judgment, whether they're from good families or not such good families. You know that. Kids have a lot of peer pressure. In my opinion, it's worse today than it was when we were teens. Between text messages, all the phone apps, and social media, they have it coming at them from all directions. Way too much information and a lot of it is harmful."

Jean cleared her throat. "I know from experience how true that is. As much as we try to protect them. I need to tell you something that heaped more guilt on me. I had a heart-to-heart with my son and asked if he had ever tried vaping. He said he had, for about a month. *Justin.* And he is in *three* sports. I went through a whole litany of reasons he should never do that again. All he said was, 'I know, Mom, that's why I quit.'"

"That's good then," I said.

"I asked him why he did it in the first place, and he said it was no big deal, almost all the guys on his team tried it." Jean drew in a noisy breath then muttered, "No big deal? Right."

"The tough part. Someone convinces them it's fine and it's goes on from there."

"Someday I may confess to my children I tried weed back in the day because my boyfriend smoked and basically shamed me into it. But I couldn't stand that weird, sweet way it smelled. And I broke up with him that night," she said.

"There you go. You can tell them you know what it's like to get persuaded to do something you don't want to do. Then you made a better choice and said goodbye to the persuader."

"Yeah, good advice. Thanks, Corky. I'll let you go," she said.

"Take care, Jean. Bye for now."

I stayed on the couch to check my emails and text messages. Queenie perked up and let out a single woof the same time I heard the garage door open. She beat me to the kitchen door and was first in line to greet Smoke and Rex. Rex rubbed his snout against her head and Queenie returned the gesture.

Smoke pulled me into his arms for a kiss that held sweet promises of things to come. "You look sleepy and tousled and sexy as all get out."

"I can't even keep a short nap secret from you, can I?"

"You cannot." He slid an arm down my back, rested it on my waist, slipped a finger under my chin, and took a closer look at my face. "You're troubled about Rebecca."

"I am."

"How about we sit down and talk it through? I'm gonna grab a beer. You?"

"I think I'll stick with water for now," I said.

Smoke got our drinks then followed me to the living room where we settled on the couch. I rested the cold water bottle on the side of my face to help clear my sluggish head for a moment, then removed the cap and took a long drink.

Smoke tipped his head back for a sip of Stella, set the bottle on the coffee table, and shifted to face me. "Tell me."

I walked him through the day, and he stopped me here and there to clarify facts. "That about sums it up. I know kids do dumb things, but this vaping thing caught me off guard. In spite of the fact that she was raised by a mentally ill grandmother, Rebecca's always been level-headed. Normal," I said.

"You've said it before, Alvie was sick, but she somehow had sense enough to let Rebecca spend time with friends who had good families."

"I think about that a lot, that she's been part of the Brenner family since she was in kindergarten. Went to camp with Tina in the summer. I guess with the way things turned out, her early connection with them was meant to be. They had an established relationship that made the adoption process go way smoother," I said.

"Not a doubt in my mind." He took my hand in his and gently squeezed. "When I think of the things I did as a teenager, I haven't a clue how I made it to adulthood."

I squeezed back. "You were a guy who had eight or ten guardian angels around you at all times."

"That sounds about right. And let's not get into the fish house incident." Smoke had been making out with a young lady and accidentally kicked over an oil lantern. It started the house on fire and earned him the nickname, "Smoke."

"If you say so, *Elton*." I snickered then shook my head. "With Mother being such a worrywart and freaking out whenever she heard what other kids got into trouble for, I wanted to keep her stress level as low as possible and did my best to stay out of trouble. Or at least did my best to keep Mother in the dark when I did."

Smoke's baritone laugh filled the room, and my heart sang with its melody. "And you still do," he said.

"Oh my gosh, my poor mother would need to go on meds herself if I drilled into the details of my job on any given day."

"I give her credit that she's held up as well as she has throughout your years of service. Especially the critical incidents you've gotten caught up in."

"'Caught up in, huh?' That's one way to put it." My mind raced through a few. "I'm convinced she gets help from above when big things go down. You know how weirdly calm she gets. Clear-headed, like then is not the time to panic. She melts down later." I gave him a nudge. "How about you? Anything new on Tad Michels' death investigation?"

"His body is with the medical examiner who plans to do the autopsy this afternoon. Sheriff said I've put in too many hours the last few days, so he sent Harrison to witness it. They'll get Michels' blood to the lab for the tox screen. We started searching his phone, checking numbers. And see if it leads us anywhere interesting."

"At least one good lead, right? After the tox report we got on our OD last week, I can only hope we haven't got another dealer selling fatal combos. Like last year," I said.

"Our whole department hopes that's not the case. What a cluster for a couple months there. Six people died, including the young woman who had somehow managed to hide her addiction from her husband."

"Yes, Doctor Watts's wife. He's Queenie's veterinarian. I took her in for her annual checkup a couple months ago and he didn't look like his normal healthy self. He was thin and haggard. Effects from his grief, I figured. He was also noticeably uncomfortable around me and that made me uncomfortable. I wondered if it was because I work for the sheriff. I didn't work his wife's case but maybe it brought back the ordeal he went through when she died."

Smoke poked my ribs. "Could be. Or it could be because you resemble his wife who was also a gorgeous blonde."

I poked him back. "Yeah, that's probably it." We jostled back and forth until Smoke put me in a hold I didn't want to escape from. One thing led to another and another and another and ended in a sweet victory for us both.

As we lay in bed later that night, while Smoke slept, I pondered when our engagement would take us to the next level, a trip down the aisle. He was still working through unresolved issues from years before. Add to that his concern about the large gap in our ages. His biggest hang-up, I surmised.

He had confessed he was worried I would regret marriage, that I would find someone better, but would remain faithfully committed to him. How many more months would it take to convince him he was my breath and life on earth?

7

Blake

Blake took a quick glance at his image in the mirror then shifted his concentration to the faucet on the sink instead. Anything was easier to look at than his face. It had undergone drastic changes in the year since his wife died. His appearance had declined from what she described as, "the most handsome man in the world," to a far less comely version of his former self.

He had dropped weight and his sunken cheeks made the bones protrude in an unattractive way. The deeper frown lines were more pronounced because he rarely smiled. He couldn't force one half the time, even when he tried. Aside from the deep creases between his eyes, his affect appeared on the flat side.

In the early days when he turned his depression inward, he sought the help of a psychologist. His medical doctor wrote a prescription for a medication he didn't fill, as much as he was tempted to, over and over. But he would not take the pills as directed to ease his pain, to make him feel better. Rather, he would swallow the whole bottle to end his life and his misery.

Blake braved another look in the mirror. It was evident why acquaintances and clients he hadn't seen for a while didn't readily recognize him. His colleagues had witnessed the gradual changes over the course of the year. "You don't look well. Are you sure you're okay?" and similar comments that grated on him, pushed him to the edge.

Blake had blown up at the last person in his office who asked him if he was all right. "Do NOT ask me that again." The other veterinarians, technicians, and office staff gave him a wide berth after that, likely figured he would get through the stages of grief eventually. They ceased giving him advice and pep talks.

The one and only thing that sustained Blake in the early days was his practice. He performed his work duties, not with the same enthusiasm, but with close to the same professional level.

His friends no longer contacted him; he had not returned their calls or messages. The animals he treated for a variety of conditions and concerns, and restored to better health, was therapeutic for him. When he cared for patients, sometimes his grief lifted an inch. But the moments were short-lived and dissipated like smoke when he was alone again.

Blake had endured a lengthy interview with Winnebago County Sheriff's Detective Dawes after his wife's autopsy and toxicology report came back. She had died from an overdose of heroin laced with carfentanil. He was stunned. When the doctor said evidence showed she had snorted a substance, it jarred him. Heroin was bad enough, but carfentanil? What would possess her to use that?

"Any idea where your wife got her drugs?" Dawes had asked from across his kitchen table.

"No. *No.*" He made fists under the table.

"She never mentioned anyone's name that wasn't familiar to you? Male, female?" He took a minute to wrack his brain for the thousandth time since his wife died. "No." His fists tightened.

"How about her friends, her regular contacts? Anyone you suspected might be using drugs?" Dawes said.

Blake thought through her list of friends. Not a suspect among them. Then again, he didn't know his own wife was using illegal drugs until after her death.

"Do you ever use carfentanil in your practice?"

Blake was stunned and stammered out, "Um, I . . . on rare occasions, yes." They could *not* think he had anything to do with her death.

"Did your wife have access to that drug?"

"No. It's in a locked room with other medications."

"She didn't have the key?" Dawes persisted.

Blake shook his head. "We use an access code to get into the room, and a key for the cabinet where the opioids are kept. Only the vets have a key. So, no. Besides, she wasn't at the office all that much." He used carfentanil so seldom, he tried to remember if he would ever have had reason to mention the drug to his wife. "She never asked me about drugs I gave the animals, and it's not something I'd talk about in specifics to her, anyway."

"We found several snack-size baggies containing powdered substances in your wife's glove box." The detective pulled a photo from his pocket and slid it toward Blake.

"What?" He glanced at it but could not touch the photo. Baggies with powder.

"Each one was tested. The heroin's purity varied from bag to bag. Two were cut with baking soda, one with milk powder, and one with fentanyl, another deadly combo, depending on how much is added."

Blake braved a look at the detective. "I don't understand. Baking soda, milk powder?"

"It makes the heroin or cocaine go farther if it's mixed with other substances. Trouble is, folks can never be sure of the purity," Dawes said.

Something about the mixes he described did not make sense. "Why would a dealer mix different things with the drugs? Wouldn't they stick with either milk powder or baking soda?"

"Could be that's how the dealer got it from his supplier. Could be the drugs are from different dealers."

Different dealers? His wife had more than one dealer? The pulses in Blake's temples started to throb.

"Doctor, your wife's cell phone was not among her personal effects when she died. Nor was it in her vehicle. Do you know where it is?" Dawes leaned in closer.

Blake drew back a tad. "She forgot it on the charger that morning."

"With your permission, I will collect the phone, check her calls and contacts. Does she have a personal computer, or did the two of you share one?"

"We each have our own laptops."

"All right. Her cell phone and computer, then. We'll interrogate her database, check her search engines, hopefully get the answers to our questions." Dawes paused and studied him. "Doctor Watts, it's important to uncover the events that led up to your wife's death, find out who she bought the drugs from. For the sheriff's office, sure. But most importantly for you, to help you heal."

Blake did not believe that was possible in his lifetime. He felt numb—a programmed machine—when he retrieved his wife's laptop from their office and turned it over to the detective. The sheriff's office would uncover what her search engines revealed. He never thought he had a reason to take a look but kicked himself now. *Why hadn't I thought of that myself?*

Her cell phone was on the counter where she had left it. He had seen it light up with calls and messages but didn't have the wherewithal to touch it, to check who was trying to reach her. He pointed at it and the detective nodded as he picked it up with a gloved hand and dropped it in a plastic evidence bag. "Doctor, we will do our best to track down the dealer who sold her the drugs," the detective said.

Weeks later, Detective Dawes returned the laptop and phone. "Your wife did a fair amount of research on opioids, but never typed the word 'carfentanil' into a search engine. We chased down every person in her contacts and checked each phone number that did not have a name assigned to it. We didn't identify a single suspect in the lot."

The information gave Blake no reassurance he would ever find out who killed his wife or that his wooden state would change.

For a long year he struggled to climb out of bed each morning, navigate his way through the day. The medical examiner's report haunted him. He could not grasp why his wife had heroin and carfentanil in her system. He had argued with law enforcement, denied that she used street drugs. How had he not known? He had a busy practice, but was he so occupied with it that he was blind to his wife's activities?

She was a fit and healthy person who exercised daily, ate well, rarely drank a glass of wine. Until a car crash rocked her world and changed her life. Their lives. The narcotic pain medication a doctor prescribed after her back surgery sunk its sharp teeth into her. When her primary care doctor would not give her a third refill, she changed doctors. He found that out after her death.

At the time she told him a friend had recommended a female physician at a different clinic, and she decided to make the switch. The new doctor wrote her a thirty-day script, but when she burned through the pills in a week, the doc refused to order a refill and recommended she seek treatment. He learned that after her death, too.

Blake believed anything his wife told him and hadn't recognized her addiction or newly acquired deception. He had never seen her swallow a pill after the first bottle of narcotics was empty. The need to maintain the façade that their life together was perfect must have governed her, dictated her actions. Had she confessed her addiction to him, it wouldn't have changed the depth of his love for her. Not one iota. He would have supported her, found the professional help she needed to recover. Done whatever he could, no matter the cost, to get her healthy again.

Blake finally worked up the courage to sort through his wife's clothes and purses and other belongings stored in her walk-in closet to donate to her favorite non-profit that had a retail store in town. They gave the proceeds to families in need. He checked pockets of her coats and pants and emptied remnants like lip gloss and combs and tissues from her purses. He found wads of cash in one and figured it was unspent drug money she had squirreled away. Blake tossed it aside and would donate it somewhere sometime.

He was perplexed when he flipped one purse over on the bed and a small case fell out. His fingers trembled as he snapped open the latch and spotted a cell phone inside. What in the hell? His wife had stashed a secret cell phone in a purse and hid it at the back of her closet?

It took him long minutes to find the inner strength to pick up the cell phone and its charger. He stared at its dark face a minute then carried it to the kitchen and plugged it in. When it reached sixty percent, he waited no longer. He turned it on, correctly guessed the passcode on the second try then scrolled through the list of contacts and calls. The contacts were noted by initials only: GH, KP, PB, TM, WE, WS. His wife had carved out a secret life with druggies and dealers. He felt gut punched.

The beautiful woman who made their house a home had managed to worm her way into, and navigate her way around, an underground illegal drug world to feed her habit. *And he did not know it.* And neither did her friends. After her death, he asked them questions about her activities, ad nauseum, until he finally believed their answers. His wife had curtailed her social life, and they were giving her time to recover from the wounds she had sustained in the crash. She was not able to go on runs, or play tennis, or do her usual volunteer work until her vertebrae fully healed.

She could not have kept her drug use hidden forever. Her behavior and appearance would have changed as she fell deeper into the abyss. It turned out her habit was short-lived.

She died a few months before the first anniversary of the accident that had set into motion the tragic turn of events.

Blake went through the list of contacts' initials and numbers a score of times, memorized a few. She made four calls the morning she died, and one of them must have sold her the lethal fix. He agonized over who the unnamed people were. Which one had supplied his wife with the lethal drug? GH, TM, PB, KP?

As he fretted, a thought struck him like an unexpected lightning bolt from the sky. It disturbed him at first and he rejected it, tried to banish it, pushed it to the back of his brain. But the thought persisted and tempted Blake for days. Finally, he gave it consideration, mulled it over, and a rudimentary plan took shape in his mind.

It was a call to action that shifted the blame and anger and despair he had directed at himself to others instead. Where it belonged. To the one who was personally responsible for his wife's death and to the others who killed vulnerable drug seekers when they sold them deadly, illicit drugs.

8

When I was on patrol Thursday morning, my work cell phone rang as I approached Whitetail Lake. I pulled my squad car onto the shoulder. Smoke. "Hello, Detective, what's up?"

"Mornin', Sergeant. We got the tox results back. Tad Michels died from the same cocktail that claimed our last victim's life. Cocaine and carfentanil."

"You have got to be kidding. Not another rash of ODs because some lowlife is lacing coke with carfentanil now."

"Major concern. In fact, I had a talk with the sheriff about ramping up our drug task force, try to get better intel on where the stuff's coming from," he said.

"Did you come up with a plan?"

"I suggested Weber and Zubinski. They did a fine job last year making contacts in the drug underworld. You had a year of experience yourself. If you're up for the challenge."

"I couldn't do an extended assignment," I said.

"Fair enough. Sheriff will talk to the deputies, work on the schedule with the chief to get their patrol shifts covered. I'll let you know."

"All righty."

I pushed the phone's end button and knocked my head against the backrest. *Really?* The year I spent on the drug task force was long and filled with stress. The least favorite assignment of my career. By far. I found the drug world a dark and dismal place. I had to pretend the parties I attended were fun instead of big downers. I felt depressed half the time and the weight of the world lifted when I went back on patrol. In the years since, I went undercover from time to time on a drug case investigation and still maintained contact with two trusted informants.

I pulled the memo pad from my pocket and flipped back a few pages. Two overdose deaths in a seven-day span from cocaine mixed with carfentanil. The first on Sunday, September tenth and the second on Sunday, the seventeenth. They both died on the Sabbath. Was that significant or happenstance? Young men. Twenty-seven and twenty-four. Add deadly to dark and dismal drug world.

We had never discovered the person, or persons, responsible for the lethal drug combination that caused six deaths the previous year, despite exhaustive investigations. When the deaths from that mix stopped, we figured the supplier had moved on, or changed to a less lethal combo. After all, why bite the hand that feeds you? In a lucrative illegal drug business, to lose one client necessitated finding another to replace him or her.

The sheriff's office had a few confidential informants we supplied with cell phones to communicate with our officers and drug dealers. The phones also served as tracking and recording devices when activated. I lifted my phone and scrolled through the contacts until I located Mac's number. I had known him since junior high school, and in high school heard he sold marijuana from his locker. Back then, they didn't bring dogs in to sniff students' lockers like they did nowadays.

The second time I saw Mac after graduation, I was on the drug task force and arrested him when he sold me drugs. He later accepted a plea deal and avoided incarceration when he agreed to provide inside information to our office. Mac had been clean ever since but maintained his cover as a user to stay connected to dealers. A sense of civic duty is what he told me. And the money the sheriff's office paid gave him extra cash.

I hit the call button and Mac answered on the third ring. "Hey, Sergeant, you must be calling about the latest drug deals gone bad."

"You're good."

"I got a little somethin' for you. Been in touch with a couple guys and word is there's a new guy in town, bringing the stuff directly from Chicago, bypassing the locals, selling it cheaper," Mac said.

"Why do they think that?"

"They got wind one of the bigger dealers got a call to that effect, said the guy got his number from a friend, but he wouldn't say who that friend was."

"Do your contacts have a clue who it might be?" I asked.

"No. No one's admitted to being that friend, from what I hear, so it's generated some curiosity trying to figure it out. They all want to protect their businesses, not let an outsider move in and steal their customers."

They must not have read the law breaker section where it says there is no honor among thieves. "I appreciate your help, Mac. How is everything going for you, otherwise?"

"Can't complain. Still got a job that pays the bills. Sober friends help keep me on the straight and narrow when I want to veer off," he said.

"Good and important things to have in your life. I'll tell you this again, I am proud of what you've overcome, how strong you've been. If you need an ear or a shoulder, you know you can contact me, day or night."

"Yeah, and I guess I have."

"Let me know if any new info pops up, will you?" I asked.

"Sure thing."

"Thanks again, Mac."

There's a new guy in town. Did the dealer from last year make a comeback with a new drug mix this time around? The thought gave me a start. The local dealers were a tight-knit community. They had reason to be on the lookout for cops, mostly. But other threats were present, like the confidential informants, or spies. I dropped the phone into the center console, replaced the memo pad in my pocket, and rubbed my arms to get my blood moving, to warm up.

After what Mac said, I considered the level of trouble yet another dealer in the county would add to the plight we already faced. Drug runs from the Twin Cities metro area to Chicago and back were continual, and a market for illegal drugs thrived anywhere dealers set up shop.

I thought of Rebecca, Emmy, Wyatt, and a young man named Kelvin who wasn't listed as a student at the school. That reminded me I hadn't heard back from Principal Goldin or Officer Dey. I dialed the principal's number.

"Missus Goldin." She sounded slightly out of breath.

"Hi, it's Corky Aleckson. Are you in the middle of something?"

"Always, but not too busy to talk with you."

"Thank you. To let you know, I checked Winnebago County records for anyone with a first or last name of Kelvin. None in the county. I found a few in the state, but not in his age group. There are two on Facebook, both in other counties. May not be his real name."

"Oh, my," she said.

"I was wondering what Emmy and Wyatt had to say about Kelvin and the vape pen, how he'd gotten access into the school."

"My apologies. I intended to call you but hadn't gotten that far yet. Rebecca didn't tell you?"

My heart picked up its beat. "No, what happened?"

"Not to worry. Emmy may not have talked to Rebecca about it. We met with Emmy and her parents, and they were as shocked as the Brenners were. Emmy said she had no idea who Kelvin was before that day and didn't know he was going to give them a vape pen. She admitted she was curious to try it. And promised not to do it again, so I hope that's true."

"Me, too," I said.

"She and Wyatt had just noticed each other and started hanging out. He's a year older so she thought he was a sophomore. Her parents said she isn't allowed to go on 'real' dates until she's sixteen," Goldin said.

"Good, and I hope Emmy stands by her promise. What did Wyatt and his parents have to say?"

"Single parent. His father. They didn't have much to say. I told you they moved to Oak Lea last spring. Mister Crocker got a manager position at a hardware store here. He is almost as quiet as Wyatt is, has a weary look about him. He's been the only parent to his three boys for years. Wyatt's the youngest and the easiest, according to Mister Crocker. He was quite upset Wyatt was involved in the vape pen incident and doesn't know either Emmy or Rebecca."

"Hmm, father and son should be less quiet to each other. What did Wyatt say about Kelvin?" I asked.

"His older brother met him first, but Wyatt didn't know where. Kelvin hung out at their house a few times and that was how he met Wyatt. Wyatt said Kelvin is easy to like, outgoing, and friendly. Like his older brother. Kelvin gave Wyatt fifty bucks to open a side exit only door here so he could see some old friends. Said he graduated last year and missed being here. A lie that Wyatt believed. He didn't know Kelvin was going to give his new girlfriend a vape pen," Goldin said.

"Sneak into your old school to see friends, really?"

"Kids don't always question things like that."

"True."

"After lunch, on his way to class, Wyatt saw Kelvin talking to kids in the hallway."

"Was he selling them drugs?" I asked.

"A major concern. We've been going through footage to see if we can capture him on one. If we get a good image, we should be able to identify him. And find out if there have been transactions happening in our hallways."

"Sounds like Kelvin is a brazen one. Maybe he's been in your school before," I said.

"That crossed our minds, too."

"If you get a good image, the sheriff's office will need a copy."

"Of course."

"What about Wyatt's brother, the one who knows Kelvin? Did Officer Dey talk to him?"

"Believe it or not, he left for basic training last week," Goldin said.

"I believe it. We run into brick walls more than we like in this business."

We disconnected and I sat for a moment to absorb the implications our conversation had revealed. I looked across the lake, and as I worked though my thoughts, took a moment to admire the trees on the hill with their brilliant-colored canopies. In autumn, daylight hours were shorter, and temperatures were cooler, so the chlorophyll in the leaves broke down. That made the green color disappear and revealed the reds, oranges, and yellows hidden underneath.

Besides the vivid colors the season brought—as much as I loved summer—I appreciated relief from the hot, humid days and nights. Daytime temperatures in autumn were often warm then turned cool and refreshing in the evenings. So when I went on longer runs, I didn't resemble a drenched rat like after my summer runs.

I got back on the road and saw a farmer at work harvesting his field corn, another raked leaves from his lawn, still another stacked wood to burn in a wood stove or fireplace. It often struck me how normal life went on for some while others were caught up in bad situations. Like the Brenners, the Nelsons, and Mr. Crocker were with their children.

When I was young and thought my brother got preferential treatment, I would whine to my mother, "That's not fair." She would tousle my hair and say, "Life is not always fair." She was right, but I had a strong, inborn sense of justice. In my vocation, one of my prime goals was to track down bad guys and lock them up. For their victims and to protect others.

The overdose deaths of two victims prompted the sheriff's office to ramp up their efforts to flush out the one who supplied the deadly combo. Smoke wanted me to go undercover. I needed to talk over logistics with him, change my attitude, and get into the right mindset to deal with dealers again.

9

After work, I drove home, parked the squad, and depressed
the radio button. "Six oh eight, Winnebago County."

"Go ahead, Six oh eight." It was Communications Officer
Randy.

"I'm ten-seven." Off duty.

"You are ten-seven at fifteen ten. Have a good night."

Queenie barked from her kennel, and I headed back to
get her. "Hi, girl. How was your day?" She ran back and forth
until I opened the door and let her out. She stuck her nose in
my side, so I petted her a minute. "You go run off some energy
while I change. Then we'll go on a run together, maybe stop
and see Gramps." She barked when I said his name.

Queenie took off toward the woods. I let myself in the
house, jogged up the steps, removed my duty belt and hung it
up. I changed into running clothes, headed downstairs to my
office den, retrieved my personal sidearm from the safe—a
Smith & Wesson in its pancake holster—and slid it on the
waist of my pants. I grabbed a lightweight jacket from the

front closet and went to the back yard for Queenie. But she was nowhere in sight.

"Queenie! Time to go." When she didn't come, I called again and looked around for her. I heard a mix of growls and cries coming from the woods. I sprinted toward it, a football field away.

The closer I got, the more vicious and hostile the deep guttural noises sounded. And the louder Queenie cried. When I finally got within eight feet, I spotted a coyote between the trees with its teeth embedded in the back of Queenie's neck. She was on the losing end of the attack. The coyote shook its head back and forth, intent on killing my pooch. I stopped, drew my weapon and aimed, terrified I might hit Queenie. I went for a spine shot, but the coyote's body moved, and the bullet struck him in the gut instead. The coyote reacted, let go of his grip. When he lifted his head, I steadied my hand, aimed at a spot an inch below his spine, and shot. The bullet struck its mark and the coyote dropped like a rock. I holstered my weapon.

Queenie wailed and so did I. Blood from wounds on her ears, back, and leg ran down her body. "Oh, my dear God, dear God." I bent over, and as she nuzzled her nose into my neck, I offered what sounded like weak assurances. I pulled out my phone and called Smoke. It went to voicemail, and I remembered he had an interview scheduled with a victim. I didn't leave a message. I tried my brother John Carl next. When he picked up it was the answer to my prayer. "Tell me you're home."

"I am. What's wrong?"

"I need you. Grab a blanket and drive to the woods behind my house. Queenie needs medical care *now*. A coyote attacked her."

"On my way." John Carl lived a mile from me, and his truck came bouncing across the field minutes later. He backed up close to where we were and jumped out. "What should I do?"

"Open the tailgate and we'll lift her in. I don't know if she'll feel like walking. We'll lay her on the blanket. I'll ride in the back with her to the vet's office."

"I don't think you can do that," he said.

"I *need* to do that."

Queenie had weighed forty-two pounds at her last visit to the veterinarian, light enough for either of us to lift. But with the two of us, we could do it with greater care. I folded the blanket in fourths for a softer ride and laid it on the back end of the truck bed. She hurt but trusted us to protect and tend to her. We gingerly got a hold under her belly and lifted her onto the blanket. Queenie's legs collapsed and she rested her head on her crossed front paws.

"Let's slide her closer to the cab." We did that with smooth enough moves so she didn't protest or cry out in pain. Thankfully. "You know where the vet clinic is, in Oak Lea?" I called to John Carl as he headed to the truck's cab.

"Yes."

I half sat half sprawled next to Queenie. "Drive carefully back over the field, and not too crazy when you get on the road." John Carl never drove like crazy, not like I might. But in case he got nervous and did.

I examined Queenie as best I could. She had a tear on her face, a rip in her ear, deep teeth marks in her leg and on the back of her neck. I swallowed hard, rested my hand gently on her back, found the number for the clinic with my other hand, and pushed the call button. I told the receptionist what happened, that we were on our way in, would be there in about ten minutes.

Queenie was quiet and I wondered if she was in shock. That would help numb the pain. A new fear hit me. What if the coyote was rabid? A single coyote rarely attacked a larger dog. Usually a pair, or even a small pack did that.

Did coyotes carry rabies? A wave of dread washed over me at the thought, and we could not get to the clinic fast enough.

After the longest five-mile ride of my life, John Carl pulled into the Oak Lea Veterinary Clinic. He slid out of his truck. "What now?"

"Go see if they've got a gurney for her. And someone to help."

Soon after, John Carl emerged with two assistants and a gurney. I slid the blanket with Queenie on it toward the tailgate. John Carl opened it and the four of us laid Queenie on the gurney. I kept my hand on her side as they wheeled her into the clinic. "We'll go directly to the emergency room," one said.

"I'll wait out here." John Carl veered off into the waiting room. He had trouble with sick or injured animals. Growing up in the country, we'd had funerals and buried plenty of pets and other animals that didn't survive from their illnesses and injuries. He hated that task even more than I did.

I stayed with Queenie and the attendants. We went down a hall, through an outer door, then an inner door to a white, sterile room. At least it looked and smelled that way. I heard someone come in and snap on gloves. "Doctor Watts," an attendant said.

As he approached the gurney, I glanced over my shoulder. "Hi, Doctor."

He started a careful visual and tactile examination. "I understand she suffered a coyote attack?"

"It scared me half to death. Thank God I got there before it killed her."

"It ran off when it saw you?"

"No. I had to shoot it. With my thirty-eight."

He raised his eyebrows and said, "Oh. Well, that's good then."

"Do you think the coyote had rabies, is that why he attacked?" I asked.

"We could test it to find out, but rabies is rare among coyotes. Distemper is more common. But not to worry, your dog is up to date with her vaccines and that includes rabies and distemper."

I reached up and pulled at my ponytail. "Of course. Sorry, I'm not processing things very well right now."

"No need to apologize. It must have been a terrible thing to go through," he said.

"Worse than terrible."

"Coyotes usually go in for a neck attack, compress the windpipe. It looks like Queenie put up a fight or moved around enough to escape serious injury until you came to her rescue."

"She must have fought for her life. The coyote wasn't much bigger than her, but it was vicious. And Queenie is not," I said.

"We'll get her sedated, on an antibiotic, get the wounds cleaned. She will need stitches for the shoulder and leg wounds. After we've finished, we'll assess whether she should stay overnight. Meanwhile, you can wait in the waiting room. If you need to leave, make sure they have your current phone number at the front desk."

I turned to the doctor. "Please. I'd feel better being with her through this." I didn't realize I had put my hands on his arms until he glanced down. I dropped them to my sides.

"I, um, I understand how you must feel. But we need to follow the standard protocols that we have in place for good reasons," he said.

I respected the need for policies, procedures, and protocols, and nodded. Queenie gave me a hangdog look when I bent over close to her ear. "They'll fix you up, girl." Then I made my way to the waiting room. John Carl was in a chair reading something on his phone. Three others were seated with pet carriers by their feet. They watched me as I sat down next to my brother.

John Carl turned toward me. "How does it look?"

I rubbed my temples. "She'll be okay. Needs her wounds treated and stitched up. Man alive. Two days ago, I was stressed about something with Rebecca; now it's my poor Queenie. This has been a tough week."

"Sorry."

"I know." I folded my hands in my lap and noticed blood on my jacket, pants and hands. No wonder our waiting room neighbors had stared at me. "I better go wash my hands. At least."

"You should."

Why did John Carl wait for me to see the blood? My brainiac bro had been an enigma most of my life. I loved him for who he was. And, confession time, I was almost as happy as my mother and my best friend Sara—who was smitten with him—when he moved back to Oak Lea. He was a rock when I needed his help or advice.

I washed my hands and face but figured it would make things worse if I tried to rinse the blood out of the jacket. I took it off, inside out. Then stretched my shirt so the Smith & Wesson on my hip was less obvious. We had a high number of permit-to-carry license holders in Winnebago County, but it made some people uncomfortable when they spotted someone with a gun. I tied the jacket around my waist, and it covered my holstered gun well.

I returned to John Carl more presentable, but before I sat down, a front desk staff called me over. "Sergeant Aleckson, Doctor Watts asked me to call the DNR to see about what to do with the coyote that attacked Queenie. I just got off the phone with the district conservation officer. He said the chances the coyote was rabid is very slim, and you could either leave the remains there as food for other animals or bury it if you would rather do that. Doctor Watts said since Queenie is up to date with her vaccines, there is no reason to test the coyote. Even if it did have rabies, or distemper, it can't hurt anything else anymore."

"All right, thanks. That works for me," I told her.

John Carl heard our conversation and squirmed a little when I sat down. "So, what are you going to do? About the coyote?"

"Leave it for food. Hungry critters will be happy to have a convenient meal. Owls, eagles, even other coyotes."

"I suppose," he said.

"If the coyote's remains are still there after Queenie recovers, I'll have you bury them, so she doesn't eat it herself."

His eyebrows shot up so fast and so high, I thought they might disappear into his hairline. I patted his bicep. "Just kidding. Couldn't resist." It was easy to get a rise out of John Carl and I gave in to the temptation more than I should.

About twenty minutes later, Dr. Watts emerged from the bowels of the surgical suite located somewhere in the building dressed in scrubs, complete with head and foot coverings. That's when I noticed he looked healthier, less pained, than the last time I brought Queenie to the clinic. Like he had a more positive lease on life. Shakespeare's King Oedipus said, "Time is the great healer," and it appeared that was true for the doctor in the year-plus time since his wife died.

I stood up and so did John Carl. The doctor looked from me to him and frowned slightly. "Mister Aleckson?"

He nodded. "John."

Dr. Watts cast his eyes downward for a second then landed them on me. "Um, well, Queenie's procedure went well, and she did just fine. She is sedated, and with the fresh sutures, it's best if we keep her here until tomorrow. We don't want her tearing the bandages off and chewing on her stitches. She won't even be aware of her surroundings tonight, won't notice that she's not at home."

"I hate to leave her."

"Corky, you have to work tomorrow anyway, and won't be home to watch her," John Carl reminded me.

"I suppose." I turned to the doctor, "What time do you think she can come home?"

"Some time after noon. Um, we'll be sure to let you know if something changes."

"Corky, I'll pick her up and keep her at my house if you need me to." John Carl worked from home.

"Your house?" Dr. Watts must have assumed he was my husband.

"John Carl is my brother and my neighbor."

The doctor nodded. "Okay. Well good then. Do not worry about Queenie. We'll take good care of her and will let you know when she's ready to go."

"Can I peek at her before we leave?" I asked.

"I think that would be all right," he said.

10

Blake

When Blake got home, the afternoon's events played through his mind. In the middle of Corinne Aleckson's crisis, after her beloved Queenie was attacked and injured, he was struck with a ray of hope. He had noticed her beauty the last time she brought Queenie in. Then today, being near her and physically touched by her, it stirred something deep inside him. When she grasped his arms and searched his face with her luminous gray eyes, his heart skipped some beats. He was caught off guard by how sexy she looked, despite her messy ponytail and bloodied clothes, and that he *noticed* her appeal.

Blake moved through a range of emotions in those few moments, desires he had buried from his former life with his wife. He wanted to pull Corinne's body against his, taste her lips, nuzzle his nose and mouth into her neck . . .

It had taken Blake a minute to leave the unexpected fantasy and get back to the reality of the injured animal on the table. She needed his skills to mend her, start her healing process. Poor doggie. Queenie would recover, with a few battle scars.

Blake almost relented when Corinne begged him to let her stay and was grateful his office had protocols in place he needed to adhere to. He believed her presence would have distracted him, not let him do his best job for his patient. What was it about her that drew him in, made him want to know everything about her? He figured it was her confidence, her compassion, the way she cared for her pet. And more.

She shot a coyote as it attacked her dog, for God sakes. That took clear-headed courage.

His wife had a long list of fine, endearing qualities, but courage wasn't one. Guilt and shame washed over him when he realized he had compared his wife to Corinne. His wife had been his everything for almost twenty years and Corinne was a woman he had known only as a client for a few years. On top of that, she worked for the Winnebago County Sheriff. A red flag. A major warning to avoid her if there ever was one.

After Blake sutured Queenie's wounds, he went to the waiting room to update Corinne. She stood up and so did the tall—maybe two inches taller than his own five foot eleven— good-looking guy next to her. They looked like the dolls his mother had kept from her youth, a slightly disheveled blonde Barbie and a buff brunette Ken. It was obvious they were close the way she bent her head near his as she spoke. The wind went out of his sails. He had wrongly assumed she was single. No wedding ring, at least.

New hope was born when he learned John, or John Carl, as she called him was her brother. Lord, he needed to put Corinne out of his mind for the rest of the evening. He had business to attend to, plans to lay out. Dealers to contact.

Blake dropped to the floor, did fifty push-ups, then two minutes of jumping jacks. He smiled with each jump. When he finished, his breaths were short puffs. He took in a deep one and let it out slowly.

He contemplated how many burner phones he had left and how many he would need. How long could he keep going? All things come to an eventual end. Would he know when to quit? When he started his quest with his wife's phone full of dealer contacts, he had no clear idea where it would lead him.

Blake had never bought an illegal drug in his life and did not know how or where to start. It concerned him a dealer might turn out to be someone he knew. Would word somehow get out into the community that he had been seen with a dealer who later died from an overdose? If he got arrested, his practice would be over, no doubt about it.

The irony? When he started working his way into the underground world of drug addicts and their suppliers a couple months back, he didn't care one iota about what happened to him personally. If he died, he died. If he got caught and was sent to prison, so be it. It was his clients, his patients, the animals he cared for, and the other veterinarians in the clinic that concerned him. He didn't want them to suffer any consequences because of things he needed to do.

11

John Carl pulled into my driveway. "Do you need anything?"

"Thanks, nothing I can think of at the minute. Queenie will recover, and that gives me huge reassurance."

"Yeah, me, too. Well, let me know," he said.

"Actually, can you tell Mother and Gramps and Grandpa and Grandma what happened? Without getting into too much detail. I know, Mother will coax it out of you no matter what. It'd just be hard for me to tell the story right now."

"Sure."

"It'll be hardest on Gramps, so keep it high level, brief. Queenie got bit by a coyote and is at the vet," I said.

"Okay."

"Thank you, brother. I appreciate it."

I climbed down from the truck then John Carl turned around and drove away. When I stepped into the house it hit me how lonely it was without Queenie there to greet me. I had lived my first thirty years without her and didn't know what was missing from my life.

My phone rang. Smoke. Finally. "Corinne?" I teared up when he said my name and it was difficult to talk. "What's wrong?" he said.

I stumbled through a play-by-play as I wandered around the house.

"Oh, my darling. I'm so sorry I wasn't there for you. And Queenie. Poor thing. She'll be okay, but what about you? Holding up all right?"

"Pretty much, and not to worry. Really. I think it made John Carl feel good to help us. Queenie will be fine. With a few battle wounds."

"It was a stroke of luck you had a sidearm with you," he said.

"Not luck. It was you who insisted I carry it when I go on runs. That likely saved Queenie, so thank you. If I would've had to go back to the house for my gun, it probably would have been too late." The thought choked me up again.

"If I didn't have to follow up on a lead I got in that interview, I'd come home," he said.

"I know that. I'm going to take that run now, work off some tension."

"Sounds like a plan, little lady. I love you."

"You, too."

We disconnected and I headed to the laundry room next to the kitchen. I laid my holstered gun on the counter and took off the bloodied clothes. *Man alive.* I treated the spots with stain remover, threw the clothes in the washer to soak in cold water and detergent, and headed into the adjoining half-bath where I washed away any leftover traces of blood.

I wanted to shut off the coyote attack video that played in my mind again, as it had a hundred times already. From the time I heard the growls and cries, to the first then the second shot that killed the coyote, to my frantic attempts and actions after that. It was difficult to believe only two hours had passed.

I had experienced grave fear many times in my life. Like when someone I cared about or was responsible for was in danger. Or when my own life was on the line. Each situation, each occurrence, was unique and called for a different response. Yet the end goal was the same: to save lives.

I was trained to mitigate critical incidents for the best outcome possible. Of course, that wasn't always the case. Incidents that had ended in tragedy would haunt me forever. But with professional help and therapy, I was able to continue to serve in my career.

I picked up my Smith & Wesson from the laundry room, changed into clean clothes, clipped on the holster, and took off. The temperature was in the mid-sixties with a whisper of a breeze. The sun's rays made it feel ten degrees warmer. I walked down my driveway then fell into a gentle jog for a half mile past Gramps' house. After John Carl told Gramps about Queenie, when the pain of the attack had eased, I would pay him a visit. I picked up my pace and turned west when I reached County Road 35.

As I neared Smoke's driveway, I stopped and sent him a text. *I'm by your house. Should I check on Rex?* He responded in seconds. *I was home at noon and he's good for the next hour. Thanks.* Good news times two. Rex was fine, and Smoke would be over after he picked up Rex in an hour or so.

I ran another half mile then turned around for the trip home. A white Ford F-150 with a back bed cover passed me, pulled over to the shoulder about a hundred feet from me, and stopped. I had seen the same truck minutes before headed the opposite direction. Someone I knew? I slowed down and my heart speeded up.

When Dr. Watts climbed out of his vehicle, I didn't know if I should feel relieved or alarmed. Had something happened to Queenie? Did I miss the call? He stopped and smiled at me when we were about six feet apart. That allayed my fears somewhat. "Ms. Aleckson, um, I hope I didn't scare you stopping like this."

"It's fine. Is Queenie okay?"

"Yes, um, she is. When I saw you, I thought you would like an update on her condition."

I nodded and waited.

"The sedation is doing its job and she has been sleeping well. We put a cotton recovery suit on her—much more comfortable than a cone around her neck—to keep her from biting at her stitches. We could also try an inflatable collar if you'd rather."

"What's the recovery suit like?" I asked.

"Actually, I have a photo of her in it. It will go in her file." Dr. Watts pulled out his phone, found the picture, and held it up. It looked like a close-fitting body sweater.

"I like it, a much better alternative than those cones. Dogs don't seem to care much for them," I said.

"I never did either, but sometimes cones are the best and necessary choice, like when a dog has eye surgery."

I managed a smile. "I'm glad Queenie can wear the recovery suit instead. Thanks for trying it out on her." I felt a bit chilled after I'd worked up a sweat then stopped. Even with the warm sun. "Well, I better shove off, finish my run."

"Oh. Of course. Unless, um, I can give you a ride home."

I shook my head. "Thanks, anyway. Running is a good stress reliever."

"I, ah, like to exercise, too, so I know what you mean. You went through a scary time with Queenie. I hope you know that if you need anything, we'll do whatever we can to help."

"I appreciate that," I said to be polite. He was being kind, but if I needed that kind of help, I would call my therapist and not Queenie's veterinarian. No offense, Dr. Watts.

His lips curled up slightly and he nodded but made no attempt to move. I lifted my hand in a goodbye wave and took off at too fast a pace. I felt an urgency to put some distance between the good doctor and myself. It made me wonder why. About an eighth mile down the road my lungs begged for more oxygen than I could pull in at that speed. I started to pant and slowed to a realistic stride. One I could maintain for the distance.

Dr. Watts's truck drove past me then turned around in the next driveway. He waved as he passed by again. When he had stopped to talk to me his face brightened, and his pupils dilated when he looked at me. Signs he found me attractive and that made me uneasy.

Something else about the doctor concerned me and I couldn't put my finger on it, pinpoint it. He had an odd duck thing going on. Did he not pick up on social cues, or did he choose to ignore them? Was he eccentric by nature, or was there something secret about himself he kept hidden?

When I got home, I showered and changed into sweatpants and a t-shirt, the third outfit for the day. I paced around the house, too wired to sit still. I hadn't told Rebecca about Queenie and wondered how to break the news to her.

She and her now sister Tina had gone with me to pick up Queenie after she was weaned.

Before her grandmother's arrest, Rebecca had lived on a farm with her and some cats. I knew she missed that part of her old life. The day we picked up Queenie, Rebecca and Tina had a blast. They ran around the farm and played with the puppies. We all agreed Queenie was the best choice, the smallest, cutest, and most energetic one in the litter.

I sent Rebecca a text. *Hope all is well. I love you and remember I am here for you whenever you need me.* I didn't mention Queenie's injuries.

A minute later I got her reply. *Thanks.*

My phone buzzed. I pulled it from my pocket and hoped it was spam so I could ignore it. Nope, my mother. "Hi, Mom."

"Oh, Corinne, I'm *so* sorry. I can't tell you how much."

The emotion in her voice filled my heart with sadness and my eyes with tears. "Thank you. I know you are. The good news is that Queenie will be fine."

"I'm relieved, glad to hear that. John Carl told us they're keeping her overnight at the clinic. The right thing to do, I'm sure. Corinne, how about I bring over some supper?"

"Thanks, but we have leftovers in the fridge. Plus, I need a little more time alone to process what happened, to debrief."

"I understand. A coyote, oh my. Remember to eat something nutritious, with protein. You'll feel better, and it'll help you sleep tonight. I love you, dear." She had been a fierce protector all my life. Of my personal life that is. When it came to my professional life, it was my turn to protect her. From too much information, too many details.

"I love you, too," I said.

"Bye for now."

I hung up and marveled that Mother had given up on the meal delivery offer without protest. She would suffer along with me through Queenie's plight. "It's just about impossible for a mother to be happy if her child is miserable," she had told me many times. The most notable time I witnessed that was when John Carl's marriage crumbled. The whole family was sad, but Mother's sorrow matched John Carl's. When he moved from Denver back home to Oak Lea, our family cheered, and Mother was ecstatic.

I contemplated whether to check on the dead coyote, but the memory of the attack gave me chills. It was too soon to return to the scene alone. I wandered around some more and wondered when Smoke would be home.

Home. The decision loomed about our permanent living arrangements after we officially tied the knot. We each owned a house. Smoke lived on a forty-acre wooded piece of property, complete with a private lake and duck slough. He built a log home fifty feet from the lake and enjoyed seasonal evenings on his dock, or in his boat, as he cast for fish. It was fun for Smoke when they bit. When they didn't, he relaxed on his dock chair or boat seat.

I built my house, a one-and-a-half story, on the twenty acres Grandpa and Grandma Aleckson gifted me. The house sat on a small hilltop that overlooked fields and pastures, with a wooded area on the back line. From there, the land sloped down to a small, clean lake at the bottom with a public access on the opposite side.

A farmer had deeded that, and a dirt road to it, to give others the opportunity to fish in the lake. It wasn't widely known outside the area, so it was rare to have more than a handful of people there, even in the height of fishing seasons.

In the winter no full-time houses sat on the ice, but I would see an occasional portable one. On warmer days, people sat on chairs holding a line through a hole in the ice.

I loved living in the same neighborhood I had grown up in, where John Carl and I played and explored, and four family members still lived. Smoke and I were at home in either place. Both settings were picturesque, each held their own distinct beauty.

Smoke's log home was more unique, reminiscent of a small-scale ski lodge. What I didn't like about his house was it sat on lower ground than the county road, and the woods between blocked a view of the road. Rex alerted when a vehicle came down the driveway, but a few times people had approached on foot and Rex hadn't heard them.

Smoke and I couldn't keep going back and forth between our houses forever. We needed to share one, create a life together we would love and feel comfortable in.

The sun was about to disappear beneath the western horizon when I heard the overhead garage door open. Smoke and Rex came into the kitchen a minute later. Rex ran off, no doubt to search for Queenie. Smoke wrapped me in his arms like he would never let go. My tightly held tension lifted, and my body relaxed. He noticed my response and eased his grip, slid his hands down my arms, took my hands in his then stepped back and studied my face.

He leaned in for a light peck then said, "You had a tough day."

I nodded. "It really caught me off guard. And the whole thing keeps running over and over in my mind. If I could just shut it off before I go crazy."

"I know that feeling." He rubbed my arms. "How could you expect a coyote attack? It's rare for them to go after dogs near their own size. That said, there are hundreds of coyote attacks reports on pets and the owners trying to rescue them. Or worse yet, small children."

"Awful."

Rex started to bark, and I followed Smoke into the living room to check on him. He stood in front of the glass patio doors and barked away. "It's okay, boy. You wonder where Queenie is, don't you?" Smoke said.

I petted Rex. "You want to go out and look for her, but not a good idea with that attacker's body lying out there in the woods. Too gross for you to get at."

"You think the coyote is still there? How about I go take a look-see?" he offered.

"It would make me feel better, knowing one way or the other. I'll grab my mag light and go with you."

We left Rex in the house and trekked to the crime scene. The air had cooled to around fifty degrees after the sun set and added to the chill I felt when we reached our destination. It was still light enough to see evidence on the disturbed ground, the broken twigs and flattened brush from the tussle, and the spot where the coyote had fallen dead. Its body was gone. Smoke flashed the light around the general area, and I didn't spot any signs of blood on the ground either.

"Could be another coyote took it home to eat," Smoke said.

"And something else cleaned up the leftovers?" I said.

"A good assumption. You can rest easier now that it's gone."

"Yeah, I won't have to make John Carl bury it."

"He offered to bury it?"

"No. I just had him going for a minute thinking he'd have to."

He put his arm around my shoulder. "The way you tease your brother."

"He's so serious, I need to shake things up here and there."

"My brothers and I just beat each other up instead."

12

Smoke had scheduled a meeting in the sheriff's conference room with deputies Amanda Zubinski, Vincent Weber, Luke Andrews from the drug task force, and me. Andrews looked like he'd lived on the streets for an extended time period. Stringy, oily light brown hair, dark circles under his eyes, and baggy clothes he must have pulled from a dirty clothes basket. What sealed his authentic druggie look was a missing front tooth. It was knocked out when he took a hockey stick blow. Luke wore a partial plate, but when he was in the drug seeker world, he took it out.

"You ready to join the team?" Luke said.

Ready, or not. His eyes landed on me like he had heard my thoughts.

"You all know I've had this assignment for almost two years, and I'm on the brink of aging out, so to speak. Word is getting around that I'm a snitch. Not a good thing, any way you look at it."

"Word is out on you, huh?" Weber said.

"One of my informants told me some guys started to question it after we took down that meth operation last month. You know it was a long investigation. Ended up arresting six suspects. Four males, two females. And me. Of course, I never made it to jail, got dropped off a minute later. They kept the guys in separate cell blocks, but after they all bailed out, one of them wondered what in the hell happened to me and asked a corrections officer. He knew what to say to protect me, told him I had a warrant in another county, so they had picked me up."

"Nice to know we can rely on our officers to tell the made-up truth, and nothing but the made-up truth," Weber said.

That got some chuckles from the group. Zubinski elbowed him, per her frequent response to his quips. I had yet to figure out their relationship status. They were good friends and hung out together a lot, but neither was inclined to admit they were a couple. Even though they acted like an old married one half the time.

Andrews went on, "At any rate, there's enough suspicion out there and I can't be bumping into guys who might finger me. Plus, it's time. I'm burning out. I cannot tell you how many hundreds of times I've asked myself, 'Do I hate to love this stint, or do I love to hate it?' Depends on the day."

Different concepts to think about.

Weber nodded. "Yeah well, me and Mandy had that short gig as a drug-buying couple when Coop flew the coop a couple years back." Cooper was on the drug task force when he left Winnebago County for a city police job.

"Sure, not long after I was assigned here." Andrews looked at me. "And you were on the task force before that, right Sergeant?"

"I was."

"Still got your same getup?" Weber asked.

"Yep. In a box somewhere." I had stuffed it in the back of a closet with the hope I would never have to wear the disguise again, even to a costume party. If I threw the clothes, wigs, and accessories away, per Murphy's law, I would need them again. For sure. I'd kept them, and now had less faith in Murphy's law.

"The sergeant can pull off a decent grunge look," Smoke said.

"Yeah, who'd a thunk?" Weber again.

"How about you, Vince?" I asked.

"I still got that stupid wig that makes me look stupid," he said.

"Not that stupid, just less bald," Zubinski put in.

I laughed. Weber had a shaved head all the years I'd known him. "And you, Mandy? The blonde bombshell again?" I said with a grin.

She smiled back. "Not sure about bombshell part, but yes to the blonde part." Her natural shade was a striking auburn. Blonde was a decided difference.

Smoke tapped his pen. "Getting yourselves into the right mindset for the drug task force is an important part of the process. Like what you do every day when you put on your uniform and gear."

We all nodded or shrugged.

"Yeah well, at least the sergeant here has some acting experience," Weber said.

I shook my head and laughed. "Me singing and dancing in high school musical productions is a little bit different than acting like a druggie desperate for her next fix."

"Yeah, but you learned to be a different person when you were up on that stage," Weber said.

"Okay, I'll give you that," I said.

Unknowns sprung up every day in our world. A sudden threat dropped from nowhere at times. Not that I believed a drug buy posed greater danger than a domestic assault call, or a shots fired call, but it pushed me further out of my comfort zone.

Smoke picked up after the digression, "What we got is two drug dealers who died from the fatal combo of cocaine and carfentanil. Griffen Houser and Tad Michels. Evidence indicates each one was alone when he snorted his final dose. That begs the question, where did they get the drugs, who supplied them? We need to nail that down, find the answer a-sap." He stood, walked to the whiteboard, picked up a black dry erase marker, pulled off the cap, then jotted key information on the board as he spoke.

"Griffen Houser lived in an older farmhouse with his wife in Emerald Lake Township. No kids. She had the tax paying job as a server at Perkins. Their pole shed served as a garage, where they parked their vehicles. Big shock when she pulled in after work that Sunday afternoon and found his body on the ground in front of his car. Powder traces on the hood of his old Chevy. The sniffing straw was next to his body.

"Wife believed he was more of a dealer than a user. Houser kept his business dealings on the downlow, never went into details with his wife, and she didn't ask questions. Had no idea who he bought drugs from or sold drugs to. Never joined him at any parties he went to. She wanted no part of that life. Stayed with him because she loved him. But thought about leaving him a dozen times. He told her he looked at his illegal operation as a way to help people in need." Smoke closed with a shake of his head.

"What kind of crazy logic is that?" Weber said.

"A crazy way to justify his actions to his wife. I would venture to say the truth was it supported his habit and gave him spending money. A common story," I said.

"Yeah," Weber said.

Smoke jotted more info on the board. "Tad Michels lived in an Emerald Lake townhouse, about five miles from Houser. His sometimes girlfriend found him two days after he died. The memory, how he looked and how he smelled will follow her to her grave. Truth be told, it will follow me to mine.

"Houser and Michels knew each other, according to their significant others and phone records. And I think it's a given they turned up at the same party now and then. We learned they had phone calls from three of the same numbers, unknown persons. No doubt burner phones."

"Yeah, good old burners to drive us bananas," Weber said.

Smoke continued, "No doubt. Their call histories showed that in the last year, Houser called Michels three times and Michels called Houser once. Not many phone conversations between them unless they utilized burner phones besides. I think it's safe to say that one did not sell the drug combo to the other. Unless Michels sold the stuff to Houser and was so guilt ridden when he died that he killed himself," Smoke said.

"Michels would have had to be there when it happened. Otherwise, how would he know for sure?" Andrews said.

"Correct, and the chance that scenario happened is slim to none." Smoke drew some bullet points on the board, followed by questions he had.

"Did the dealer know the cocaine was laced with carfentanil?

"Does the fact that Houser and Michels knew each other mean anything to the supplier? Chances are, however, a lot of dealers in the county know each other.

"Did someone target them, or was it happenstance?

"They both lived in the same area. Was that a factor, or not?"

Andrews pointed at the board. "Good questions and ones your new team here will work on, find the answers to."

Smoked nodded. "Yep. Another thing, and this may be key to getting those answers. One of Corky's informants told her that word on the street is there's a new supplier in the county."

"I hadn't heard that. Not surprising, since I have limited contact with my peeps," Andrews said.

"He allegedly brings the stuff directly from Chicago to Winnebago County. Not what the usual suspects around the county do," Smoke said.

"That's true. Dealers I know get their stuff in the Twin Cities and sell it here. Or get it from meth labs right here in the county," Andrews said.

Smoke puffed out a breath. "With the growing drug crisis we got, last thing we need is a large-scale supplier setting up shop in Winnebago County. That brings another scenario to mind. We got two dead dealers in a week's time, makes me wonder if he's deliberating eliminating his competition." He wrote the last four words as a question.

"Geez, Detective, your questions and scenarios are starting to make my head spin," Weber said.

Andrews scratched his beard. "Hmm. So Detective, you mean he is trying to scare others into buying directly from him, or else?" Andrews said.

"One possibility, it's happened before. Houser and Michels were small scale as far as dealers go, the reason they flew under our radar for so long. In fact, after Michels ODd a few months back, it sounded like he had a Come-to-Jesus-epiphany moment, said he'd cleaned up his act, quit dealing," Smoke said.

"And that's when—and how—we found out he'd gone back to dealing. He wouldn't say how long he had been at it. He was off probation and off the grid for over a year. That much we know," I said.

"One of those bad apples ya haven't seen in a while that bobs up to the surface every so often, reminds ya he's still around," Weber said.

For me, it was like radio waves in the universe. When a violator came to mind, when I wondered how he or she was, nine times out of ten that person would appear. Or I would hear something about him or her. And not always in a good way.

"Michels told us he attended NA meetings twice a week and they'd kept him on the straight and narrow for months. After we revived him with naloxone, he was grateful, gave the poor excuse he had a bad week, caved in for one last high. I believe he'd convinced himself it would be, too. Like too many addicts. Michels would still be alive if he hadn't given in to another 'last high.' Nobody with him to call nine-one-one," I said.

"Ah geez, it gave him three whole more months to live until he died from the next overdose," Weber said.

"Have you counted how many times someone you've arrested tells you, 'I learned my lesson, I will never do that again.' And then he gets arrested again. And again, and again," Zubinski said.

"I can't count that high." Weber raised his eyebrows.

"Vincent." It was my turn to elbow him.

Smoke shook his head and drew his eyebrows together. "When addicts love their drug of choice more than anything else in the world, when the need is that strong, they can be clean for months, years, and it's still a daily fight."

"Sometimes it's an hourly fight, or a hundred times an hour, I've been told," Andrews said.

"How sad is that?" Zubinski said.

"A girl I knew who got hooked on meth said the first time she tried it was like when she was a kid and got that one Christmas gift she really wanted, but never thought she would get because it was expensive, and her parents didn't have extra money. When she opened the gift and saw it was what she had wanted forever, it was magical. Her elation, her excitement gave her a high that went on for hours.

"And the first time she used meth, that's how it was. Like getting that one magical gift, only better. And every time she used after that she craved the same high she got the first time. Never happened, but she kept trying until nothing was left of her. She was twenty-four and looked fifty, weighed maybe sixty pounds, sores all over her face and body, very few teeth. I saw her shortly before she died and went home and cried," I said.

"Is anyone else feeling depressed here?" Zubinski asked.

"Sorry, Mandy," I said.

She shrugged. "Some parts of this job are harder than others. I've been feeling extra emotional about the kid we lost to heroin six months ago."

"Ah geez, Mandy, you were practically in spitting distance from her house when you took the call, got there in a minute tops, gave her the nose spray then did CPR till the EMTs got there," Weber said.

Smoke nodded. "The doc said she was most likely dead a while before the nine-one-one call came in. It was too late for the naloxone to wake her up, or the life-saving efforts to bring her back."

Zubinski pulled a wallet-size photo from her breast pocket and held it up. A bright smile shone on the dark-haired beauty's face. "I got this in the mail yesterday from her parents. And a note with it that said, 'Cara would have been eighteen today. Here is a picture from her last birthday. Please remember her this way. We want to thank you for all you did.'"

"No wonder you feel like you do, Mandy. But wow, the fact that her parents care that much and felt the need to send you her photo and a note says a lot," I said.

"It does, and I'll carry this with me for a long time." She put the photo back in her pocket.

"Hey, like the sergeant here who keeps victims' photos with her, too," Weber said.

"Yep. Cara wasn't a victim in a case we were working, but she was a victim," Zubinski said.

The room went quiet until Smoke cleared his throat and broke the silence. We all had raw emotions to come to grips with. "How about we take five. Use the facilities, grab a beverage," he said.

On the way out, I put my arm around Zubinski and squeezed gently. She lifted her eyebrows and gave me a nod in return. We had a rough time when she started with the sheriff's office but had smoothed things out over time. She'd had a crush on Smoke and for some reason started the rumor that he and I were lovers. Years before we were.

I did my best to avoid her but was polite and tried to be inclusive when we worked together on an assignment. A few critical incidents we shared changed that, and our relationship took a dramatic one-eighty. Life or death crises can make or break a bond. In our case, they made it and strengthened it besides. I wasn't as close to Mandy as some of the other deputies, like Vince Weber, but I respected her and had grown to like her a lot.

I went into the squad room and saw reports in my inbox that needed review. As I picked up the top one, a text message from John Carl came through. *Queenie is ready. On my way to pick her up, will take her to your house.*

A feeling of relief rushed through me. I replied, *Thanks, bro. Catch you later.* Then turned my focus back to the report. I read it, and the next one, and put them in the next-in-command's box. Smoke popped his head into the squad room and pointed his thumb the conference room direction. I replaced the unread reports then trailed behind him to where the others waited, seated at the table.

Andrews held up a phone with a skull face on its black cover case. His undercover cell. "I'll let my confidential sources know I'm leaving the task force and they can expect to hear from at least one of you in the next day or so. You can tell them Butch told you to call. I'll forward their contact info to your new cell phones."

"Butch, huh? Well geez, since I kinda look like a bulldog, I'll go with that alias. Bulldog," Weber said.

"I like Bulldog, but no, you do not look like one, Vince." Andrews turned to Mandy and me. "Corky, Mandy, I think you could go by your own nicknames if you want."

"Sounds like a plan to me," Smoke said.

Zubinski and I looked at each other and shrugged.

A plastic shopping bag sat on the table in front of Andrews. He reached in and pulled out three cell phones. They had post-it notes stuck to them with our individual names on each and he handed them over. Personal cell, work cell, drug work cell. Check. Should I buy a distinctive case to put the new one in? One outside my normal character or usual choice?

"Your phones have the Bluetooth recording capability. The number to call is in your contact list as Pete, and on the post-it note. Here are your microphones. Hide them as close to your mouth as you can. In the brim of a cap, your wig." He passed them out.

Smoke pulled out a stack of bills and divided them up. "Five hundred each to start. If your informant does a buy for you, give him a hundred for an ounce of meth, one fifty to two hundred for an ounce of coke."

Smoke and Andrews led the charge to formulate a plan and the rest of us followed along. They spelled it out. Sometimes we would go solo with a confidential informant, other times we would pair up with another deputy. Our purpose, our goal, was to flush out the mysterious dealer, find out who was selling fatal drug combinations that caused the two dealers' deaths.

13

When I got home, John Carl was on the couch in the living room with a book in his hand. Queenie was wrapped in her recovery suit at rest by his feet on the blanket-covered rug. I dropped down beside her and rested my head on her back, careful to stay clear from her injuries. Her eyes fluttered open for a few seconds then closed again.

"She's been okay for you, John Carl?"

"Yep, resting the whole time. The vet sent along a sedative, and I got her to take a dose a half hour ago. I wrote the time on a notepad and put it next to the bottle on the kitchen counter. Doctor Watts said it would be good to give her another dose at bedtime to help her sleep. Tomorrow, if she gets agitated, try half a dose, see if that helps. And any questions, call the clinic. Watts also gave me his cell phone number if you need to reach him. It's on the notepad, too," he said.

I stood up, leaned over, and gave him a hug. "Thank you, John Carl."

"You're welcome. It's been nice having another English Setter in the family, and Queenie's a good dog." Our Gramps had one on the farm as far back as we remembered, until about eleven years before. John Carl was ten months older than me, and we had a long list of shared memories.

"Why don't you get a setter? Queenie can use another friend besides Rex."

He shrugged. "Maybe. I've been thinking it's too bad Rex wasn't here when that coyote showed up. He must be twenty-five pounds heavier than the coyote was and could have taken it down," he said.

"It wouldn't have attacked if Rex was with her."

"That's true. A lone coyote wouldn't have attacked two dogs in the first place, especially one Rex's size."

"I have to admit the whole thing has got me pretty spooked. I'll be afraid to let Queenie run freely, even knowing the odds that it would happen again are about a gazillion to one. And don't check my statistics," I said.

"I won't." But I knew he would. He was a knowledge nerd to the core.

"I have a work assignment tomorrow afternoon, into the evening. Might you be available for doggie duty?" I asked.

He thought for a moment. "Sara and I are cooking dinner at my house, so no problem." Sara had been my best girlfriend for over twelve years, and John Carl's fiancée for a few months.

"You sure?"

"Sure," he said.

"I'll bring her over around two. And thank you." I waved my hand in front of me like a fan. "You're welcome to stay,

John Carl. But I need to shed my uniform. I can't tell you how good it feels to lose twenty pounds when I get off work."

He leaned his head a tad to the side. "That's what your duty belt weighs?"

"Or more, and you can look that one up," I said.

"I didn't realize it was that heavy."

"You get used to it. It doesn't bother me, not as much as my Kevlar vest does. Especially in summer."

"In your line of work, everything you carry is important. You've had things happen." Things had happened, all right.

"True." Another consideration about undercover work. I would be without most of my tools.

"I'll take off then," he said.

"All righty. And think about it. A dog might be good for you."

"We'll see," he said on his way out.

I knelt beside Queenie and checked her breathing. It was regular and even, so I went upstairs, lost twenty some pounds then changed into jeans and a light pullover sweatshirt. As much as a run would have lifted my spirits, I couldn't leave Queenie alone, even for a short time.

"Well, no time like the present." I went to the closet in the upstairs hallway where my druggie get-up was stored, pulled tubs from the first shelf, and set them on the floor to access the one at the back. When I picked up the tub, it felt heavier than I knew it was. Perception was an odd thing at times. I replaced the other tubs then carried the one I needed to my room and set it on the bed.

As I lifted the lid, I instinctively held my breath against any unpleasant smells. But when I inhaled, I didn't detect any offensive odors. Surprise. The clothes were clean when I packed them, but somehow thought a pungent marijuana odor might have woven its way into the fibers of the jeans and shirts and jacket. I shook the clothes out one by one and laid them on the bed.

The plastic bag with the enclosed long brunette wig was next. I untwisted the tie and when it opened, I caught a mild stench, a combination of hair, elastic cap, and a musty odor. I would hang it outside to absorb the fresh autumn air scent.

Low top black boots with a leather strap across the tops and clunky three-inch heels sat next to the bag filled with chains and jewelry at the bottom. What the real life Corky would only wear in costume or undercover.

The doorbell's ding-dong-ding startled me. It was rare that anyone used it. My family members and closest friend had keys and others sent me a text when they stopped by, to see if I was home. Every so often a package was delivered, but nothing was on order. I ran down the steps and glanced out the front window. A white Ford F-150 sat in the driveway and Dr. Watts himself was at the door. He held Queenie's collar and leash in his hand.

I released the lock and opened the door. Watts smiled as he held up the items. "We, um, forgot to send these with your brother."

"I hadn't even noticed they were missing. Thank you, I surely could have picked them up."

"No, it ah, was our mistake, and I'm glad to drop them off. How is Queenie?" he asked.

"She's been pretty zonked out since I got home from work. My brother gave her a sedative."

He nodded. "Would it be all right if I took a quick look? Checked on her?"

"Please do. Come in." I pointed at the back of the couch. "She's on the blanket on the other side."

When he walked past me his damp hair and clean fresh scent told me he had showered a short time before. I hoped it was because he had attended to sick or injured animals and needed to clean up or was on his way to meet someone. Not because he wanted to impress me. Watts made his way around the couch. Queenie was lying on her uninjured side.

The doctor bent over and placed a hand on her stomach, near her heart. "Nice. Strong, steady beat. Very good." He stood and turned toward me. "Another day of quiet rest will go a long way in her healing process, help her make a complete recovery. With, ah, a few scars, that is."

"I'll do my best to keep her quiet. We don't have a very wild household here," I said.

He nodded, walked over to the glass doors, lifted his arm, and pointed toward the back yard. "Where did the coyote find Queenie, out in the field, or in the woods?"

"The woods. Queenie likes to run back there, sniff the ground, chase squirrels and chipmunks."

"Did you happen to check on the coyote's remains?"

"We went back there last night, and nothing was left of it, so John Carl dodged that bullet," I said.

He turned around with his eyebrows drawn together. "What do you mean?"

"I told him he'd have to bury the coyote if the critters didn't eat it first. It was more of a joke, anyway. I wouldn't have made my brother bury it. I guess I'm better at things like that than he is."

Watts nodded about six times, like he needed to process what I had said. Why had I told him that dumb tidbit anyway?

Nervous chatter sometimes popped out of my mouth in uneasy social situations. Dr. Watts had brought me to that state. Again.

"Well, thank you for dropping off Queenie's things." Would he take that as his hint to leave?

"You're welcome. Well, um, we will see Queenie next week for her check-up, look at her stitches, check on her healing progress. You can call the office to set up an appointment," he said.

"Will do." I walked to the front door and Watts followed. "Enjoy the evening," I said.

"You, too." And out the door he went.

I slid the deadbolt over then turned and leaned my body against the door. He made me want to shout, "No more surprise visits. You need to keep your distance." It was the way he fixed his eyes on me, like he needed to memorize what I looked like so he could paint my portrait. Plus, he stood too close to me, inches closer than Minnesota social norm.

If Dr. Watts had a crush on me, I needed to nip that in the bud. The problem was I couldn't call him up and say, "I'm engaged so don't get any ideas." Maybe he was awkward around women, wasn't sure how to interact. He was an animal doctor, not a people doctor after all.

As I made my way back to the bed stacked with my undercover clothes, I determined the best course of action was to bring Smoke with me to Queenie's next appointment, introduce him to Dr. Watts as my fiancé. It would be out in the open, in case. Potential future awkward moments would be averted. After that, I would transfer Queenie's care to another veterinary clinic. Decision made.

I took off my jeans and pullover and slipped into the tight black jeans with a dozen horizontal slits across the thigh area, a black fishnet long-sleeved top, and an acid washed gray t-shirt with a Pearl Jam logo front and center. Then stepped into the clunky boots. The only thing I liked about them was the three-inch height gain. I would add jewelry and chains for the real deal, but the clothes were enough for now.

"Corky!" Smoke called from the lower level. I hadn't heard the garage door open.

"Upstairs. Queenie is by the couch," I called back and navigated my way down the steps as best I could with the clunkers.

"Hey," I said.

Smoke smiled. "Rex found Queenie in about a second and took up guard duty next to her on the blanket." He greeted me with a sweet kiss. "You look like the queen of grunge."

"I have a date tomorrow night and needed to figure out my wardrobe," I said.

"Date, huh? A grunge fest?"

"Ha. It's a buy with Mac to wiggle my way in with dealers, start making contacts."

"What a fun way to spend a Saturday," he said.

"Yeah. Hey, whose idea was it to include me on the task force?"

"With the Bluetooth recording your every movement, and backup close by, I gotta say it makes me less jittery."

"Me, too. John Carl and Sara offered to take Queenie for the evening, so that's a load off my mind," I said.

"Good. Any plans for supper?"

"Gosh, I hadn't thought that far." I glanced at the pendulum clock on the wall. Five fifty-six.

"I would have suggested dinner out, but with Queenie needing care, we'll find something here. There's bound to be something tasty in the freezer," Smoke said.

"I think we have a few choices left."

We checked the frozen dishes and agreed on baked ziti in a marinara sauce.

"I'll go slip into something more comfortable," I said and left Smoke to thaw and heat it in the microwave while I changed back into Corky clothes.

When I returned the ziti was still heating. I got out French bread and a salad mix purchased a few days before.

When the meal was ready, we settled at the table to eat.

"So. Doctor Watts stopped by to drop off Queenie's collar and leash, and I gotta say he sends off weird vibes. Intense ones."

"I agree that he is a different animal. No pun intended."

I groaned then smiled. "Uh huh."

Smoke swallowed a bite of crusty bread. "When I interviewed him last year, he was in genuine denial. Could not come to grips with his wife's cause of death, that she had a drug problem. Total disbelief. He had a busy practice, put in long hours, but it makes you wonder.

"All I could figure is she must have been one hell of an actress. I think he saw what he wanted to see. His beautiful wife healthy again, fully recovered. He had never heard her on suspicious phone calls, hadn't checked her computer search engines. Didn't think he had reason to.

"And it's a big mystery how she made contacts with dealers. Somebody got her introduced somehow. But nothing on her phone. No deleted calls or text messages."

"Burner phones," I said.

"No doubt. Maybe she used them once then dropped 'em in garbage cans or threw 'em in a swamp or some other disposal site along the way."

I shook my head. "She was clever, unfortunately, for her and her husband. How long do you figure she lived her secret life before her death?"

"Four months, by my estimates after conversations with the doctors who refused to write her more opioid scripts. Watts was in the dark about that, too."

"Smoke, you said Watts sees what he wants to see. I wonder if he is ready to move on and just noticed me because I kinda resemble his wife."

Smoke leaned forward and put his hand on mine. "Could be, and I don't like that thought at all. You think he has designs on you, engaged woman though you be?"

"I'm not sure. What I do know is there isn't another man on this planet you need to be jealous of. Because I only have *designs* on you."

He stood, moved in behind me, and nibbled on my neck. "Prove it."

"With pleasure. Meet me in the bedroom after I check on Queenie."

Half an hour later, we lay on our sides, our faces inches apart, and our hands clasped. "You proved an important point, all right," he said.

"There is no doubt."

Smoke kissed me until Rex barked from downstairs. "I better check, in case something's up with Queenie." He pulled on jeans and headed downstairs.

"I'll take a quick shower and be right down." I was in and out and dressed in no time flat.

Smoke sat on the couch, talking to Queenie and Rex. Queenie didn't appear to be in any discomfort as Rex licked her face. I took a seat next to Smoke and gently scratched Queenie's neck. "Hey, girl. You woke up. Your friend Rex is happy to see you. You look really good, all things considered."

"That's a slick wrap they put her in," he said.

"I think so, too. It's a recovery suit and she can't scratch or bite her stitches. I'll get her food and water." I retrieved her dishes with fresh food and water. She got to her feet, lapped up some water, took a few bites of food, then dropped down again on the blanket.

"Not hungry, Queenie?" Smoke said.

"She's on meds to keep her calm and sleepy today. More tired than hungry."

Smoke and I chatted and watched the dogs until my phone rang at eight thirteen p.m. It was Rebecca. "Hi, Rebecca. How are you?"

"Not too good, Sergeant Corky."

My muscles tightened and I stood up. "What's up?" I somehow kept my voice even.

"Tina and I had to leave a party, so we walked to the Holiday station. Mom and Dad are out for their anniversary dinner, and we didn't want to like bother them. Justin isn't answering. Do you think you can come and get us?"

Not the time to press for details. "I'll be there in about eight minutes. Hang tight." We disconnected.

Smoke rose, too. "What?"

"All I know is something happened to make Rebecca and Tina walk away from a party. They're at Holiday. Jean and

Dale are out, so I need to pick up the girls." I gave him a quick peck, jogged to the kitchen, grabbed my purse from its hook, and was on my way to Holiday in the GTO.

14

The girls stood outside by the tire air pumps. Neither was happy, evidenced by the creases between their eyes. Rebecca had a double frown mark and Tina's was a single line. I pulled up to the curb, got out, but left the door open. When I smiled, they managed small ones in return. I reached in and pushed the bucket seat forward. "Climb in and I will be your chauffeur."

Tina climbed in first and I gave Rebecca a pat on the back as she got in. When we were buckled in, I said, "So what happened?"

"A bunch of us were at Catelyn's down in the rec room playing pool, having fun, and then like a few kids started vaping," Rebecca said.

"It's a walkout basement, so mostly they were in the back yard, but some came in with the stuff," Tina said.

"Where were her parents?" I asked.

"Upstairs and didn't know about it. We don't think," Rebecca said.

"Who was there?" They were silent for a minute, so I added, "Emmy? Her boyfriend Wyatt?"

"Yeah, but we kinda stayed away from them. Like, just because," Rebecca said.

"Were they vaping?"

"Not that we know of. Not that we saw," Tina said.

"What about Catelyn?" I asked.

"We don't think so, but she didn't like kick anybody out," Rebecca said.

"We snuck out the walkout door," Tina said.

"That's when we saw Kelvin," Rebecca said.

My heart rate doubled. "Kelvin? Is he still there?"

"Maybe. It's nice out so a bunch of kids were outside," Rebecca said.

"What's Catelyn's address?" I said.

Rebecca checked her phone. "Two-two-zero Fourth Avenue Northwest."

"I'll swing by there, take a look," I said.

Both girls gasped.

"What if they see us?" Rebecca said.

"We'll make sure they don't," I said.

I backed out and drove the four blocks to the address. It was a two-story house on the corner. "Duck down," I told the girls as I took a right and cruised past to observe the back yard. A sizable group, ten or twelve kids, were gathered. I pulled over at the next block, out of their sight. "What was Kelvin wearing?"

"Um, like jeans and a hoodie with some kinda logo on the back," Rebecca said.

"Color?"

"Gray," Rebecca said.

"And the logo was a man on a horse and said Polo," Tina said.

"Thanks." I phoned 911.

"Winnebago County, is this an emergency?"

"Randy, it's Corky. Can you connect me to an Oak Lea police officer?" The girls groaned from the backseat.

"Sure, Sergeant, here you go."

A few seconds later the officer was on the line. "Officer Raab. Sergeant Aleckson?" he said.

"Hi Jim. I'm here in Oak Lea and drove by a house where it looks like a bunch of underage kids are vaping in the back yard."

"No adults home?"

"Not sure."

"What's the address?" he said.

After I told him I added, "Tell them a concerned adult saw them and reported it. Oh, and Jim? If there is an older kid there, he would be a good one to talk to. Tall, lanky, name's Kelvin, wearing jeans and a gray Polo hoodie. He may be an adult and the one who got the vaping stuff for the kids."

"Good to know. I'll get my partner to meet me there. We'll park down the street, but they'll probably take off in all different directions when they see us."

"Yep. Will you call me later, let me know how it went? You have my number."

"Sure." He disconnected.

We needed to get a bead on Kelvin, lock him up if he was eighteen, or older. If I had my badge and sidearm on me, I could have helped, in an unofficial capacity. If I were alone. Without Rebecca and Tina in the backseat. Or at least hung around and watched the action. I turned to the girls. "They will never have to know you were involved in the call to the police."

"Okay," Rebecca and Tina said as one.

"Hang tight, girls." I left the car and jogged to a spot where I could see into Catelyn's back yard. I counted five girls and four boys but didn't spot a young man with a Polo hoodie among them. Some minutes later I saw Oak Lea Police Officers, Raab and Carter, come around the house from opposite directions. It was a cluster when the officers crashed Catelyn's party. I heard girls scream and saw kids crowd together, but didn't see anyone run away, unless they had escaped into the house.

I went back to the car and looked at the girls crouched down in the backseat. Their pale, frowning faces told me how upset they were. I understood. "Everything will work out fine. The police are breaking up the party."

"We feel so stupid," Rebecca said.

"Don't. You're the smart ones for leaving when you did," I said.

"But what if they figure out that we told on them?" Tina said.

"You didn't. I did. Remember that. I'm the one who called the cops."

"I guess," Rebecca said.

"Okay," Tina agreed.

"Ready to go home?" I started the car.

"Would it be okay if we went to your house instead?" Rebecca said.

"Mom and Dad were going to pick us up at the party at ten, after their date. Justin's out with some guys from his football team and has a midnight curfew," Tina added.

I got the hint they didn't want to be home alone, knew the incident had left them unsettled. Afraid.

"Sure thing. Off to my Blackwood Township country home we go. I'll give Smoke a quick call first." His name topped my favorites list, and I hit the call button.

"Corinne?"

"Hey. Rebecca and Tina are going to spend a little time with us until their parents get home."

"Sounds like a plan. On your way now?"

"Be there in a few," I said, pushed the end button, shifted into drive, and away we went. The girls filled me in on more details.

"We got scared. Rebecca was already in trouble, and this would mean bigger trouble. For both of us," Tina said.

"We didn't know what to do at first, like we wanted to tell Catelyn's parents, but how could we?" Rebecca said.

"I think Catelyn was embarrassed, but she didn't want to be a big tattletale," Tina said.

"She's trying to fit in with some cool kids," Rebecca said.

"When kids came inside and were vaping, I heard her say something to Paddy, like they had to go outside," Tina said.

"We told Catelyn we had to like go so she knew for sure and then we took off," Rebecca said.

"You girls did the right thing. You said older kids were there, like Kelvin who might even be an adult?"

"He was the oldest one there, probably," Rebecca said.

"A few sophomores that I know, and maybe a couple a juniors, but mostly it was us freshman," Tina said.

"Any idea why Catelyn's parents let older kids come?"

"I don't think they knew for sure. A bunch of kids were mostly outside. And some just came in the back door with them," Tina said.

I attempted a casual tone when I said, "Did the parents pop in downstairs at all, see how everyone was doing?"

"They brought pizzas down maybe an hour ago, but that was before a lotta the kids got there," Rebecca said.

Catelyn's parents were no doubt surprised when the cops showed up and broke up the party. Winnebago County had a social host ordinance that held adults in a household liable if they allowed underage kids to drink or smoke on their property.

"Girls, before we get home, I need to tell you Queenie got hurt yesterday and is in what's called a recovery suit. But not to worry because she will heal just fine." I gave them a played down version of the incident.

"Queenie must've been so scared," Rebecca said.

"For sure. She's such a sweet dog. I'm glad she's okay," Tina said.

Rex greeted us when we stepped into the kitchen. The girls giggled when he gave them each a friendly lick. Smoke wore a warm smile. "Good to see you, girls. Come in. I started a fire to take off the evening chill and keep the furnace from running as long as possible."

"Nice, thanks. Would you girls like something to eat, or drink?" I offered.

"I'm good," Tina said.

"Me, too. Where's Queenie?" Rebecca wondered.

"On her now favorite blanket by the couch," Smoke said.

The girls headed into the living room and plopped down beside Queenie. She seemed content when they spoke soothing words and gently petted her. Smoke and I sat in armchairs opposite the couch. We highlighted what happened Catelyn's that prompted Rebecca and Tina to leave the party.

"I'm proud of you girls for getting the heck out of Dodge when you did, not giving in to peer pressure. I speak from experience when I tell you too many kids have ended up in the hospital because they got sick vaping. You know what THC is?" Smoke said.

They both nodded.

"It's like the drug in marijuana," Rebecca said.

"Correct. When there is a high level of THC in the vape, kids don't know it and they're getting poisoned, dropping like flies," he said.

"Eew," Tina said.

Both girls squirmed and shuddered.

"Kids, and adults, too, think that since they're sucking in a vapor instead of smoke that it's better. But it lands lots of people in the hospital with what they call lung injury. Thousands," I said.

"Really?" Rebecca said.

"Some people think smoking cigarettes is gross. But with one vape product, there is as much nicotine in one pod as there is in twenty regular cigarettes. Think about that. Twenty. Another reason why kids get sick, throw up, pass out," I said.

"I can tell you a lot of folks are having a heck of a time quitting. It's a fact that kids get addicted to nicotine much easier than adults do." He clapped his hands together. "Well, that's the end of the lecture. Think about what we said. And tell your friends when they try to talk you into doing something because everyone else is doing it. Prosecutions are *way* up for people caught in possession of THC cartridges. If people continue using those drugs, they will get caught at some point. That's a given," Smoke said.

I slid off the chair, crawled over and gave Rebecca and Tina hugs. "We want to watch you grow up, follow your dreams, make good decisions. Because we love you."

Rebecca smiled. "You, too." Tina nodded.

I glanced up at the clock. "It's nine thirty so you may want to let your folks know where to pick you up."

"I'll text them," Tina said.

Officer Jim Raab phoned me at nine forty-six p.m. I went into the den office to take the call. "Hey, Jim."

"Hey. Long story short. Carter and I crashed the party, collected the names of everyone who was there and who had been there. And confiscated four vape pens. We talked to the Werners and their daughter Catelyn. Parents said when they checked on things, brought food down, nothing suspicious was going on. Catelyn said kids started vaping 'all of a sudden.' That's how she put it, and she didn't know what to do."

"Lots of pressure to fit in when you're fourteen, fifteen. How about Kelvin? Did you catch him?"

"Nobody named Kelvin there. Catelyn said she heard someone call a guy that name before we arrived and saw a tall, skinny guy with a gray hoodie on. His hood was up so she didn't get a good look at him. Didn't see when he and a couple others left," Raab said.

"Kelvin wasn't on her guest list?"

"No. Catelyn's account was that kids she didn't invite showed up with friends she did. No one we talked to admitted knowing Kelvin, so it could be he showed up with kids who had already left. Catelyn gave us their names. The Werners seem like decent people and were upset they didn't know what was going on in their own home. We gave them a verbal warning, no charges, and will talk to the parents of the other kids there, the ones who Catelyn saw vaping. Thanks for alerting us," he said.

"Thank you. We need to track down Kelvin. He was in Oak Lea High School on Tuesday and gave away at least one vape pen to minors," I said.

"I heard about that incident from Casey Dey. We'll do what we can to help, Sergeant," Raab said.

"Appreciate it."

The Brenners arrived at my house a few minutes after ten. They listened to the party story—not the way they hoped their celebration night would end. After Smoke and I offered our congratulations, they thanked us and left with the girls.

"Having teenagers is not always easy," I said.

Smoke raised his eyebrows. "Ya think?"

"What I think is this day has gone on forever. Or is it just me? It still is Friday, right?"

"Long day, longer week. Since I'm on call this weekend, I am ready to turn in. Catch a few winks in case I get called out in the wee hours. Even if I don't."

I put my arms around him. "I think I'll crash on the couch. It'll make me feel better being near Queenie in case she needs anything."

"She has her protector right beside her."

"Her pooch protector. But I can get her a drink or tend to her if she needs something besides moral support."

"I'll give you that."

"I need my pajamas and pillow and blanket," I said.

Smoke and I headed upstairs, prepared for bed, then I tucked him in and kissed him good night. "I love you."

"I love you more than my own life." I felt the same way about him.

We held each other a moment and shared a last kiss. "Sleep well."

15

On Saturday morning I opened my eyes to find two dogs' snoots near my face. Queenie laid her head on my arm, and Rex let out a woof. It took me a second to remember I'd slept on the couch. I rolled toward them and rested my hand on Queenie's head a minute then scratched Rex's neck.

"You look good, Queenie. How do you feel?" She perked up at her name and tipped her head to the side.

Smoke came in with a mug of coffee and the rich aroma filled the room. "Good to see you're back among the living, little lady."

I sat up. "That for me?"

He handed me the mug and took a seat next to me. "The dogs already ate and drank and did their business."

"I can't believe I slept through it all."

"You crashed hard last night. You even snored," he said.

"I did not."

"Next time I'll record you."

"You will not."

He leaned over for a good morning kiss.

"Don't you think Queenie looks better?" I asked.

"A whole lot better. The note says you can give her a pain med if she needs one. But she doesn't act like she's hurting much. Hardly has a limp."

"I think the recovery suit helps a lot. Seems to hold the stitches in place. We'll keep an eye on her, monitor her. She needs to take it easy for a while."

"That's a fact. I'm going to head home, take Rex with me. That will help keep Queenie quieter for the day."

"You don't have to."

"I do, for other reasons, too. To take care of some neglected household duties, pay bills, gear up for later when I hover in the background, make sure you and Mac remain healthy," he said.

The new assignment on the drug task force. "Yeppers, it'll be good to know your team is hovering nearby." I gave him a kiss on the cheek.

He smiled, squeezed my free hand, and got up. "Rex, time to go home."

Rex's ears perked up and he ran ahead of Smoke to the door. When Queenie didn't follow, I knew it was for two reasons: she wanted to stay with me, and she wasn't her normal energetic self. I had a laundry list of things to do, but they could wait. Especially the house cleaning part. Why perform an unpleasant task today you can put off until tomorrow?

I finished my coffee then rolled off the couch. "Well, girl, how about we chill out for the morning. I need to call Gramps and Grandma and Grandpa, and you can hang with me and rest when I do."

By two p.m. I was dressed in my grunge outfit, had fought my wig into place, put a thick layer of black liner on my upper and lower eyelids, added a long chain around my neck, another around my waist, and had the drug phone in my jacket pocket. In other words, ready to report for duty. I dropped Queenie off at John Carl's, then stopped at Gramps' house to borrow his car. I used his old Buick when I needed a vehicle that didn't draw people's attention, unlike my own car often did.

People knew me and if they spotted a brunette behind the wheel, they might wonder. I was the only one who had driven Gramps' Buick for several years and finally convinced him to let me pay for the annual license tabs. But he wouldn't let me pay the insurance because he "might drive the old girl sometime."

Gramps gave me his extra garage door opener some time back, along with permission to use his car whenever I needed it. I used the remote opener, drove into the garage, and parked my car in the open stall. The door to the house led into the front entry and I found Gramps in his usual recliner chair. He held the local newspaper high in front of him, so it covered his face.

"Hi, Gramps," I called out.

He lowered the paper and blinked in a double take when he saw me. "You sound like my granddaughter, but I'd a forgotten you told me you'd be all disguised up today."

"How do I look?"

"Different."

I laughed at the way he summed it up in a single word. "I have to agree with you, Gramps. Not my usual style, but kinda cute, huh?" He stared at me without a reply, so I said, "It's probably best if we skip our hugs for today, what do you think?"

"I'd say so. All that black stuff on your eyes might get smeared." He shook his head and frowned. "I miss our Queenie."

"I know you do, and I know she misses you, too. I'll bring her over in a few days."

I drove the Buick to the sheriff's impound lot where the undercover vehicles were kept, along with towed vehicles that would either be returned to their owners or sold at public auction. I used my ID badge to access the building where the keys hung, selected the set for an older Chevy Trailblazer, filled in the date, time, and my badge number on the sign-out form.

When I opened the Chevy's driver side door and pushed aside some papers and fast-food containers, a rotten odor spilled from one or more bags. I went around to the passenger side door and pulled out a handful of junk, carried it to the trash barrel by the door and repeated with a second load. Must have been a recent impound vehicle of a guy who lived on junk food and had no sense of smell.

Mac had asked me to pick him up at a regional park a mile from Little Mountain at three that afternoon. Smoke and Weber would join us, then Mac and I would head to the first dealer's place in Emerald Lake, twelve miles southwest from there. The park was a popular biking and hiking destination with its miles of wooded nature trails, next to a pristine chain of lakes.

Mac stood by a tree at the appointed spot. He wore sweatpants with a quilted flannel jacket. I scanned the area for his truck, but no other vehicles were in sight. I parked the Chevy, got out, and joined him under an oak tree's cool shade.

"Hey, Mac. Where's your vehicle?"

"North parking lot. I hiked down here. After our visits, you can drop me off near there." Mac was cautious about who he might be seen with.

We made small talk until Smoke pulled in behind the wheel of a rusty Ford Ranger. Vince Weber was his passenger. It gave me a lift knowing they would back us up. Both had brains and brawn. Smoke higher up the scale for brains, Weber for brawn.

We moved in close to work out the details. Smoke and Weber wore jeans and zippered hooded sweatshirts with their badges and handcuffs tucked away in pockets, and sidearms in shoulder holsters inside their hoodies. The only weapon I had at my disposal was the defensive tactics I practiced over and over in preparation for whatever came my way, on and off the job.

Smoke and Weber would be within a block of the meeting places Mac had set up with dealers. I had a Bluetooth microphone clipped in my wig and would activate the receiving and recording app on my phone before we went in for the drug buys. Smoke and Weber would monitor us closely, keep tabs on every word, every move.

"Corky and Mac, a reminder that once you're recording do not make any side comments until after it's turned off. The tape will go into evidence for the sheriff's and county attorney's offices as we build the cases," Smoke said.

"Understood," I said.

Mac handed a piece of paper to Smoke. "Names, addresses, and phone numbers. First guy is Kip Lewis. Pretty new to dealing. I knew him back when we both used and partied together. Mostly sells meth and weed, but he's got other stuff, too. No clue if he's selling the laced cocaine, but we should be able to find out after a couple of buys."

"Yeah, huh. Kip Lewis was a frequent flyer back when. Just when you figure the guy musta got clean or died 'cause you ain't seen him around, he pops up as a dealer," Weber said.

Mac nodded. "It's a vicious circle for a lotta guys. Second one, I only have his first name. Percy. Showed up on the scene sixteen, seventeen months ago maybe, from what I hear. Cocaine, heroin, meth. Doesn't bother much with weed, I'm told. When I called them, I said my friend was looking for meth and coke."

"I was never in on a bust with Lewis, never arrested him, so I hope he doesn't recognize me from when I ended up on the news with other cases," I said.

Smoke made a humph sound. "No way. Just lower your voice, talk slower than normal. You'll be fine."

"You think Lewis checks out the news?" Weber quipped.

Smoke glanced at his watch. "It's about that time." He looked at me and a little butterfly flitted its wings in my stomach.

Mac and Weber each muttered something indiscernible, then we climbed into the vehicles. Mac's face scrunched up when he sat down. "Your rental has a bad smell to it."

I didn't get into the details. "It needs a good cleaning. Next time I'll do a smell test before I sign one out."

"That'd be good." I learned something new about Mac. He had olfactory sensitivity.

Kip Lewis lived in an apartment building in Emerald Lake where I had responded to calls over the years. The building's exterior screamed, "Spruce me up or tear me down." The bricks needed to be tuckpointed, the roof called for new shingles, and the siding had places where it had rotted through. Without a complete overhaul, it faced demolition in the not-too-distant future. The interior was in even worse condition. Dated. Worn carpets, held together at the seams with duct tape. Dirty walls that hadn't seen a new coat of paint in decades. No security entry system, a relief for Smoke and Weber in case they needed to get in there fast.

"All right, I'm activating, so no word until we have contact with Lewis," I told Mac.

He nodded and I made the call then followed him into the building. He found apartment 109 and delivered four knocks to the door. Kip Lewis, a man of average size and looks, opened it a minute later. "Hey, man. How's it hanging?"

"Cool, it's all cool," Mac said.

Lewis looked me up and down. Literally. "Welcome to my humble abode. No apologies. It's what I can afford until I get on my feet again."

"Thanks." I glanced around. "It's not that bad. I've been in way worse."

"Corky here is new to the area and doesn't wanna travel back to Wisconsin every week for her stuff." Our cover story.

"What part of Wisconsin?" Lewis said.

"Eau Claire."

"Far enough."

I nodded.

"You're not a minor, are you?" Lewis asked.

"Nope. Over twenty-one." Thirty-three, in fact.

"I got jammed up once when I sold to a kid that I swear I didn't know was a minor," he said.

I nodded again. "Mac says you sell quality stuff."

"Yeah. I do. So you want both meth *and* coke?"

"Cocaine is my first choice, but my income says I can't use it all the time. Meth takes care of the in between times," I said.

"I get that. Totally get that. And to let you know, I don't scalp people," Lewis said.

"Good to know."

"How much you need?"

"How much for an eight ball of meth?" 3.5 grams.

"One fifty," Lewis said.

"And the cocaine?" I asked.

"One twenty a gram."

"I got two fifty with me. I'll go with an eight ball of meth, and would you take a hundred for a gram of coke?" I asked.

Lewis studied me a minute, crossed and uncrossed his arms. "I suppose." He left the room for a few minutes and returned with five two-by-three-inch self-sealing baggies that contained white powder. Three were marked with an M, two with a C.

I pulled the four bills from my pocket and handed them to Lewis. When he gave me the baggies, I slipped them in my jacket pocket.

"You know, you could stretch your dollars with PCP, or acid, or 'shrooms," Lewis said.

"I know. Thanks. You get your stuff from Chicago, like my dealers in Wisconsin?" I asked.

"No, I got more of a local connection. From the Twin Cities. He's got a runner from Mexico, and I got no interest in them kind of headaches. My business is easier to manage, and I mean to keep it that way."

"Sounds smart to me. He gets you quality stuff, who can complain?" I said.

Lewis smiled. "That's right. Well, thank you for your business and I hope to see you again." He wouldn't be happy to see me if the next time was because I got called to testify against him in court.

I had taken care not to smile during the buy and nodded yet again. We said our goodbyes then Mac and I headed out the door. I took a quick glance and saw Smoke and Weber were in the same spot down the block. Before I got into the Trailblazer, I pulled the phone from my back pocket and pushed the button that stopped the recording. It was no big deal if Lewis happened to see me. He would figure I was checking for missed calls or new messages.

Per our arrangement, I drove back to the park for the meet up with Smoke and Weber before we headed to the next buy. We stood under the same tree as before and I handed the illegal drugs over to Weber. He was ready with an evidence bag and opened it for me. I dropped the baggies in, and after he sealed it, he recorded the assigned case number, the contents, who collected it, the date and time. Then Weber and I added our signatures.

Smoke pulled out a one-hundred-dollar bill and handed it to Mac. "That's what we agreed on for your help this afternoon, right?"

"Yeah, thanks."

"We did a property search on Percy's address and got his last name. It's Bennet. Percy Bennet," Smoke said.

Mac turned to Smoke and Weber. "Okay. I told Corky about this, but I gotta warn you about this Percy character. Besides drugs, he's addicted to porn. And he seems oblivious that not every one of his clients wants to see and hear that shit. So if you hear something, it's not people in the room, it's coming from his computer."

"Good to know when we write up the search warrant, when it comes to that point," Smoke said.

"Geez, I hope the guy shows some common courtesy with the female sergeant here at his place," Weber said.

"Hope so. It was like background noise that he tuned out when I was there. What happened before I got there or after I left, I didn't want to think about. Could involve children," Mac said.

"None of us can handle child exploitation. Another illegal business he may be running? Maybe some of his clients who are also porn addicts ask about it, want to find out what he's got?" I said.

"Sicko stuff. Don't ya sometimes wonder how these birds of a feather manage to flock together?" Weber said.

"All the time. A whole different world," Smoke said.

16

Percy Bennet lived in a 1960s rambler a block north of the Mississippi River in Little Mountain. Mac told me he heard Percy did some off-site dealing to keep traffic down at his house. The neighbors were older folks for the most part. I had called Communications and asked about calls there and learned there had been no unusual or suspected criminal activity reports at his residence.

It seemed to me Mac and I stood out like sore thumbs when we parked in Bennet's driveway, as he'd requested. I activated the recording app, and Mac and I walked into the garage through the service door. The garage was devoid of the usual tools and lawn equipment. No mower or snow blower. Shelves filled with storage tubs, a gray Honda Civic hatchback, garbage and recycle bins were about it. Mac delivered five rapid taps on the door that led into the house.

"Give me a minute." We heard a series of beeps that indicated Bennet was turning off the security system. A deadbolt lock clicked and a skinny man, maybe forty, with thinning hair and facial and arm sores—likely from heavy meth use—let us in and led us to the living room. The house was clean with vinyl plank floors, and not an abundance of furniture. A couch, coffee table, armchair and side table was about it. He didn't offer us a seat; this was not a social visit.

Bennet's laptop computer sat on the coffee table with a porn movie playing. Mac pointed at it. "You mind? There is a lady present."

Bennet looked at me and shrugged. "*Ladies* like this stuff, too." I stared back and maintained a blank look. He shrugged again then closed his laptop. I fought the urge to kick him where it hurt to wipe the smug look off his scabbed face.

"You need some fine coke, I hear," he said.

Mac answered for me. "Corky needs a local supplier for coke. And I need some weed for myself."

"How much for an ounce of coke?" I asked.

"A C-note is good. I usually get more, but I like to give first time buyers a deal."

"And the weed?" Mac said.

"By the ounce or joint?" Bennet said.

"Joint."

"Seven bucks each."

"A hundred gets me what?" Mac said.

"Fourteen."

"Let's go with an ounce of coke and the fourteen joints. Okay with you, Mac?" I asked him.

Mac nodded. "Sure."

After I handed Lewis two bills, he keyed open a drawer in the coffee table. We stood some distance back but were close enough to see dividers inside the drawer that kept the illegal substances separated. Eight balls, and smaller amounts of meth were in different sized baggies. It appeared cocaine was packaged by the ounce in two-by-two-inch baggies. The joints were in a pencil box-like container that latched. And on down the line with other drugs.

Two things surprised me: he let us see his cache, and he had everything organized to that degree. By the order of the garage and house and the drugs, I suspected Bennet had obsessive-compulsive disorder, made more pronounced by his drug use. He pulled out two baggies and passed them to me. Then he counted out fourteen joints, put them in a bag, and handed it to Mac.

"Thanks," I said for both of us.

"It's a done deal. When you find out how top grade that coke is, I know you'll be back for more," Bennet said.

Laced with carfentanil that might kill me instead? "Cool. Where'd it come from?" I asked.

"My guy gets it from Colombia."

"Nice. Your guy from the Twin Cities?" I asked.

"Chicago." A bigger operator.

Mac cut in, "Well, that's why we're here. Top-grade stuff."

We were there mainly to build trust, form a relationship of sorts to get more information from him on our next visit. Half the battle was done. Bennet had let us into his house, unlike some other dealers did.

"Hey, you wanna stay, do a line?" The way Bennet stared at me made me think he could imagine me in an offensive video. Maybe I had acted too friendly. I managed to suppress a shudder.

Mac shook his head. "Appreciate it, but we got plans."

"Maybe next time," Bennet said.

Or sometime after hell froze over.

It was a relief to get out the door. I held up my hand so Mac would hold tight for a second. The deadbolt lock clicked followed by a series of beeps. Bennet was cautious and had reason to be. I pointed my thumb toward the service door, and we were outside and in the Trailblazer in seconds. I shut off the recording, then I got a text from Smoke, *See you at the park.*

I responded with, *10-4.*

I recorded the time we arrived at Bennet's house and the time we left in my memo book. "I feel like I need a cleansing shower."

"Me, too, and he didn't leer at me the way he did you."

"You noticed, huh?"

"I don't know how you kept your cool. I about lost it," Mac said.

"If he had touched me, it's possible he would have suffered an injury."

Mac laughed. "I might have enjoyed that. He is one of the sleazier guys I've met, and that's saying a lot."

"Man. Well, despite Percy Bennet's major creep factor, I appreciate you introducing me to both him and Kip Lewis. It's important to get an in with them. And you take so little pay, for heaven's sake." I backed out of Percy's driveway.

"It's plenty. Really. If I didn't need the cash, I'd volunteer my time. You saw how I got my life back when I got clean. It is only by the grace of God that I'm not six feet under instead of sitting here with you today. I'll keep doing what I can to help cut down on drug traffic around here," he said.

"Thank you. You know what? I feel a little bad for Kip Lewis. He's messed up, working to build an illegal business so he can get out of that dive. Thinking backwards. If he put half that much energy into a legal business, he'd have something."

"Agreed. I gotta admit I feel a little guilty setting him up, but it's only a matter of time before his world crashes down around him. It's the nature of the drug addiction beast," Mac said.

I was a couple blocks from Bennet's house when I noticed a gray SUV behind me in the rearview mirror. I was navigating my way out of the neighborhood to get to the main county road. When I turned, it turned, and that struck me as odd. I took a left that kept me in, instead of out, of the same neighborhood. And so did the SUV. "Mac, do you think Bennet has someone that keeps tabs on people that buy from him?"

"What do you mean?"

"It might be a coincidence, but someone's followed me since we left his house," I said.

"Are you kidding me?" He started to turn in his seat to look.

I reached out my hand to stop him. "He might see you and I don't want to alert him. He's stayed behind me on every turn around these blocks."

"That is strange. I kinda wondered why you took those extra turns."

"I can't quite read his license plate. Can you see it in the sideview mirror?" I asked.

"Not really."

"That's okay. Could be a coincidence. I'll head over to the Legion. There is a back way out through the alley there. See if I can lose him," I said.

"Okay. And here I thought we'd had enough excitement for one day."

"Welcome to my world."

I took a non-signaled turn into the parking lot halfway up a block then drove around the parked cars to the alley entrance. It ran to the block's end and through the next. Instead of going back to the county road, the shorter route, I went south on State Highway 25. "I don't see the SUV behind us anymore," I said.

I didn't stop Mac when he turned to look out the rear window. "Do you think he's gone?" he said.

"As far as I know. With the line of cars behind us, I can't be sure. We'll find out when I take the next right."

It was the road that went west to the park. After I made the turn, Mac checked the rear window again and I glanced in the rearview mirror for the umpteenth time since we'd left Bennet's.

"Don't see him. I think that shortcut through the alley did the trick. Good move," Mac said.

"After years on patrol, I have gotten very familiar with the highways and byways and alleys in Winnebago County. And it's come in handy in all kinds of situations."

"I bet it has."

We entered the county park and parked near where Smoke and Weber stood. We got out and joined them. The late afternoon wind had picked up, and the mid-fifties temperature felt ten degrees cooler.

Smoke raised his hands, and we did high fives all around. "Fine job, team. Both buys went along without a hitch."

"The second was a more disgusting experience, but we got it done," I said.

"Percy the porn king?" Smoke said.

"He is also OCD and paranoid and has meth sores on his face and arms. Probably on the rest of his body, too," I said.

I pulled the baggies of cocaine from my pocket and Mac got the marijuana from his. Weber had the evidence bag ready, filled in the information, and we signed off.

"We might have been followed when we left Percy's place," Mac threw in.

Smoke looked at me. "Explain."

"After a couple blocks, I noticed a gray SUV behind me. When I turned, it turned, several times. Didn't make sense. We couldn't get the plate, but we lost him."

"By fast thinking and a quick maneuver," Mac said.

I had to further "explain."

"Huh. Detective, I saw a gray Kia sitting in the driveway where that house is for sale," Weber said.

"Sure, I noticed it, too. Figured he was waiting for the realtor. He pulled in shortly before you two wrapped up at Bennet's, was still there when we left. That must've been shortly before you did," Smoke said.

"Maybe it was the same one. I didn't see it, but I had other things on my mind," I said.

"I didn't either, but like you said, Corky, other things were on my mind," Mac said.

"If they're house hunting and not from the area, they could have gotten confused about getting back to the main drag and followed you," Smoke said.

"Who knows? Could be. This assignment has put me more on edge than usual," I said.

"Understandably so. Well team, we have reports to write, evidence to turn in. Thanks for all your help, Mac. Appreciate it, once again," Smoke said.

"Glad to do what I can. Until next time," Mac said.

"See you back at the ranch, Sergeant," Smoke said.

"Okie doke, sir. After I trade vehicles at the impound lot," I said.

"We need to do an exchange at the lot ourselves," Smoke said.

"Ah geez, we've only been sitting in that old thing for four hours. Can't we keep it a little longer?" Weber wisecracked.

"It's a good thing we weren't stuck in that beast as long," Mac pointed at the Trailblazer.

Smoke raised his eyebrows.

"It stinks. Forgotten food bags," I said.

I dropped Mac off at the park's north entrance then headed to the sheriff's impound lot in Oak Lea. I looked forward to trading it in for Gramps' cleaner and fresher Buick. When I pulled in, Smoke stood outside, leaned against his Ford Expedition. Weber had already left for the sheriff's office. Smoke waited for me to park, return the keys, and log in the returned vehicle. I also left a note it needed to be aired out, at a minimum.

"Sounds like Percy Bennet was all Mac had warned you he would be," Smoke said.

"And more. Gross. I feel like I need to be disinfected."

"We heard the moaning sounds from the video before he shut it down. Wrong time, wrong place."

"What a clueless guy," I said.

"On the next buy, hopefully he will be more clued in. And more comfortable with you, trust you more, show you some respect. We need to find out who he buys from, see if he knows anything about the new supplier in the county. And that goes for Kip Lewis, too."

"Yes. It would be great to get the info on the next buy. Lewis is not as disgusting as Bennet, but the fewer visits to either place the better," I said.

"You got that right."

"I feel worse for what Lewis is caught up in than I do for Bennet. Bennet is a bigger threat to society and needs to be locked up for a long time."

"Something to look forward to when we surprise Percy Porn with a search warrant in the near future," he said.

I smiled and nodded. "Yep."

That was the plan. But plans go sideways in the worst way possible at times.

We met Weber in the sheriff's office squad room. He sat at a computer typing up his reports. Smoke had the two bags of drugs, along with the recorded evidence tapes, the conversations between the dealers, Mac, and me. "Hey Vince, want to join me, be my witness when I turn this stuff in?" Smoke asked him.

"Sure, boss."

I sat down at another computer when they left the room. For my first report, I gave my play-by-play version of what happened, from the time I picked up Mac to what transpired at Kip Lewis's place, then the meet up with Smoke and Weber where we handed the drug evidence over to them.

Smoke and Weber returned before I started on the second report. Weber sat back down at his computer and Smoke headed to his cubicle to work on his.

"Hey Sergeant, do we know how to have fun on a Saturday, or what?" Weber said.

"What."

He snorted. "Ha! Yeah well, I gotta say I was pumped how everything went down today. I admit I was getting close to the edge when you were with the porn guy. The other guy seemed decent enough, but ya never know in these deals when something out of the blue happens, and it goes south in a split second."

"It was a huge relief things went as well as they did. No need for your team to rush in and intervene. We need to keep it that way," I said.

"Yeah," Weber said.

17

Blake

Tomorrow is Sunday. The day Blake was set to meet the third dealer for the third time for the third overdose for the third Sunday in a row. It took time to build a level of trust with the dealers, prove that he delivered high quality products at a more than fair price.

He could not take a penny of profit from a sale. The thought made his stomach churn, so he offered the cocaine for the same price he had purchased it. If any balked, he hemmed and hawed to seem legitimate, then lowered it further. Blake wanted them to be putty in his hands until their last moment on earth.

Had he been looking for a fix instead of approaching dealers as a supplier, a seller, it would have been less involved. Hell, he wouldn't have had to pose as someone else at all. A lot of professionals used illegal drugs for any number of reasons. Like his wife. Dealers didn't care who they sold to as long as it wasn't the cops. In the months he had courted dealers, something they mentioned a dozen times was that wealthy people did not dispute the cost of high-grade stuff.

Blake's top priority was to eliminate the four dealers his wife had contacted the day she died. One sold her the fatal mix, but every dealer played a part in her death, as far as he was concerned. He had first names for three of them and had yet to learn the fourth's, a guy that went by KP. KP said he wasn't available until Tuesday, so their first in-person meet was set for that afternoon. It would be a tighter time frame working to gain his trust in five short days. But that's all the time he had to deliver the fatal overdose on the right day. Blake would make it work. Percy tomorrow, KP next Sunday.

When the four had paid the ultimate price, he could start to court the rest of the dealers in his wife's secret contacts' list, see if he wanted to carry his mission to the next level.

When he could work it into his schedule, Blake had fallen into the habit of watching the comings and goings at the drug dealers' places in the week before his last encounter with them. He wanted to see what their clientele was like, who they were. Some surprised him. They were men mostly, along with teens of both sexes, and women, too. Young, middle age, older. Some professional, well-dressed. Others looked like they had crawled out of holes to get their next fix. Depending on their degree of addiction and frequency of use, some had high-cost habits.

A real estate house for sale sign sat in a yard two doors down from Percy's. The window coverings were open, and the house looked vacant from what Blake could see. He had used the driveway as a parking spot a few times. He let the car run in case a realtor showed up with a client. He figured if that happened, he would back out and wave, like he was taking a closer look at the house. The neighborhood had little traffic, in general, and on that street in particular. Probably why

Percy chose it. Blake sat there for ten, twelve minutes and not one vehicle passed by. There wasn't a steady stream of buyers at Percy's house, and that lessened his stress.

When he parked in the house for sale driveway the day before his last trip to Percy's, Blake saw an older Trailblazer in the driveway. Not long after, a couple came out the garage service door, the one he had been instructed to use on his visits. The male looked to be in his early thirties, average build with a beard and shaggy light brown hair. No one he recognized from previous visits.

Something about the petite brunette seemed familiar. Her size, the way she carried herself, lifted her arm, her gait pattern. Damn if she didn't remind him of Corinne Aleckson. Corinne had occupied much of his thoughts appeared in his dreams when he was able to sleep. He must be hallucinating to see Corinne in that girl beneath the dark hair, heavy makeup, and weird clothes.

The woman got into the driver's seat and the man climbed in the passenger's side. They sat for a few minutes, maybe to get their fix. When the old Trailblazer left Percy's and drove past him, Blake could not stop himself. He backed out the driveway and followed it, with a block or so between them. The woman appeared lost because she took a couple extra turns from what he could tell. When she crossed a main city street where he had to wait for a stoplight, he lost her. He cruised around a while but didn't spot the Trailblazer again.

Blake headed back to Percy's and witnessed two more people go into his garage, the second one thirty minutes after the first. Percy had been specific about the times Blake had to be there. Tomorrow it was set for eight p.m. After dark. When families were at home gearing up for the school and work week ahead, he would be taking care of business.

18

I woke up Sunday morning feeling scuzzy. Not clean enough. I had washed my druggie outfit, wiped down the jewelry, and taken an extra-long shower where I scrubbed and rinsed twice before bed.

It was a less than pleasant experience with Kip Lewis in his rundown living quarters, but whenever I thought of the minutes spent in Percy Bennet's house and the imagined activities that had occurred there over time, I cringed. No one had ever called me a germaphobe but being in Bennet's house made me feel like one. As a deputy, some unpleasant interactions brought out that notion now and then. Too many people lived in unhealthy conditions. And with Bennet it wasn't because his house itself was dirty.

I longed to be near Smoke and picked up my phone to call him. He had kept Rex at his place so Queenie would have another night to heal.

He answered with, "Mornin', darlin'."

"Good morning, my love. Out on a call?"

"No, they let me sleep the whole night. How are you and Queenie?"

"We're good. She did fine with the steps up to the bedroom and slept on her usual rug by the bed. She also did well for John Carl and Sara last night, seems to be on the mend. I feel comfortable leaving her for an hour or so when I meet my family at church."

"I'd join you if I knew I wouldn't get called out in the middle," he said.

"No worries. I better get a move on, catch you later."

"Promises, promises."

I chuckled and disconnected.

It pleased Mother when I attended church, as my work schedule allowed. Every important religious milestone in our family had happened there: baptisms, confirmations, weddings, and funerals.

My mind and spirit needed to be uplifted and renewed given Rebecca's problems, the coyote attack on Queenie, and the afternoon and evening spent with drug dealers.

I slipped into church and saw Gramps, Mother, and her boyfriend David, John Carl, and Sara sitting in the back pew. Gramps' preferred spot. All five smiled at me when I took a seat beside Gramps. He reached over and squeezed my hand.

I felt the tension in my body and mind dissipate as the service went on. The music, scripture readings, prayers, and sermon on forgiveness restored my strength and encouraged me that all would be well in the long run.

Pastor Hobart, a kindhearted older soul, added a little hug with his handshake on my way out the front door. "Always a pleasure to see you, Corinne."

I returned his smile. "You, too. I appreciated your message this morning. Especially so."

"Glad to hear that. We've had our talks about things that happen in your job, and you know who to turn to for help."

"I do."

My family greeted Pastor Hobart, then our group moved together and formed a loose circle on the side lawn.

Mother put her hand on my arm. "Can you join us for dinner, Corinne? We're eating at noon. Elton, too, of course. And bring Queenie, if she's up to it."

Dinner with the fam and my best friend, soon to be sister-in-law, sounded like a fine choice. A chance to forget about things for a time. And enjoy a good meal besides. "Sure. But I don't know about Smoke. He's on call. What can I bring?"

Mother kissed my cheek. "Thanks, but we're all set. See you there." We chatted a few minutes then the five left in their vehicles, and I drove away in mine.

David Fryor had been there to pick up the pieces when Mother's fiancé—and our former sheriff—broke off their engagement. The sheriff suffered a stroke, and had made progress in his recovery, but secrets he had kept hidden surfaced, and hindered Mother's trust. It was best they parted ways.

David was an all-around great guy who divided his time between his home in Texas and his hometown in Minnesota because his father needed help with his care. As Gramps did. Mother and David had that responsibility in common. And both were widowed, David more recently than my mother.

When I got home, I sent Smoke a text. *Dinner at Kristen's, noon.*

Good deal. Hope to make it. The menu?

Didn't ask. Does it matter?

No, my now growling stomach says anything will be good.

I spent time with Queenie, and we took a walk around the back yard for some exercise. She loved the security of her kennel but leaving her in the house another day made me feel better. It also signaled her I wouldn't be gone long.

The mixed barbeque ribs and baked potatoes aromas in Mother's house reminded me it had been over a day since I'd had a decent meal. Or any meal at all. The whole gang was at Mother's.

"No Queenie?" Gramps asked me.

"She needs another day or two to heal."

"Well, the food is ready. Let's get it dished up and on the table," Mother said. We filtered into the kitchen and had vegetables in serving bowls and the meat on a platter in no time. Ribs, baked potatoes, carrots with butter and mint, and steamed broccoli. The tossed green salad with a vinaigrette dressing, a mixture of olives, hard rolls, and butter were already on the dining room table.

We sat around the table, gave our thanks, and the feast began. Each one gave a synopsis of life's happenings. Mother had a dress and accessory shop, and the winter stock had arrived. "I don't know where the summer went."

David had lived in Texas for many years and flown to Minnesota often the last years to be with his elderly father. He had known my mother from high school and when they reconnected, a decided spark between them grew brighter as time went on. "Dad would have joined us, but couldn't muster the energy, said he'd better take a nap instead," David said.

John Carl spoke next. "Work is going well. I like the remote option and the ability to reach clients anywhere in the world." He was a business analyst, but I didn't understand the scope of his job, all it entailed.

Sara smiled. "Things are always hopping at work, but I have a number of good clients who toe the line. They make up for the ones that don't."

Grandpa Aleckson never had a lot to say. "Kristen, this is a fine meal. Thank you."

Between the two, Grandma was the talker. "Grandpa and I will head to our winter home in Arizona in about six weeks, and we hope you will come visit. Grandpa still likes to golf a few times a week. After all his years doing nothing but farm from sunup to sundown, sometimes earlier, sometimes later, I'm glad he's found something fun to do."

Grandpa nodded then turned to Gramps.

"I get by just fine, mostly with my daughter's help." Gramps looked at me. "But I do miss Queenie."

"Here you go, Gramps." I brought up the photos of Queenie in her recovery suit on my phone and handed it to him. "She likes it. She acts like she's wrapped in love. And seems better every day."

"That is a fine suit. And a good way to protect those wounds of hers," Gramps said and passed the phone to Grandpa to send it around the table. "And I sure am glad you got all that goop washed off your face, and you're back to your own hair color, Corky," he added.

Mother's eyebrows rose. "What makeup, what hair color?"

I lifted my fork. "I had to do a little undercover assignment yesterday, so Gramps saw me when I borrowed his car."

"Corinne, not more drug undercover assignments?" Mother said.

A knock sounded at the front door and Smoke called out, "Anybody home, or is that good food I smell all for me?" Saved by my man. He stepped into the dining room with a broad smile. "Hello, everyone. Thanks for the invite, Kristen. That empty chair for me?"

"Yes, Elton, of course it is," Mother said.

"Thank you." His eyes captured mine and my heart did its usual ping-ping. "Next to my darlin'." He gave me a peck on the cheek and sat down. People passed dishes his way, and it was a good thing Mother had made enough for twenty because Smoke had an appetite. He may have missed a few meals himself.

I nudged him with my elbow. "We were doing a little round robin, and I'll go next so you can eat. You all know about Queenie. Mother, I'm on a temporary assignment, nothing to worry about. But the sheriff's office *has* been investigating two overdose deaths that happened a week apart. It's kept Smoke and others busy. Remember last year we had six overdose deaths within a short time, and we're concerned there could be more than the two this time around. It's a priority to find out who the seller is and stop him."

Grandma leaned forward. "That's right, and you weren't able to uncover who the seller was last year, so I'll pray you find out this time." Grandma was the one who understood me best and shared the love I had for my career. She would have been a cop herself if her life hadn't taken a different path.

Mother didn't press me for more details and the two hours spent with loved ones relaxed me, helped ease my stress.

Smoke followed me home, and I found Rex on the rug with Queenie. He was there for her, knew Queenie needed to lay lower than normal. Smoke and I sat on the couch to relax for a handful of minutes—until he got called to a burglary. "Later, my dear." His kiss told me later would be worth the wait.

I took in the back yard view from the glass patio doors and when my thoughts turned to Rebecca, I picked up the phone and called her. "Hi there, what are you up to?" I asked.

"Not much. My family went to their grandparents, but I didn't feel like going so I'm hanging out here." She sounded sad, lonely.

"I was thinking about getting some ice cream at Parlor, wondered if you'd come with me so I wouldn't have to go all by my lonesome. Can I talk you into it?"

Ice cream was Rebecca's favorite treat. "Oh, like, sure."

"Yay. Let your folks know where you will be. And if you're ready, how about I pick you up in, say, ten minutes?"

"Sure, thanks!"

Rebecca emerged from the house wearing jeans and a rose-colored jacket that complemented her light complexion and blonde hair. She had natural beauty, and the older she got, the more striking she was. And she didn't recognize it in herself.

She climbed into the GTO's front seat with a bright smile, and we drove to her favorite ice cream place housed in an old brick building on Division Street in Oak Lea. It was the place to be that day, the way it looked. We were in line when Rebecca nudged me and said, "I just saw Kelvin looking in the window."

I turned on a dime to the front window that spanned the shop's width. "Did you see which way he went?"

She pointed east. "I'll be back." I gave her a twenty-dollar bill and scurried out the door. I turned right, jogged to the block's end, stopped, and looked for anyone on foot, or for a vehicle backing out from a stall. Nothing. I crossed the street and glanced into each parked car. Aside from an older lady in a minivan the others were unoccupied.

At the west end I crossed again and checked those cars, then headed down a walkway between Parlor and another brick building. The walk led to a lower-level parking area and other businesses that were not open on Sundays. I stood and scanned the lot and vehicles parked there but didn't spot anyone in or around them.

How had Kelvin disappeared so fast, and why? I jogged back to Parlor and found Rebecca at a table with our bowls of ice cream. Chocolate with sprinkles for her, butter pecan for me. The change was on the table. "Thanks," I said and sat down across from her.

Her frown lines were evident when she nodded. "So, like what happened?"

I lifted my hands in defeat. "I hoped to spot him, see if he'd tell me who he is, or get a plate number from his car. No such luck. He must be a pro at disappearing. Or else he's a chameleon who can hide in plain sight."

"Oh."

"Did he see you in here when he looked through the window?"

"Yeah, he stared right at me. I think he saw you and didn't want to come in here, 'cause I was with an adult and not another kid," she said.

Other teens were in the shop. Kelvin may have been scoping the place for someone to sell drugs to, or listen in for the next party to crash. *Asshole.* Or he wanted an ice cream and when he saw Rebecca and her escort, he changed his mind. I was beyond frustrated trying to find out who he was.

19

Blake

Blake pulled on jeans, a smooth black windbreaker, ball cap, and his new signature sunglasses that covered half his face. He told the dealers he had an eye condition called photophobia. He didn't, but his mother had suffered from it. Light, especially bright light, brought on migraines that debilitated her until the day she died. Along with the fake beard he wore, it proved to be a convenient way to change his appearance without much bother.

He retrieved one baggie with the toxic mix, and one with pure cocaine from the covered tin cookie container he kept shoved to the back of a kitchen cabinet. A client gave him a tin filled with buttery delights for Christmas every year. The last one sat unopened until a few weeks ago. He took out a cookie, put the whole thing in his mouth and while it softened and melted, he dumped the rest in the waste basket. The tin was a great place to keep his stash.

He had gotten the name of a supplier in California from a dealer—who also served as a middleman—on Hennepin Avenue in Minneapolis. It cost him $1,000 for the tip that proved invaluable. Blake called the supplier on the spot with the dealer at his side so Blake could hand him the cash as he made the necessary arrangements.

Blake decided it was worth the risk to wire an initial $5,000 to Chance, the supplier. Chance suggested that Blake use Walmart because they had a high rating for non-bank transfers. That was a new one for Blake and he tried to remember the last time he had reason to buy anything from that retailer. He would go to a metro Walmart, or one outside of Winnebago County; less chance someone would recognize him.

Chance was reliable and shipped the cocaine in a variety of packages with different return addresses and company names on them. The stuff was hidden in the toes of shoes from an exclusive store, under dress shirts from a high-end clothing store, in a hidden layer under hot mustard from Chinatown. Chance was clever and busy, and Blake was happy to pay whatever it cost for what he needed to get his jobs done.

Blake checked his watch, and nervous energy pushed him to take it off earlier than usual. He would get to Percy's early and wait until their agreed upon hour for the buy. Blake needed to be the last one on his schedule. Indeed, the very last person Percy would ever meet with again. The sun had set an hour before. Besides the lights in homes, businesses, and streetlamps, it was an almost pitch black night. Blake sat in his wife's Kia in the shadows with a clear view of Percy's modest rambler.

Blake had been there once before, for their second meeting. The first meet had been in a city park. Percy had a disgusting porn video playing on his laptop he didn't bother to shut down. But Blake did not want to rock the boat at that point. He blocked out the sounds as best he could. No signs a wife or children lived there, thank God. If by chance, someone else—a witness—was at the house, he would give Percy the pure cocaine instead of the mix. That had not yet happened, but he had to be prepared in case it did. Pure in his left pocket, mix in his right pocket. Blake had been meticulous to a fault with his plans and preparation.

Percy's garage service door opened, and out walked a familiar-looking figure. He had his head down and when he looked up, it took Blake a minute to process who it was. Kelvin Dean. *Kelvin Dean?* What in the hell was he doing at Percy's residence? Nothing good, that was for sure. Drugs, pornography, and who knew what other illegal activity Percy might be up to. Kelvin's parents were among his top clients. They provided a large chunk of his income year after year. He genuinely cared about them besides. He didn't know Kelvin as well as others in his family. But he liked the kid well enough. Smart, personable, polite. And Kelvin had been with the likes of Percy B? It made Blake sick to his stomach.

Kelvin was over eighteen, maybe over twenty. What could Blake tell his parents? That he saw Kelvin leaving a known drug dealer's house? One who died a short time later from a toxic overdose he had given him? Blake watched Kelvin walk in the opposite direction from where he sat. He rolled down his window and listened for a vehicle to start up and drive away. It took a few minutes before that happened. Kelvin didn't drive past him, and Blake had to believe he had left the neighborhood.

Blake drove his vehicle two blocks and parked behind a closed business. Countdown time. Five minutes until he walked through the same door Kelvin had left. The service door was unlocked. He put a hankie on the knob when he opened it. The door that led into the house was locked with a security system. Percy told him to knock six times in as many seconds and then he would open the door, as before. It struck Blake that Percy was either paranoid or compulsive, or both. But his earthly trials would soon be over.

Had Kelvin left his prints on the doorknob, or elsewhere, so be it. If the authorities questioned Kelvin and his family learned he was a drug addict, it might force him to get the treatment he needed. Could save his life.

At the appointed time, Blake was let into Percy's rambler, and amid the distracting sounds of yet another porn video, Blake poured out the deadly combo onto the coffee table, watched Percy sniff it, and die. Blake covered his tracks as he had with the last two dealers. The authorities would find only Percy's prints on the baggie. He slipped out minutes later and hiked to the dark lot where his wife's SUV awaited.

Blake climbed into the vehicle and reached into his windbreaker's left pocket. The bag of pure cocaine wasn't there. He got back out and checked the car seat, the floor, then ran his hand under the driver's seat. Nothing. His jeans' pockets were next, the windbreaker again then his jeans' pockets a second time. Just vinyl gloves in a back one. He knew he had the bag with him so what in the hell had happened to it? It was a risk to retrace his steps, but it was necessary. He kept his eyes focused on the dark ground and hoped the white packet would be easy to spot. He couldn't remember his exact route across the yards, but figured he was within a few feet either way.

He got back to Percy's house, donned the gloves, and when he opened the garage side door, wished he had thought to carry a small flashlight. Blake wouldn't use it outside and attract anyone's attention, but with the lights off in the garage, it would have helped. He didn't spot the bag anywhere, and even looked under Percy's vehicle in case he had unwittingly kicked it when it fell out of his pocket.

Blake paused for a deep breath before he stepped into the house. The kitchen light and living room lamps were on. Thank God the porn video had stopped playing on the computer. He scanned the room, glanced quickly at Percy's body then crept over and braved a longer look at him. No baggie was on, or near, his body. He glanced into the half open coffee table drawer, and he didn't see the foreign bag with the others. In his fixed concentration over his third mission, had he taken the bag from his pocket and set it down somewhere? Blake had absentminded moments, and as much as he didn't believe it happened, had to admit it was possible.

On his journey from Percy's house, back to his vehicle, he scoured the ground, his eyes traveling back and forth. He checked his pockets a couple more times, and then the SUV. One thing concerned him the most: an animal would find the cocaine, tear open the bag, and consume the drug. It might kill a small dog and make a larger one sick. If it was someone's pet, it would baffle the owner about what happened.

On his drive home, Blake pushed aside his distress over the missing bag. It was beyond his control. Then a sense of accomplishment washed over him. Through his efforts, three killers had left Planet Earth and would never do harm to another vulnerable person again. He had two days before his first meeting with KP and longed to spend his free time with Corrine Aleckson. Blake had driven past her house in the SUV a few times and hoped to catch a glimpse of her.

Thoughts of her danced around in his mind as he went about his work and other activities. Maybe that was why the female client who left Percy's house the night before reminded him of Corinne. Because he wanted to see her, be with her. One thing puzzled Blake and that was why Corinne acted shy around him. Was she attracted to him as well and felt the need to hide that from him?

20

I was on patrol Monday morning when my phone rang. I pulled onto the shoulder and answered it. "Smoke?"

"You're gonna want to report to Percy Bennet's residence a-sap," he said.

"What's up?"

"Bennet's dead."

That caught my next breath. "*Dead*?"

"Zubinski discovered his body after a welfare check got called in. I got here a few minutes ago. There are traces of powder on his coffee table, a sniffing straw next to it. I have a strong hunch he died from a lethal combo of cocaine and carfentanil," he said.

"This does not seem real, at all. We were just there buying drugs from him."

"That confirms he was alive Saturday late afternoon. I would venture to say he died sometime yesterday. His body's cold and stiff, so we figure he's been dead less than thirty-six hours. Medical examiner will be here shortly, give us an estimated time of death," Smoke said.

"Three deaths three Sundays in a row."

"Cannot be happenstance."

"Someone winnowing down the competition?" I said.

"Or acting as a vigilante?"

"Or Bennet was the one with the lethal combo all along."

"Killed the others and then himself?" Smoke said.

"Nah. He acted pleased to have a new client."

"Yep."

"I'll be there in fifteen." I sat there a moment to absorb that Percy Bennet was dead. His drug dealing days were over and the case we were building against him had died with him. But his death opened a new investigation. If he died from cocaine and carfentanil, it was tied to the other overdose deaths. The cases that baffled us. Instead of using my radio, I phoned Communications and told Robin I was en route to Bennet's address. And phoned again when I arrived.

Smoke and Amanda Zubinski had parked their squad cars in front of Bennet's house. I pulled in behind them then retrieved a bag that held a coverall suit, shoe coverings, and vinyl gloves from the trunk. Items to both preserve the scene and protect me.

I phoned Smoke. "Should I come in through the garage?"

"Yes."

I pulled on the suit and gloves, entered through the garage service door, put the paper covers on my shoes, and stepped into the house. The putrid odor that permeated the living room told me Percy Bennet's bowels had emptied at the time of his death, or shortly thereafter. I kicked myself for not swiping menthol salve under my nose before I entered.

Smoke and Amanda Zubinski stood several feet away from Percy Bennet's body. Bennet was on his back, about a foot from the coffee table. His face was turned up toward the ceiling and his arms were above his head, like he was reaching for something. Maybe a lifeline as his own faded away. His legs were nearly straight on the floor with a slight bend in his knees. He must have died and toppled over.

I caught Smoke's and Zubinski's gazes then looked from one to the other without a word. When Smoke said, "Sorry, didn't think to warn you about the foul odor," I realized I had made a face. "Need some menthol?" He fished out a tube from his coverall suit's breast pocket.

"Sure." I took the tube, squeezed out a glob, and spread it above my top lip. "I somehow missed that you got called here, Mandy."

"It came in at eight thirty-seven," Zubinski said.

"Ah. I did hear the welfare check in Little Mountain call but didn't catch the address. I was on the phone with Mac about our drug deal here Saturday, ironically. He's in for a little shock when he finds out about this," I said.

"For sure. We get welfare checks about every day and most times the people are fine," she said.

I nodded. "Who called it in?"

"Anonymous male. Said his friend was expecting him but didn't answer the door when he knocked, or his phone when he called. Multiple times. The blinds were closed so he couldn't see inside the home. Person reporting said Bennet would have told him if he had to leave for some reason," Zubinski said.

"Friend, huh? I'd guess customer," I said.

"No doubt. I had Communications look up the phone number, but no owner's name was attached to it. A prepaid," Smoke said.

"Mandy, walk me through this, from the time you arrived here. I sense a hole in the caller's story," I said.

"First thing, I walked around the outside of the house looking for any uncovered windows to peek in. No luck."

"Drug dealers can't let the outside world see what's happening inside their homes," I said.

Zubinski continued, "I knocked on the back door first, then the front, rang the bell, got no answer. The garage service door was unlocked, so I rapped with my baton and went in, knocked on the inside door. Again, no answer. I opened it and announced my arrival. No one alive to hear me, as it turns out. Went into the living room and caught the stink before I saw Bennet on the floor. I felt a little creeped out being here alone with his body, so I went back outside and called Communications who called the detective."

"Nobody likes being alone with a dead body, Mandy. When we were here on Saturday, we found out that when Bennet was expecting customers, he left his garage service door open but kept the door to his house locked. When Mac set up our meeting, Bennet told him how to get in, and how to knock on the inner door," I said.

"Okay," she said.

"There is no way a friend, or regular customer, would *not* know the process. Bennet had a security system. With that turned off and both doors left unlocked, I'd say the PR must have gone in, found Bennet. But he didn't want to be identified because he's a user. The other possibility is he was the one who gave Bennet the dose and decided to report it for reasons known only to him," I said.

"That's pretty much what I came up with," Smoke said.

"I agree. Bennet wouldn't have left his house open, no matter what. Detective Dawes and I lifted prints from the garage and house doorknobs and the door frames. Got a few good ones and hopefully we'll get some hits," Zubinski said.

"Also got photos of Bennet, and the scene," Smoke said.

I peered at the drawer in the coffee table. "His vast supply is still there," I said.

Smoke nodded. "It has a lock on it, but the drawer was not locked. It was already partially open, so I pulled it a little further to get better pictures. Lots of drugs in plain sight. Detective Harrison is writing a warrant for a judge to sign so we can search every nook and cranny on his property. Given what Bennet had going on with his illegal operations, his drug stash drugs, drug money, and porn videos could be anywhere. It's gonna take the team a long time to gather and document all the evidence."

"No kidding." I pointed at the coffee table drawer. "We threw around the idea that the dealer who's supplying the lethal drug combo might be purposely killing off the competition. In that case, was he here when Bennet died? Or, like I said before, did the PR in fact enter the house and find his body when he came to buy drugs? In either scenario, you'd think they'd steal Bennet's supply," I said.

"You would think. And either scenario is possible. That being said, someone could have taken a handful of his stash and we would never be the wiser. Unless Bennet kept a log of the products he had on hand. Mandy and I took a walk through the house and didn't spot any obvious evidence of riffling or theft."

"Sounds familiar," I said.

"Yep. Same deal at the other overdose scenes. Griffen Houser was found in his garage. Kept his drugs and money in the house. Tad Michels had drugs in his kitchen drawers, money in a lockbox under his bed. Easy enough to find and take both. We don't know how many customers Bennet let his guard down with, like he did with you and Mac. Might have been a fluke, might have been showing off for some reason, might have been high and not thinking straight," Smoke said.

"With that gross porn video playing it was hard for us to think straight. And the most horrible part was I heard what sounded like children's voices in it," I said.

Zubinski made a face like she had taken a sour bite of a lemon or lime.

Smoke pinched the bridge of his nose. "I would have had great difficulty restraining myself if I'd been there. Back to Bennet and why he let you see his stash, it's too late for him to tell us."

"Did you find his phone?" I asked.

"Might be in his back pocket. We'll wait on the medical examiner to find out." Smoke glanced at his watch. "I expect Major Crimes any minute. After the ME has done her preliminary exam, they'll take Bennet's prints before she takes custody of his body. Hard to believe, but when I checked, Bennet's prints are not in the system, not under his name at least. Could be they'll come back registered to someone other than a man named Percy Bennet. We shall see," Smoke said.

We heard a large vehicle pull to a stop in front of Bennet's house. Then Deputy Brian Carlson's voice came across our radios and told Communications they had arrived at our location. I stepped into the kitchen and moved the curtain enough to see the Major Crimes Mobile Unit at the curb. And several other vehicles parked on the street. Three squad cars no doubt attracted people's attention. The crime unit would bring more.

"They can come in the front door. More convenient." Smoke walked over and opened it for them.

"Mason called in sick, Vince Weber is with Carlson today," I said as they walked up the sidewalk, dressed in coveralls. Each held a black bag filled with supplies. Both had a shiny line of menthol under their nostrils, more prepared than I was. Neither spoke until they stepped inside. Even then, they stood silent for a time as their eyes scanned over the scene and Percy Bennet's body.

Carlson's freckled face squeezed into a grimace. "I was at the first OD two weeks ago, and I gotta say this scene is eerily similar."

"Ah geez, we gotta catch the creepola who's doing this crap. We were here Saturday night, wondering if he could be the one selling the lethal stuff, and now he's dead," Weber said.

"Unreal," I added.

We moved into the kitchen to await the medical examiner.

"We'll get Bennet's fingerprints after the ME does her check. I had Communications check and there are no prints in the system attached to his name. It's possible Bennet's never been arrested anywhere, but the chance of that is slim to none, in my opinion. In any event, if Percy Bennet is who he says he is, it makes our job a lot simpler. If not, we'll have to track down who he really is," Smoke said.

"I ran the plate on the car in the garage, and it's registered to Percy Bennet," I said.

"You're right and my hunch might be wrong." Although it rarely was. "Hope his next of kin are in his phone contacts. We need to notify them, a-sap," Smoke said.

"Mandy and I will talk to the neighbors, see what they know about Bennet, what they've noticed. Yesterday in particular," I said.

"Yes," Smoke concurred.

The Midwest Medical Examiner's van backed into the driveway. "Sergeant, how about you let them in through the garage. You four can hang out here in the kitchen while the doc is with Bennet. We don't want to crowd her," Smoke said.

"We'll just hover in the wings," Weber said.

I slipped out the doors and noticed a few more vehicles had stopped along the road. A local reporter stood with a group of onlookers. Chief Medical Examiner, Dr. Bridey Patrick, and Roy Swanson got out of the van. He was a death investigator and former deputy from a neighboring county. We met him on a case last spring. Dr. Patrick was squat with spiked gray hair. She wore a serious expression, as per usual. Her small brown eyes captured mine in a look so intense it convinced me she could peer into my very soul.

Swanson had well over a foot of height on the doctor. He was lanky and gaunt looking and reminded me of Skeletor the first time I met him. But now I thought he was more of a mix between Skeletor and Abraham Lincoln. Swanson retrieved a bag from the back of the van.

"Hello, Doctor Patrick, Investigator Swanson," I said.

Patrick nodded. She rarely made small talk, even in greetings. She was focused and saved her energy for her work.

"Mornin' Sergeant. At least we got a perfect weather day, if you want to look on the bright side," Swanson said.

My lips curled slightly upward as I held the garage service door open for them. Patrick didn't notice my half-smile, but Swanson gave me a nod. Both were suited up. We all slipped on clean shoe coverings before we stepped into the house.

Smoke led Patrick and Swanson into the living room. The rest of us stayed in the kitchen as Smoke had directed. The doctor was professional and thorough, and I was always drawn in by her intense concentration from the time she entered a scene until she took custody of the body, or bodies, like in our last major case.

Dr. Patrick asked Smoke for a rundown, what he knew, who had discovered the body, what had been done since the sheriff's office first arrived on the scene. Smoke filled her in and included the drug buy on Saturday afternoon. Swanson noted the information in a memo pad.

"Thank you, Detective." Patrick held a room thermometer up in the air. "Seventy degrees."

Swanson captured photos with a 35-millimeter camera of Bennet and the surrounding area, the powder on the coffee table, and the open drawer with the baggies of assorted drugs. Then Patrick did a tactile exam of his body. "It doesn't appear his body was moved. Let's roll him over for a look at his back to check for lividity."

Patrick, Swanson, and Smoke rolled Bennet onto his right side so his back faced us.

Smoke held up his hand. "Wait a minute. Looks like a baggie full of powder got stepped on here, ripped it open. And left a partial shoe print behind." He knelt for a closer look. "Bennet is barefoot, so we have proof positive that someone else stepped on the baggie, left the print. I would say it happened after Bennet was dead. Bennet may have been holding the bag and it dropped when he went down.

Smoke stood. "Somebody was next to his body, didn't see the baggie. His foot was either under Bennet's hoodie, or the hoodie moved when that person lifted his foot to leave. Either way, he didn't hear the baggie break, probably because a damn porn video was on. If that were the case, I guess we can be grateful. Didn't notice that he left his shoe print behind. Bennet's hoodie lightly covered it, but not enough to wreck the print."

Weber elbowed both Zubinski and me. "Ah geez, tell me we just caught a break."

"That would make this a good day. Depends on how common, or uncommon, that footwear is," Carlson said.

Smoke looked our way. "Let's hope for less common. Now, the question is, was he here when Bennet ODd, or did he come on the scene after he died? We still have the fact that the door was unlocked to consider. Weber, Carlson, we need photos."

Weber had the camera strapped around his neck. He went over to Bennet's body and captured images from different angles. "Sole pattern looks like it's from an athletic shoe, but I can't tell you which brand," he said.

"Agreed. We can't preserve the shoe print, but we'll collect the baggie and powder with the other evidence, see if anything comes from it. Could be there is a fingerprint on the underside of the baggie," Smoke said.

"That would be sweet," Zubinski said.

"All right, if you are ready, we can move the decedent—carefully—a few feet over so as not to disturb the print. Then I will check his back and side," Patrick said.

Smoke and Swanson performed that task. Patrick pulled up Bennet's hoodie and t-shirt. The purplish-blue discoloration on his skin confirmed he had been in that position for hours. "Detective, go ahead and remove his cell phone and wallet, then we'll roll him back," she said.

Smoke withdrew the items from Bennet's back pockets, held them up, nodded at Carlson who took them, carried them into the kitchen, and laid them on a counter.

Smoke picked up the baggie and studied it. "Looks like a partial thumbprint was captured on the baggie."

Little cheers erupted among us.

"I'll grab an evidence bag," Weber said.

Smoke dropped it in when Weber held it open, then Weber took it to the kitchen and laid it on the counter.

"Who's got the fingerprint kit?" Smoke asked.

"I do," Carlson said, and dug it out of his supply bag. He went over to Bennet's body and Weber helped him roll the prints.

"Will you bring in the gurney and body bag, Roy?" Patrick said.

"Sure thing."

When Swanson headed out, I followed to assist. He glanced at the onlookers. A handful of people leaned against their cars. Some conversed with those around them. It was obvious there had been a death in Bennet's house, and they no doubt wondered how long it would take to get the scoop. I imagined the young reporter was chomping at the bit for it.

Zubinski and I would make the rounds among them in short order, see what they could tell us about Bennet.

"All settled in as a death investigator?" I asked Swanson.

"I am. The duties are more focused than when I was a deputy. And I like that. I help get the answers people need so they can move on after they lose someone they love," he said.

"One of the most important parts of the job, for sure."

Swanson opened the van's back door and I helped him roll out the gurney. Then he reached in for a body bag and placed it on top. "I had burned out by the time I retired, but I wasn't ready to sit on some beach all day twiddling my thumbs. Makes this part time gig perfect. I still get to see my old cronies from Carver County when we get called to a scene there. And meet some new ones from other departments. Like here in Winnebago County."

"Yeah, that's cool."

Swanson rolled the gurney into the garage, and Zubinski helped him lift it into the house. Weber and Carlson had collected the prints. They pulled plastic coverings over their coveralls to help transfer Bennet's body. He was thin, but still dead weight, and on the ground to boot. Weber positioned his arms under the upper body, Carlson the middle, and Swanson the legs. Patrick had the body bag open to receive Bennet's remains. I watched them lay him on the bag but looked down when they zipped it up. I'd had problems with that for years, and it didn't seem to get better as time went on.

"We are ready to take Mister Bennet to the office. Ray has the chain-of-custody transport form for you to sign. Per usual, the sheriff's office will retain his personal property for your investigation," Patrick said.

Swanson withdrew the form from the black case and passed it, along with a pen, to Smoke. He glanced it over, signed it, and returned it to Swanson who nodded and tucked it back in the case.

21

The Midwest Medical Examiner's van pulled away from the driveway as the audience watched. Deputy Ortiz arrived with the search warrant, written by Harrison, and signed by Judge Adams. It gave the team carte blanche to examine every square inch of Bennet's property because illegal drugs and illicit videos could be in any drawer or closet or anywhere else.

Zubinski and I took off our protective gear and headed out to canvass the neighborhood. The reporter approached us with a pad and pen in hand.

She looked at our name badges with her almond-shaped brown eyes. "Sergeant, Deputy, I'm Cheri with the Little Mountain Times. Can you tell me what happened at that residence?"

I shook my head. "Sorry, the sheriff's office will have a statement later today."

"A body was removed from the home."

"That's true, and that's all I can say."

She persisted. "The crime lab is there along with three squad cars."

I lifted my hands. "Sorry."

We walked on, and she didn't follow us. Zubinski went one way, and I went the other. We needed to learn what the neighbors knew about the resident at 603. I met Bennet's next-door neighbor; an older gentleman named Ronald Petra.

"Please tell me how well you knew Mister Bennet, your observations about him and his activities," I said.

"Percy moved here about four years ago. Seemed friendly enough. Didn't talk to him much, but when he was out and about, he always said 'hi.' Then he was gone for maybe a month. That must've been a year and a half ago. Thereabouts.

"When he came back, he looked different, not like himself. Like he had cancer or something. Lost weight, his hair was thinner and longer. Had a scruffier look to him. Mostly though, he acted different, not as friendly. Kept more to himself. Got a fair number of deliveries so I figured that's how he did his grocery shopping, and the like. Saw him drive away ever' so often.

"I went over there once to see if he needed anything, rang the front doorbell, and he opened it just a crack. Looked at me like he didn't recognize me at all. I thought that was kind of strange. Anyway, he said he was good and closed the door. Didn't even say 'thank you' or 'goodbye.' Just shut the door."

I nodded and made a note on my memo pad. *Memory issues?*

Petra continued, "People stopped by his place, I noticed. Maybe to bring him stuff, maybe to help him. I don't know. Most seemed like normal folks, but I gotta say a few looked like what I would call on the questionable side. Ever' so often I wondered if something was goin' on over there, cause Percy kept his drapes mostly closed. Not that I ever saw anything or heard anything to make me call the cops. No loud parties anyhow."

"What sort of thing did you think might be going on?" I asked.

"Maybe parties with two or three or more. Drugs. Booze. Sex. I didn't want to think along those lines, but kind of wondered. Like I said, they could've been friends who came to help him. He wasn't old. I'd say late thirties, but he didn't look well. And if he died that young, it pretty much confirms what I suspected. He was dying."

Assumptions abounded when the truth was hidden. "How many guests did Bennet have? Were there some every day?" I asked him.

"I couldn't say cause I'm not always around myself. My wife's gone, and I enjoy helping my kids out when I can. My grandkids always need a ride somewhere or help with something or other. But I would say Percy had somebody stopping there most days," Petra said.

"How about yesterday, or last night? Did you happen to see any visitors go into his house. Or leave from it?" I asked.

"No, can't say I did. I was home watching TV and went to bed early, right around nine o'clock."

"Thank you, Mister Petra. For the information and for helping your kids and grandkids. I know they must really appreciate it."

Mr. Petra nodded and smiled. "And you don't know how glad I am to have 'em."

I pulled a business card from my pocket and handed it to him. "If you think of anything else about Mister Bennet that might be helpful, please give me a call."

He studied my card. "I will."

Zubinski and I met back in Bennet's yard. I lifted my thumb toward Petra's house. "Neighbor didn't know a lot about Bennet's activities, but he said Bennet was gone for a month about eighteen months ago, and when he came back, he looked ill. It's curious, anyway," I said.

"It is." She pointed at the house on the other side of Bennet's. "Nobody home there so I'll check back later. The others I talked to didn't know much."

"Same here. Seems to me it would be a good neighborhood to run an illegal operation from your house. Trusting people who didn't see much, if anything, amiss," I said.

"Yeah, so don't go spreading that word to anyone else," she said.

I chuckled as we headed back into Bennet's garage then opened the inside door and announced we were back. The team had a stack of evidence bags on the living room floor. Smoke was putting the laptop into a large bag. "I took a look into Bennet's files and came across a familiar name."

I shrugged. "Whose?"

"Eloise W."

A sense of dread burned through my middle. "I hate to ask. Do we know more than one Eloise W?" I asked.

"As in Doctor Watts's wife, Eloise?" Zubinski said.

Smoke swiped his forehead with his sleeve. "Unfortunately. I pulled up two videos that Bennet, or someone else, made with her in them."

"That sicko," Weber said.

"As in, you don't want to see them," Carlson said.

"We viewed enough to see what they were, then turned 'em off. Appeared to be more soft than hard porn if that's any consolation. That SOB Bennet must have talked Missus Watts into an uneven exchange, modeling, etcetera for drugs," Smoke said.

The fiery sensation in my stomach spread up my neck to my face. "Yuck. That type of thing—probably more with prostitution than porn movies—happens to teens and people who don't have money for drugs. But Missus Watts had money," I said.

"She might have been spending a lot, depending on her habit, and felt the need to hide some large expenses, keep her husband's suspicions and questions at bay," Smoke said.

"Our investigators never found a connection between her and anyone we know in the drug world. Not in her phone, not on her computer," I said.

"No. This new info supports what we figured. She was cunning enough to cover her tracks with burner phones that were never found," Smoke said.

"We'll have to let Doctor Watts know about the videos," I said.

Smoke sucked in a breath. "We will. Not an easy conversation, by any stretch of the imagination. If the videos are out there in the cyber world, it's only a matter of time before someone who knows the doctor and his late wife will see them and recognize her, know who she is. Due to the content, they might not tell the doctor, rat out themselves.

"But there is always the chance the famous 'anonymous' caller would. Truth be told, we don't know if the doctor is into that stuff himself and might happen across the videos. The best approach is to bring Watts into the office for a chat. First off, we need to find out if he knew Bennet, or if their paths had ever crossed," Smoke said.

"I agree." I would not be in the interview room for that session. But I might watch from another room.

"The guy is gonna flip out, go completely wacko. Mandy, 'member how he was when we told him his wife was dead and then took him to the hospital?" Weber said.

"Something I'll never forget. He was shell-shocked, all right. I really felt sorry for him," she said.

"Watts did *not* believe his wife died from an illegal drug overdose. Makes you wonder if he ever came to grips with it. Or it could be Watts is a guy who convinced himself the evidence and the blood tests were wrong," Smoke said.

"He wouldn't be the first," Carlson said.

"No. Change of subject. I took a quick look through the contacts in Bennet's phone. A positive note is he has one listed as 'Mom' so we can make the notification. He's got a long list of others. Some by one initial only. The one listed as 'El' got my attention, of course. We'll check them all because one must have sold him the lethal dose," Smoke said.

"And will check the numbers against the ones we got from the others who just overdosed, maybe from the same combo. We have the digital file from last year's ODs and can cross-check those, too," Carlson said.

"Sounds like a plan. I'll phone Bennet's mother this afternoon," Smoke said.

"Yeah well, that's not gonna be no easy call neither," Weber said.

As it turned out, the call revealed complex implications we had not anticipated.

Zubinski, Smoke, and I carried evidence bags to the mobile crime unit. Then Zubinski and I left to assist another deputy on a domestic assault call. Smoke stayed to help Weber and Carlson finish the search and collect further evidence. We met back at the squad room at three thirty-five. The three had shed their protective coverings, and they all looked tired, with eyes and mouths that drooped a bit.

"Mandy and I have our reports written and filed. Were you able to wrap up at Bennet's?" I asked.

"The house, anyway. Finished processing, collected the drugs. Have latent prints from the doorframes and doors. Got lots of paraphernalia, the exploitive DVDs, money, three cell phones, two laptops. And photographed everything, including the large array of underclothing he had. Men's *and* women's. But it isn't illegal to have closets and drawers full of clothes, no matter what they were used for. We'll go back tomorrow and process the garage," Smoke said.

Weber scratched his arm. "Guess we all need long, hot showers."

"You know it," Carlson said.

"I'm about to call Bennet's mother and will put it on speaker phone if you want to sit in on it. You may come up with something to add," Smoke said.

Carlson lifted his hand. "I'm good. It'll take time to bring in all the evidence, get it entered."

"Yeah. I'll grab a cart for that. Detective, you can fill us in on how Mom reacts, what she says," Weber said.

"I'll help the guys," Zubinski said.

I looked at Smoke. "I guess it's just you and me. After dealing with her son, I'd like to get a sense of who she is, what she's like." I followed him to his cubicle where he took his seat at the desk, and I sat down on the other side.

Smoke pulled the memo pad from his pocket, threw it on the desk then flipped it open to about the fourth page. He picked up the landline, dialed, and hit speaker. "I recognize the area code is from western Wisconsin. Of course, folks move so she could live about anywhere."

"True."

"Hello?" It was difficult to tell it was a man's or woman's voice on the other end. Deep, froggy.

"Hello, this is Detective Elton Dawes with the Winnebago County Sheriff's Office in Minnesota. Is this Missus Bennet?"

"Not anymore."

"Are you Percy Bennet's mother?" he inquired.

"Was."

Had she disowned him?

"I am very sorry to tell you this over the phone, but we found your son deceased in his home today."

"Is this some kind of sick joke?" she asked.

"Ma'am?"

"Percy's been dead over a year. March of last year. Eighteen months ago." Her voice cracked. About the time Mr. Petra told me he had left for a month and came back looking ill.

Smoke's eyebrows shot up. "That poses a bit of a quandary for the sheriff's office here. A man named Percy Bennet with a Minnesota driver's license that matches his description was found deceased in a house in Little Mountain."

Her volume rose. "Oh. My. God. That weasel. Are you telling me he's dead, too?"

After she was silent a while, Smoke said, "Ma'am?"

"That's not Percy, it's Pearce," she said.

"Pearce Bennet?"

"Yes, Percy's older brother by a year. Evil brother, I hate to say," she said.

"And you are their mother. What is your name?" Smoke asked.

"Betty Jessen."

"Do you live in Wisconsin?"

"Wausau." More than halfway across the state.

Smoke shook his head and softened his voice when he said, "First off, you have my condolences about your sons."

"Why did Pearce die?" *Why, not how?*

"It was a drug overdose. An illegal substance," Smoke said.

"I knew his using drugs would come to a bad end someday." Her voice held no emotion and had quieted to a breath above a whisper.

"Ms. Jessen, it sounds like you've been through more than your due. If you would, take me through what happened, how Percy died, how Pearce might have ended up assuming his identity."

"First off, I didn't know he'd gone and done that. Not that it surprises me. Nothing Pearce did shocked me after a while. Getting back to Percy. He had a good job in a machine shop in Little Mountain and that's why he moved there, even bought a house. He was doing all right for himself. Lived in Minneapolis before that.

"Anyway, my son—Percy, that is—found out he had pancreatic cancer. Stage four, not even two years ago now. I told him to come home so I could take care of him. He gave his notice at work. Told me he couldn't bring himself to tell the folks at the shop why, so he said I was the one who needed *his* help. He had trouble believing he was as sick as he was, and I think he believed if he didn't talk about it, it would go away. Or something like that," Jessen said.

"Not uncommon. A lot of folks are in denial when they're sick," Smoke said.

"I suppose. Anyway, Pearce showed up at my house one day. I hadn't heard from him in I don't know how many months. When he saw the state Percy was in, he told me he would stay to help me out. Pearce didn't look so good himself. I fooled myself into believing he had reformed. Repented for his sins. And I have to say, he did help with Percy, so I give him credit for that.

"Just before he died, Percy asked Pearce to go to Minnesota, take care of his affairs, sell his house. Percy said he could keep his car in payment. It was all paid for. Whatever profit he got from selling the house would go to me. That never happened. Pearce left with the car after Percy passed, and I never heard from him again," Jessen said.

"Not in the entire eighteen months?" Smoke asked.

"Nope. He changed phone numbers so I couldn't reach him that way. I don't drive on account of spells I have now and then. I suppose I could have found someone to give me a ride, but it's a long way over there. After a year had passed, I thought Pearce must have sold the house, taken the money, and moved on. At that point, I really didn't care. Money couldn't bring Percy back, and if it kept Pearce away, that was all right by me. I admit that 'good riddance' is what I thought. Pearce was what they call a 'bad seed.' From the time he was a toddler, he was mean, dishonest, did anything to get what he wanted." Her voice faded again.

Smoke cleared his throat. "Is there someone on your end to help you navigate through all this? Family, friends? Or something we can do to assist you in any way?" Smoke asked her.

It took her a moment to answer. "Oh. I guess you need to make the arrangements. Go ahead and cremate him. I don't want the ashes. As far as the house and whatever is in it, let me talk to a friend. She used to be a realtor and is smart about that stuff. I'll call you in a day or so."

"Sure." Smoke gave her his work cell number then repeated it. "Call anytime, day or night. We all need someone to talk to at three in the morning at times."

That choked her up. She was barely audible when she murmured, "Thank you." And then disconnected.

"If Pearce—who we thought was Percy—wasn't dead, I'd be tempted to wring his neck myself," I said.

"You got that right." He looked pensive for a minute. "Add to that, it seems kinda cold giving a death notice over the phone. Betty Jessen surely has had hardships. Two sons, one like Jekyll, one like Hyde. She didn't name other family members when I asked if she had someone to help her. Seems her sons' father is out of the picture. We'll let everything sink in before we tell her that, as next of kin she's the one who will need to authorize the cremation. But that can wait. Whether she pays for it, or not. With a house and a car to sell, she is far from indigent. Another day." Smoke pinched the bridge of his nose.

"For darn sure. The bigger thing right now is tracking down the killer that gave her son the deadly combo. The third lethal dose. Not to mention the third Sunday in a row." I held up three fingers twice.

"If we had enough people power, I'd ask the sheriff to station a deputy at every known drug dealer's place in the county, but that's a—"

"Pipe dream," I finished for him.

"We need to apprise Doctor Watts of the porn videos. But Betty Jessen? I see no reason to delve into the details of her son's other activities here in Winnebago County."

"I agree. Any charges against him died when he did."

"Yep."

"The ME will do Bennet's autopsy tomorrow?" I asked.

"Doc said he'd be the first, at oh eight hundred. I'll be there to witness, along with Weber. Unless you'd rather be there instead."

"No, Weber is a better choice."

22

Blake drove by Percy's house fifteen minutes after he made the anonymous call and saw a sheriff's car parked out front. A minute later a female deputy emerged from the garage service door. It took him aback when he recognized her from the worst day of his life. A Zubinski. She and V Weber, the stocky, bald deputy showed up at his office with news that ended the life he knew and loved. He had no way to predict that day the primary focus of his new life would be to get rid of as many drug dealers as possible.

He pulled over to the curb a half a block up and adjusted the sideview mirror so he could watch the deputy. He lifted his phone to his ear with the pretense he was on it. The deputy pulled out her own phone and pushed buttons, her long legs taking strides down the driveway and then back again. It was obvious she was nervous, upset. Finding a dead body that had started to decay would do that to a person. How long would it take for reinforcements to arrive? And the medical examiner?

The day she and her partner delivered the news about his wife he hadn't noticed how attractive she was. Her reddish auburn hair had tones that gleamed in the sun, like different shades of flames in a fire. It was pulled into a tight ponytail, like last time, and he wondered what it was like when she let it loose and shook it free.

Blake scratched his head to banish those thoughts. He was exhausted and started down a mental path he should avoid. Corinne Aleckson was more his type, even though a voice somewhere deep inside whispered, "Keep your distance from her." If only his heart could come to terms with that warning. He wanted zero distance between them.

Deputy A Zubinski was still in the driveway when an unmarked sheriff's car did a sharp U-turn, pulled up to the curb behind her car, and parked. His heart picked up its beat when another familiar figure got out. Detective Elton Dawes. Blake had seen him arrive at the first dealer's death, but there wasn't a good vantage point for him to sit and watch the goings on there. Out in the open country he would have been too visible. He had to settle for a few drive-bys instead.

Then the detective was at the second overdose. And now the third. All three dealers' deaths. Maybe he was the expert who investigated what they called suspicious deaths. If so, he would be at another death scene next week. With the same unsatisfying conclusion: each dealer had sniffed bad drugs that killed him with no evidence anyone was there when he died.

It was the same thing when his wife died. Five others besides her got bad drugs and died. Yet the sheriff's office never found out who that killer dealer was. As they will not find out who the dealer killer is this time around. He smiled at his imagined play on words. Killer dealer. Dealer killer.

Blake decided to leave, check on things back at the office, and return when more authorities, like the medical examiner, showed up. It took the sheriff's office hours before and hours after the bodies were taken away, so he had plenty of time until then.

He'd told his office staff over a month ago that he needed time off here and there to attend to personal matters. He blocked out days he hoped appeared random from his schedule with the caveat that if something happened to an animal that belonged to one of his top clients, like the Deans, they should call him. He prayed it wasn't on a Sunday afternoon or evening, and so far, so good.

After a brief stop at the office, Blake returned to Percy's Little Mountain neighborhood and spotted cars lined up on one side of the street. He figured people had seen the emergency vehicles because the quiet neighborhood normally didn't have much traffic. A few people leaned against their vehicles. He pulled into the house for sale driveway and parked. With the action happening two doors down, no one would pay much attention to him.

The Winnebago County Sheriff Mobile Crime Unit stopped in front of Percy's house and two deputies emerged. One he had seen at the other deaths, and the bald one he knew was V Weber, the one with A Zubinski on that dreadful day. Someone opened the front door and they disappeared into the house. It wasn't long before the Midwest Medical Examiner's van backed into Percy's driveway.

Blake's heart rate tripled its speed when Corinne Aleckson herself came out to meet them. It struck him that it was the first time he had seen her in her sheriff's uniform. She looked sexy as all get out. Her hair pulled into a tight bun on top of her head showed off her sweet features. Blake told himself he should stop fantasizing about her but didn't want to. Not when every fiber of his being ached for her. He knew he could win Corinne over if he courted her right. She seemed cautious around him, and he guessed she had been hurt in the past and needed assurance that she could trust him. Blake would move slowly, in fact that was a good thing. He had at least one more dealer to deal with and it was smart to keep distance from Corinne until then.

After the medical examiner left, Corinne and A Zubinski came out. A woman approached them and talked for a minute before they started talking to other people. It was time for Blake to disappear. He was only two houses away from Percy's and sent up a "thank you" when neither one seemed to notice him and flag him down in his escape. It took him a split second to realize he had been careless, reckless to stay so long, this close to Percy's. He didn't want that old saying, "curiosity killed the cat" to apply to him.

23

I sat on the living room couch with Queenie and Rex near my feet, a glass of white wine in my hand, and gazed out the glass patio doors. The sun would set in about a half hour. If I wanted to watch it go down, I would need to move to another spot, face the opposite direction.

The past week's trauma was behind us, anyway. A second overdose death. Rebecca's one-day suspension. Queenie's attack. The coyote I had to kill. Dr. Watts and his strange behavior. The Saturday workday from hell outfitted with too much makeup, a tight wig, grunge clothes, and armed with only a Bluetooth recording device for the drug buys. Thank the good Lord I didn't have to run in those platform boots. It would not have been pretty.

Top that off with an elusive Kelvin at large. Chameleon Kelvin. He was at Oak Lea High, yet a substandard video didn't reveal his identity. He showed up at the Friday night party and managed to duck away without being captured. Then he was outside the ice cream shop, looking in the window, but disappeared before I could find him.

I had thought this week would be better. How could it be worse? Thankfully, yesterday was a nice break with family and friends, good food, laughter. But the morning's discovery that Bennet was dead took the sheriff's office back to square one. Another dead dealer who had sniffed a lethal drug, or drug combination. A dealer I bought drugs from on my first day as an undercover agent. I felt uneasy, more reluctant to go on another buy.

Then come to find out the real Percy Bennet had died over a year before. The man we knew as Percy was Pearce Bennet, a man who'd led a despicable existence, had stolen his honest, hard-working brother's identity. News that rubbed salt into his mother's wounds. The poor woman must have gone through a sad range of emotions after she heard what Pearce had done, how he died. Betty Jessen sounded like she no longer cared, couldn't face another tragedy. She wasn't prepared to come to grips with more dreaded news, so it was better to feel nothing. When hurt ran as deeply as Betty's must, burying feelings provided an effective, protective coping mechanism.

I knew that well. I had embraced it many times over the years, welcomed detachment, distanced myself from events or experiences and the misery that gripped me because of them. But I learned a person could not stay there forever without negative consequences. Lack of sensation led to strained personal and professional relationships, lost satisfaction, and pleasure. Pain hurt big time, but I discovered I had to accept it and deal with it, if I wanted to experience joy, too.

I swallowed a sip of the cool, buttery Chardonnay, and gently rubbed my foot on Rex's and Queenie's backs. All was right and cozy in our little world. When the phone jingled it gave me a start. I brushed away the few wine drops that had splashed on my lap and looked at the phone's face. *Should I answer it?* My respite time was over for the time being.

"Hello, Doctor Watts."

"Oh, um, Corinne, hi. And, ah, feel free to call me Blake."

I stifled a groan and rolled my eyes instead. "Thank you." *Doctor.*

"Is this, um, a good time to call? I didn't want to interrupt you over the weekend. Not knowing if you had to work, or what."

Where was he going with all this? "Actually, I wasn't on the schedule last weekend." Not assigned to a particular road shift, anyway. It must have been the wine in my system that compelled me to add, "I had a nice time with my family yesterday. How about you?"

"Oh, well, that's good then. And, um, thanks for asking about me. My weekend was good. Took care of things I needed to do."

"There is always that, right?"

"Yes. Well, um, the reason I called was to ask about Queenie, find out how she is healing, how she is doing," he said.

"Actually, I think she's doing great, all things considered. Not back to her usual energy level, but close. Her recovery suit seems to make her feel secure, so thank you for suggesting that."

"Certainly. That's very good to hear." He paused and I remained quiet so he finished with, "Well, um, I will let you get back to your evening. Let me know if any problems arise. Otherwise, we'll see you and Queenie at her appointment."

Her next—and last—appointment with Dr. Watts. *Blake.* "Thanks, night."

"Good night, Corinne."

Corinne. Okay, that's what caused my unsettled reaction. The doctor had never called me by my first name before tonight. Then said it again in closing. The inflection in his voice made it sound personal. *Intimate.* Like he had said it a hundred times before. Had he practiced it? *Feel free to call me Blake.*

It had always been Doctor and Ms. in our handful of exchanges at his clinic. Queenie's injuries had changed that. Since I left Queenie at the clinic last Thursday, I had seen Dr. Watts twice, and now spoken with him on the phone. Three interactions, all initiated by Dr. Watts. Did he see a change in our relationship, a move to add a personal side to it?

I debated whether one glass of wine was enough. It took four seconds to decide two would be better and I headed into the kitchen for a refill. The stove clock read seven ten p.m. Where was Smoke? He figured he would have things wrapped up on his end by six. I carried the wine back to the couch, slid my body onto the soft leather in a semi-reclining position, left arm over the pillows, knees bent with my legs tucked close to my chest. I took a sip of wine then reached over and set it on the end table behind me.

I stared at the back yard as the sunlight faded and half expected a coyote, or a pack of them, to bound out from the woods and add to my distress. My mind circled back to the overdose deaths. Who was the artful dodger that managed to kill three drug dealers in as many weeks? People in the illegal drug world knew each other. Yet the best intel we had on a prime suspect cited a "new guy in town." Local dealers must have had contact with him for that information to get circulated among them.

Luke Andrews had distanced himself from that world. Dealers suspected he was a cop or worked with the cops and no longer trusted him. Most would avoid him, not take his calls, open their doors to him. But there might be others who would want to harm him.

The county's protocol was that deputies in undercover operations were not to inhale or ingest drugs. But in a few instances, they did, or pretended to do a taste test. Bennet had asked us to snort a line of coke with him. I wondered if bags of the deadly drug combo were in his coffee table cache. Our investigators would find out when they were tested.

If so, it was a game of Russian roulette at his supplier's will. It didn't make sense a supplier would do that. Bennet's business seemed lucrative enough and if something happened to him or one of his clients, the supplier would have to find another dealer.

Was the new guy courting new dealers to sell to, and deliberately eliminating the ones he didn't like for one reason or another? Pearce Bennet certainly rose to the top of dislikeable people on my list. But Tad Michels and Griffen Houser? What was the connection between the three that earned them a death sentence? Again, was it related to the string of deaths the year before?

Some dealers had died in that last round, but not everyone had been identified as one. Like Mrs. Watts. Small time dealer to feed her habit, got the lethal drugs from her supplier? She had a cache of drugs in her glovebox believed to be her personal supply, but maybe she had friends she was selling to.

Her connection to Bennet and appearance in his videos made her suspect. Since no dealers' numbers were found in her cell phone, what happened to the phone she used, whether it was a prepaid or a burner? Had she run over it, then tossed it into a trash bin or a body of water? That's what I would do if I were a criminal and wanted to destroy evidence.

The wine had relaxed my body somewhat, but my mind was still in overdrive. When Smoke opened the door and called out, "Hello," Rex and I both got up and headed to the kitchen to meet him. Queenie's ears perked up, but she stayed put.

Smoke looked like he had been forced to stay awake for days. Or was ill. His eyes were bloodshot and watery, the skin on his face was pulled tight, and he wore a slight frown, like his head hurt. He smiled enough to deepen his dimples and pulled me into his arms. "Oh, I cannot tell you how good you feel. Is it okay if I fall asleep right here?"

I gave his neck a peck. "I have a better idea. Go stretch out on the couch. I will bring you food and drink."

"Be still my heart."

I stretched my arm around his waist, he dropped his to my shoulders, and we managed the short distance. As he plopped down, he noticed the wine glass. "If I needed a nightcap, that would look good."

I picked up the glass as we sat down. "Sip?" And handed it to him.

"Why not? Every day could use a bright spot." He took more like a gulp, handed it back, then reached over and squeezed my thigh. "Besides you, of course."

I leaned my head on his chest. "It was a long one for you."

"It felt good to get the evidence inventoried and turned in. And the reports written. We had a load to sort through between the drugs, videos, money, phones, laptops. We'll get forensics to start interrogating the devices tomorrow. After Bennet's autopsy, I'll call Doctor Watts, bring him in for that uncomfortable conversation."

"Not fun. The past week has churned around and around in my brain. Events, people, activities, unanswered questions. And the oddest person ever, although not the creepiest, is Doctor Watts. He called me a while ago. To check on Queenie—"

Smoke interrupted, "And her owner?"

"Probably." I pulled at his shirt. "Doesn't matter because after Queenie's appointment on Friday there will be no reason to take his calls. If he tries to make one."

Smoke picked up my hand and kissed it. "Yep."

"So, what can I get you for supper? We've got those leftovers from the dinner Mother sent home with me yesterday. Barbeque ribs, minted carrots, broccoli. And I could nuke a potato if you want."

"You have me sold, but I don't need a potato. Thanks."

"An easy sell. And a beer while it's heating?"

"I suppose one won't hurt."

After I dished up a plate and put it in the microwave, I pulled a Stella from the fridge, popped off the top, and served it to Smoke with a kiss. "That's what I was missing," he said.

The microwave oven beeped so I left to finish the meal preparation. "Would you like to eat in there?" I called to him.

"Sure."

I grabbed utensils and a napkin and set the meal on the coffee table. "Sorry, doggies, I need to move the table in closer for Smoke."

Smoke smiled. "Thanks, darlin'. I will be the first to admit I love it when you spoil me." He bent his head to give thanks for the meal, then leaned over and dug in. "Mmm, this is already hitting the spot. You ate?"

"Yeah, I skipped lunch, so I grabbed an early supper." I let him eat in silence for a bit then said, "Smoke, you know last year, when we had those overdose deaths? Four were known, or at least suspected, drug dealers. Two were not. No real pattern. This time around we got three known dealers who died three Sundays in a row. Could there be a connection between the two sets of overdoses?"

"Could be. Did the same guy make a return visit? Or has he been here all along? Back then we thought there was a chance he didn't know he was peddling the lethal combos. But had to suspect it after the six deaths. Or did he kill on purpose, then took a year off, and decided it was time to play God again?" Smoke shook his head and waved his fork. "Nah, that's too crazy. What makes more sense is, some bad stuff got here last year, made its way to a few dealers who unwittingly sold it."

"And this time around?" I asked.

"Someone is targeting specific dealers for reasons we have not yet uncovered."

"Agreed. Something hit me earlier about last year's ODs. What if Missus Watts was a small-time dealer? She had a supply in her glovebox. And she knew creepy Bennet well enough to be in his videos," I said.

"You make a point. However, I doubt we will ever get that answer since neither one is here to tell. You never know, something could turn up in Bennet's phone or computer records. His recent conversations are top priority. Eloise Watts has been dead over a year, and whether or not she did any dealing back then no longer matters."

"No reason to bring that possibility up to Doctor Watts. What you have to tell him tomorrow will be bad enough," I said.

"You got that right."

24

Smoke left bright and early to pick up Vince Weber and make the forty-mile trek to the Midwest Medical Examiner's Office in Ramsey.

I was in the office mid-morning when my contact, Mac, phoned me. "Hey, Corky."

"Hey. What's up?"

"First off, I gotta say I'm a little freaked Percy Bennet bit the dust after we were just there, just bought drugs from the guy."

I didn't correct Mac, tell him that it was Pearce Bennet we had been with. Or other details I would share when I could. "I know. It will take a while for the whole thing to really sink into my brain."

"Same here," he said.

"We witnessed Bennet's behavior, knew he had issues. Not to mention the things he was involved in."

"Issues. Damn straight on that one. And drugs made them worse." Mac sneezed.

"Gesundheit," I said.

"Thanks. I don't know where that came from. Anyhow, the main reason I called was to tell you I set up a meet and greet for you and Mandy with a dealer. He goes by the initials KP."

"KP. Where and when?"

"Tomorrow afternoon, four o'clock, Henry Olson County Park. From what I hear, KP is a guy who does *not* meet people at his residence. Just off-site transactions. I understand he's been dealing for over a year, maybe closer to two."

Henry Olson sat by the south fork of the Crow River, in western Winnebago County. "Did he name a particular spot in the park?"

"Yeah, he'll be on the second pathway that leads down to the river."

"Any idea what he looks like?" I asked.

"Never met him, just talked to him on the phone. Sounds like he's on the younger side with plugged up sinuses, maybe from smoking, maybe from snorting. Told him my usual guy was low on his cocaine supply, so he gave me his number. And that me and my girlfriend were hosting a little party and looking for sniff. She'd be the one buying, and her friend would be with her. Because my girlfriend had a bad experience once and won't be alone with dealers she doesn't know. Told him I was out of state, or I'd be the one buying."

"Quite the story, Mac. I like it, makes me sound like I'm on the vulnerable side, nobody for him to worry about. That's what we are aiming for. An in with another dealer. I've been in that park a hundred times, but I'll scope it out later, figure out the best place for our backup team."

"Just so you know, I gave him your cell number, the new one you're using. He'll probably call you at some point to confirm. I'll send his number to you," he said.

"Good. Mac, once again, I appreciate you and all your help."

"You bet. Have a good one."

After we hung up, I called Zubinski. "Sergeant?"

"Hey, Mandy. Mac arranged a drug deal for the two of us tomorrow."

"Oh, boy, I can't wait."

"No more than I can." I filled her in on the details, then said, "How about we meet at the impound lot at three to pick up our ride? We'll look for a decent vehicle this time since this KP thinks we're having a drug party, and they can't be cheap."

"Yeah. A decent ride and a decent amount of money for the party drugs," she said.

"Copy that. I'll put in the request."

It was almost noon when I pulled into Henry Olson County Park off County Road 6, to have a look around and eat the lunch I'd picked up at The Sandwich Shoppe in Oak Lea. It was among the smaller parks in our county system with a few picnic tables. It was a popular spot for fishers who cast for large catfish, northern pike, and crappies in the Crow River, a tributary of the mighty Mississippi. It also had a few shorter hiking trails that wound through the wooded areas.

It was sixty-seven degrees and sunny, a great day to be outdoors and enjoy nature. Two vehicles, a Honda and a Dodge pickup, were parked in the designated area. I ran both license plates. The Honda came back to a woman I didn't know, and the Dodge was registered to Kendrick Dean. That made me curious.

Dean's family owned a renowned horse farm where they raised bucking quarter horses, sought after by rodeos across the United States and around the world. I had never had a call for service there but stopped in to introduce myself sometime back. Mr. Dean was proud to give me a tour and show off his beautiful beasts. They lived on the other side of the county, but maybe it was a favorite fishing spot for him. He might enjoy the challenge of landing fighting catfish from the river.

I set off to I explore. KP planned to meet Mandy and me on the second pathway. I bypassed the first, walked thirty feet to the next, and followed it down to the river. I thought Mr. Dean might either be fishing there, or from the first path. But neither Dean nor the person who owned the other vehicle was anywhere in sight. A third pathway ran close to the river then turned and headed into the woods.

In addition to being a good spot to hike, fish, and picnic, people also launched kayaks or canoes from the park. Or did drug deals, an unfortunate occurrence at most county parks. I had happened upon surprised dealers and buyers a few times myself and needed to call for backup.

I headed back. Smoke and Weber could station themselves anywhere along the first pathway or stand by the river with fishing poles in their hands. If anyone spotted them, they would blend in, not stand out. As I reached the open area, a gray Kia SUV pulled into the park then did a quick U-turn and left. The sun reflected off the vehicle so I couldn't see the driver or read the plate. I had an eerie flashback to the gray SUV that followed Mac and me after we left Bennet's house on Saturday.

I walked to a hilltop on the opposite side of the parking area and looked around. Trees with their brilliant-colored leaves would accentuate the décor of most homes built in the 1970s, and many today. The maples with their shades of gold, orange, red, yellow, purple. The quaking aspens' trembling leaves rivaled the color of the sun. The sumacs with bright red and orange leaves looked like burning bushes.

There were countless sights to admire in Mother Nature. The vehicles' owners were likely on trails in the woods. It was apparent why KP had chosen this park for a meet. Fairly private with secluded areas, the perfect public place to conduct a drug deal.

I snatched my sandwich and water from the squad car and sat down, the lone diner at a picnic table. Birds landed in the trees and hopped around the ground in search of seeds. Squirrels scampered about. I lifted my face to the sun and enjoyed its warmth. The chicken and avocado sandwich was seasoned to perfection and hit the spot.

A vehicle slowed and caught my attention. A gray Kia SUV looked like it was about to turn into the park then speeded up and continued down the road. The same one that had pulled in earlier? If so, why did he rush away both times? Maybe he was looking for someone and didn't spot their vehicle in the lot. If my squad car had scared him, that meant the driver had something to hide. A dealer or buyer, perhaps? Had I been in my car, I would have followed him, looked for unusual behavior, run his plate to see who he was, in case he had an outstanding warrant.

When my phone rang, it took me a few seconds to swallow a bite. Sara. "A call in the middle of your workday. What's up?" I asked.

"Wondering if you're gonna take a lunch break?" Her voice was thin, strained.

"Actually, I'm at Henry Olson Park eating lunch as we speak."

"Seriously?"

"I can't get into it right now, but I picked up a sandwich and here I am."

"All right, I'll let that go until you can fill me in. I'd rather have this talk in person, but I need to tell you I'm worried about you," she said.

"Worried how, why?"

"Saturday when you dropped Queenie off with John and me you were in your little druggie outfit. You are out there with desperate and scary people, and people are dying. Every week. Three overdose *deaths*. Two of the victims had been on probation in our county, are in our system. Tad Michels was my probationer."

"I knew that," I said.

"All of us here in Court Services are wondering if there will be another victim. And who that might be. Another one we've worked with, tried to help, worked to steer to a better life? I'm hoping against hope last weekend was a one-time assignment for you. You know how much I hated the last time you went undercover into that world. I hate it even more now," she said.

"Whoa. Sara. I think my worrywart mother and serious-minded brother are influencing you. I know the drug world is dangerous, at times. Not always. And you know that if I get assigned any undercover work, whatever that may be, I will not be out there alone."

"Okay, my brain knows that, but something in my gut is screaming 'danger ahead,'" she said.

"Sara, outside of Smoke, you are my dearest friend in the world. We have shared our ups and downs for over twelve years. We have a long list of kept secrets between us. I trust you completely and you trust me. Right?"

"You know I do."

"Every day I report for duty, I believe it will turn out fine, but nobody knows what might happen any given day," I said.

"If that was supposed to make me feel better, it doesn't."

"I don't know what else to say."

"Promise me you'll be okay," she said.

I crossed my fingers when I said, "Promise," because it was something I could not swear to. And Sara knew that, too.

After we disconnected, Sara's words and the emotions behind them made my body tense up and filled me with apprehension. Fear. Of what? The meeting with KP, or was there something else I needed to be aware of, to watch out for?

I chewed on another bite of sandwich, but it had lost its gourmet appeal. I wrapped the paper around it and stuck it back in the bag then took a gulp of water to wash away an unpleasant taste that had settled in my mouth. Sara wasn't psychic. However, she did have spot-on intuitions about who she could trust, and when she needed to watch her back.

No question my law enforcement/public safety mindset was off kilter with the undercover assignment. That must have been why Sara had passed on her unsettled state to me. I needed to press a refresh button and bring my focus back where it needed to be. For my personal protection and the wellbeing of others. I rubbed my arms with as much vigor as possible in the hope the bleak feelings would dissipate like the clouds overhead.

As I stood and stretched, Smoke phoned. "Detective?"

"Doc Patrick's team wrapped up Pearce Bennet's autopsy," he said.

"Seems like it took longer than normal."

"We got a later start. Long story short, Doc said Mister Bennet wouldn't have lived to be an old man. His heart, lungs, sinuses, circulatory system, and brain all showed damage from excessive coke and meth use."

"On the outside, it showed up on his skin as sores," I said.

"Yep. Lots of sores and scabs. Those nasty meth bugs, crank bugs. Bennet must have felt a whole lotta critters crawling on his skin, under his skin," he said.

"What torture. The one time I got bit by sand chiggers I couldn't believe how much those bites itched. I thought I would go crazy. At least Mother's home remedy of apple cider vinegar and baking soda gave me some relief."

"I can relate. Chiggers got me back in my teen years. They were bad one summer at the Pacer Lake beach. Lots of welts on my legs and the worst itching that went on for days. Well, we got off track there," he said.

I gave a little laugh. "Hey, we just learned something new about each other, right? Getting back to Bennet. Did Doctor Patrick identify a cause and manner of death?"

"Presumed overdose, and the lab will run blood tests this afternoon. Manner could be accidental, suicide, or homicide."

"And it's up to us to prove it was a homicide," I said.

"You got that right. That's why they pay us the big bucks."

I heard Weber let out a loud "huh."

"Are you finished at the ME's office?" I asked.

"Yeah, my driver is cruising down Highway Ten as we speak. The way he drives we'll be at the office in about thirty."

I heard another "huh."

"Your driver sounds like Johnny one-note," I said.

"Could be worse."

I chuckled again. "I guess. We'll touch base later, and I'll fill you in on tomorrow's planned activities."

"Later then."

I felt calmer after we disconnected. Smoke had the ability to allay my fears even in a conversation about an unrelated matter. It reminded me he was there for me and would do anything to help in times of trouble. Grandma Aleckson was another who had talked me off the ledge more than once. She had instilled bravery and confidence in me from the time I was a toddler and on through the years.

Grandma was the one who recognized Smoke and I were in love before either of us was ready to admit to it. She was blessed with emotional intelligence and wisdom and had innate investigative skills. Grandma guided me onto a clear path more times than I could count and helped get me back in the field after a critical incident landed me behind a desk in the sheriff's office for months. When Smoke coaxed me back to help with a case, Grandma convinced me I could do it. Not an easy feat. After that, I secretly considered Smoke and Grandma as my crisis tag team.

She answered after the first ring. "Hi, Grandma."

"My Heart. How are you?"

"To be honest, I'm a little stressed." Okay, a *lot* stressed.

"What happened?" she asked.

"Sara called to tell me she's worried about me. It's a case I'm working on."

"What's going on? Have you been threatened, dear?"

"No, no, nothing like that. I told Sara it was Mother and John Carl with all their worrying that's impacting her thinking," I said.

"I don't believe that's the case. Sara thinks for herself. She has years of experience with felons and other miscreants."

"She does."

"If Sara's worried about you, she may have good reason," she said.

That did not reassure me. I countered with, "But she couldn't put her finger on it. Said it's a gut feeling."

"Ah, hmm. How about you and your gut feelings?"

"Okay, I admit I have felt off since Queenie got hurt. It actually started two days before but got worse after that." I told her about Rebecca's ordeal. About Kelvin, without giving his name. The three overdose deaths, without getting into details. Then finished with Dr. Watts's behavior and the extra attention he showed me.

Grandma's sigh came through loud and clear over the phone. "My Heart, my dear Heart. Why didn't you call before this?"

"I should have and thought about it. But you know how I usually need to process things before I can talk about them. Even to you. Even to Smoke."

"Yes, and you know we share that trait." Along with many others. "Let's examine some things. Queenie is doing well now," she said.

"Thankfully."

"Things are better with Rebecca."

"Again, thankfully."

"But this drug boy who is on the loose is a major concern."

"He sure is," I said.

"And the veterinarian is also a concern."

"Yes. There's something about him that gets me. And like with Sara and her fears, I can't put my finger on the exact reason why."

"You're smart, but more importantly, you have good instincts. You made the decision to change vets after Queenie's next visit. And to avoid him in the meantime," she said.

"You agree I should not take his calls, or answer the door if he stops by?"

"Definitely," she said.

25

Blake

What in the hell was Corinne doing at the Henry Olson County Park? He pulled into the park before he noticed her sheriff's car. Seconds later she walked from the treed area into the clearing with her uniform on. And looked right at him. Had she recognized him? Was she there because someone reported something she needed to check out? Was KP a known drug dealer they were tracking, and she had followed him there? No. She wouldn't be alone if that were the case. Other deputies would be there, too.

As he drove away, he struggled to catch his breath, could barely see to drive, and pulled over before he crashed into someone. He thought he might suffer a heart attack. When he regained some composure, he chided himself, mentally kicked himself a dozen times.

Guilt settled in. He should not have acted like he had anything to hide. It was normal for people to go to parks, that's what they were there for. For the public to have places to recreate. What was suspicious was that he took off when he saw Corinne.

If she had seen him and asked about it, what would he say? That he liked the park and stopped there sometimes because it was a good place to think? But as he pulled in, a meeting reminder beeped on his phone, one he had forgotten all about? Yes, he had seen a sheriff's car but not her. Or he would have at least said hello before he left.

Blake scrubbed his face with his hands. He had been a truthful person in the past. Before his mission started, he could not remember when he told a lie, other than a white one to protect his wife's feelings. Like when she asked how he liked an outfit she bought, and he told her it looked good on her. That part was true. Like all the clothes she wore. Everything looked good on her model body. That he liked a particular outfit was not always true. Since his mission began, Blake had been forced to lie to the dealers and hide his actions from the authorities to accomplish his tasks. But the thought of telling Corinne a bald-faced lie poked holes in his gut. What would he say to her?

He had noticed at least two other vehicles at the park but couldn't say what kind or color they were if his life depended on it. He figured one must be KP's. Blake drew a breath and dialed his number.

"Where are you?" KP said.

"There is a sheriff's car and a deputy at the park. Didn't you notice?"

"No. I'm down the path near the river and the sheriff's car wasn't there when I got here."

"I'll give them a little time and then swing back in. If that's okay with you." He didn't want to identify Corinne by name.

"Sure, I got an hour before I gotta be somewhere."

Blake waited eight minutes. The trees blocked view of the parking area until he was by the turn-in access. Damn. Corinne's car was still there. What could she be doing there? He sped up past the park then pulled over to let KP know the coast was still not clear.

"How about I hike up to get a view and let you know when the sheriff's car is gone?" KP offered.

"That'd be good. Thanks." Blake could not blow this contact, this deal. KP may have killed his wife. He was the last of four suspects she had called. Blake had been up in the air about whether to continue his mission, eliminate more dealers after KP. But he decided right there on the spot that KP would be the last dealer to die at his hands. Blake couldn't continue to handle the arrangements, not with the hoops he had to jump through, the pressure he was under, the stress it caused to arrange his schedule around drug deals, the lies he told. Especially since he had fallen for a sheriff's deputy sergeant. That made everything more complex.

After KP was taken care of, he would go back to his single vocation as a veterinarian, the job he loved. Moments of tension or anxiety were nothing compared to what he had experienced the last months in the illegal drug world. Where he had to be polite to dealers who sold his wife drugs and live with the knowledge that one was her killer. At least it gave him peace that in a few days, the last of the four suspects would be facing his maker.

Blake drove his vehicle partway down a long driveway to avoid being spotted by Corinne if she went south on County 6. He let the engine idle in case someone appeared, and he needed to leave in a hurry. When his phone rang, Blake's hand trembled so much, he had trouble hitting the green talk button. Finally. "Yes?"

"The deputy's car is still here, but I don't want to go wandering around in case they see me," KP said.

"I agree. I would think they'd be gone soon. And I have some really good stuff for you after they leave," Blake said to keep KP patient and interested.

"Well, man, I got about forty-five minutes left. We should be okay."

Six minutes and twenty-eight seconds later, KP called to let him know the deputy's car had just left. "I'll be there in a few minutes." Blake watched the road for a bit to see if Corinne drove past the driveway where he sat. With no sign of her, he knew she had taken the north route. Blake returned to the park and saw only one vehicle there, a Dodge Ram pickup. Must be the man's and he could finally meet up with KP after all the unexpected hassles. He pulled the SUV to a stop and willed his body to relax. He needed to project a cool and collected presence.

Blake pulled the sun visor down to glimpse himself in the mirror. He had been using his wife's tanning bed every day and his skin had darkened to a strong black tea color. He had paid a lot for his fake beard, well worth it. It had gray strands mixed in with the dark brown that gave him a distinguished look and covered his sunken cheeks. The change in his appearance from a year ago was extraordinary. And not all bad. He slid his sunglasses from the top of his head to rest on his nose.

Blake left the vehicle and once again patted his windbreaker pocket to be sure the packets were still there. KP had told him to follow the first pathway toward the river, the eastern most one in the park. Blake was halfway down it when a man stepped out from behind a tree and gave him a second near heart attack that day.

For two reasons. He was already tense enough, and that element of surprise spiked his heart rate to a number off the charts. But the more critical reason was that KP was none other than *Kelvin Dean*. Damn it all. There he stood with the Deans' son on an illegal drug deal. What were the chances? He thought for a second the man on the path was an optical illusion. That he imagined it was Kelvin because he had seen him leaving Percy's house Sunday night.

Blake was caught between a rock and a hard place. Turn tail and run or follow through with the deal and decide what to do about the whole issue later. He jutted his chin out and frowned to alter his appearance a bit.

"First things first. You carrying?" Kelvin asked.

"No."

"Can you lift your jacket and turn around?"

Blake did so then shrugged.

"You look kinda familiar," Kelvin said.

Blake shrugged again, stuck his sweaty hands in his pockets, and was grateful when he came up with a lightning-fast response, his voice a raspy whisper with an accent. "I do? I didn't know there was another guy out there as good looking as me."

Kelvin laughed. "I like a guy with a sense of humor. And who still has smarts even after he's been using long enough for it to show up on his looks."

"It's that obvious?" Blake said.

"Yeah, man. A little, anyhow."

Blake pulled four baggies from his pocket and passed them to Kelvin. "Here you go. You won't find better sniff than this anywhere."

Kelvin opened a bag, wet his pinky finger, dipped it into the powder, pulled it out and stuck it on his tongue. He closed his eyes and smiled. "Yeah, man. This is gooood stuff."

"I know you have to get somewhere, and so do I. How about this? Those are your first complimentary samples. I'll get you a couple more in a few days. And if you're interested, we can talk terms after that. What you might want, how much it will cost."

"I can't argue with free, man." Kelvin studied Blake for a second. "Are you sure we don't know each other from somewhere?"

"My memory isn't all that great, but I think I would have remembered you," Blake said.

"Ha! Likewise. I guess I'll take off then. Call me, or I'll call you."

Kelvin headed up the pathway and Blake sank his weight against a tree. Kelvin Dean was not just a drug addict, he was a damn dealer. And one who might have killed his wife. He knew Kelvin sold her drugs because there had been several calls between the two. Could Kelvin have known who she was, that she was his wife? He didn't think that was possible. Not unless she told him who she was, and why would she reveal her identity to her suppliers? She had turned into a clam, at least to him, those last months.

Until Blake spotted Kelvin leaving Percy's house, he had not seen him for some years. But Kelvin had a distinct look that Blake would know anywhere, a combination of his parent's looks. His mother was petite with small, attractive facial features. His father was a big guy with large features that fit his face. Kelvin had smaller eyes, mouth, and chin like his mother, a bigger nose and ears, and was tall like his father. Somehow it worked and gave him a comely look.

When Blake began his mission, he hadn't fathomed he would land in such a bizarre predicament. How many other people he knew, or at least thought he did, were drug users and abusers? He had lived in a bubble with his blinders on, that much he had discovered in the last months. If he didn't know what his own wife was up to, why would he think he knew what anyone else might do in their personal lives?

At least Kelvin seemed to trust him and without a doubt liked the free cocaine Blake had paid big bucks for. He would call Kelvin in a couple days and arrange the next meeting for some time on Sunday. How busy would the park be on Sunday? Not like in the summer, he figured.

He knew why Kelvin didn't want to meet at his house if he lived with his parents. Blake had five days to make the big decision. Give Kelvin the fatal dose and settle his wife's score, or let him live out of respect for his parents? They entrusted the care of their valuable horses to Blake and had paid him a ton of money over the years. He wished he had someone to consult with in his decision. Unless his wife's spirit whispered in his ear, there was no one. It was all up to him.

26

I walked into Smoke's cubicle and Weber was there, too. When Weber spotted me, he raised one eyebrow in a look I recognized, one that told me he was up to something. He started scratching his face, his arms, his chest. "Oh, these damn chiggers are driving me crazy."

I reached over and gave his bicep a backhanded tap. "You are one funny guy, Vince. Not." But he was and looked goofy enough to make me laugh.

Smoke tapped his pen. "Sergeant, you have another meet up with a dealer scheduled?"

I nodded. "Tomorrow. Mandy and I will meet a guy called KP in Henry Olson Park at sixteen hundred. Mac says he does not meet buyers at his house. You two available to serve as our backup?"

"Lord willing and the creek don't rise," Smoke said.

"River. The park's on the river," Weber said.

I shook my head. "Vincent."

He raised his hands. "What?"

"Let's get a hold of Mandy, see if we can pull our plans together for tomorrow," Smoke said.

I fished out my phone and called her.

Zubinski answered with, "Sergeant?"

"Hi. I'm with Smoke and Vince. Can you meet us at the office to run over tomorrow's deal?"

"Sure. In about ten, if that works."

"Yep, in the detective's cubicle."

I pushed the end button. "She'll be here in ten. So. Any surprises at Pearce Bennet's autopsy?"

"Not really. Just a sad reminder how drugs can damage a human body," Smoke said.

"Yeah well, if the druggies out there sat through an autopsy, saw what their insides looked like, that might shake somethin' loose in their brains to make them wanna quit that shit," Weber said.

"When drugs are that important to them, scare tactics only go so far," I said.

Weber leaned his head toward his shoulder in a stretch. "Yeah."

Smoke picked up the receiver on his desk phone and glanced at his memo pad as he punched in the numbers. "I'll let Bennet's mother know her son's body can be released tomorrow morning." He hit the speaker button.

"Hello?" Betty Jessen answered.

"Ms. Jessen, Detective Dawes, Winnebago County. We spoke yesterday."

"Yes."

Smoke's eyebrows drew together. "I'm calling to let you know your son's body will be ready to go to the funeral home of your choice in the morning."

"I told you to cremate him." Her voice was flat.

"I'm sorry, but I'm not able to authorize that. I can, however, give you some names of local directors to choose from."

"I can't do that. I can't do anything." She let out a loud wail that made all three of us jump.

After listening for a minute to sobs that changed in timbre like clashing symbols, Smoke said, "How about I do some checking, see what we can work out on this end."

The voice that held no emotion the day before exploded with it now. "I still have trouble believing Percy is gone, and then Pearce goes ahead and kills himself with drugs. Before he reformed. All these years, that's all I wanted. For him to reform. To feel bad for all the wrongs he did to everyone who loved him. Instead, he just kept going further down the toilet. That's what he did. Right into the sewer." Her new howl was deafening and made the hairs on the back of my neck stand on end.

Weber clapped his hands over his ears and Smoke pinched the bridge of his nose, looked at me and mouthed, "What now?"

"Ask her who we can call to be with her," I mouthed back.

Smoke gave her a minute, then asked the question.

"No. I will . . . call . . . my friend." And disconnected.

"Ah geez, that woman has one set of pipes. I think she mighta popped my eardrums," Weber said.

"Frightful, no doubt," Smoke said.

"I'm worried about her. Yesterday she acted like she didn't care and today she totally fell apart," I said.

"Boss man, maybe you should call the cops out there, ask them to knock on her door," Weber said.

"Thinking the same thing." Smoke turned to his computer and struck some keys. "Checking what county Wausau is in. Or if they have their own PD." He typed some more. "Marathon County, and Wausau does have its own PD. It's business hours. Good deal. I'll try that number."

Weber and I waited when Smoke placed the call. "Yes, this is Detective Elton Dawes, Winnebago County, Minnesota. . . . Yes, I have been in your state's Winnebago County. . . . The reason I'm calling is to request a check on one of your residents, Betty Jessen. I don't have her address. . . . Oh, you do. Good. Yesterday we delivered the news her son had died in our county, and when I followed up with her a few minutes ago, she didn't sound like she was doing well. . . . I appreciate that. And if you could let me know? . . . Thank you."

Smoke relayed his contact information then hung up. "They are very familiar with Ms. Jessen. On account of her son Pearce." He raised his eyebrows.

Amanda Zubinski joined us. "You all look like you got bad news," she said.

"Sorta." I filled her in on the Betty Jessen conversation.

"And we lost half our hearing during the poor woman's breakdown deal," Weber added.

"Wow. Not to sound selfish, but can't say I'm sorry I missed it," Zubinski said.

"Nope. Mandy, ahead of our meeting tomorrow, I went to Henry Olson Park to scope it out. It was quiet. Only two vehicles there and one belonged to Kendrick Dean. That surprised me for some reason," I said.

"The horse guy, that Kendrick Dean?" Weber said.

"Yeah. Anyway, I didn't see him, or anyone else while I was there, so they must have been off on the trails. Doesn't matter." I turned to Smoke and Weber. "It will be easy for you to hide, or at least to blend in there. Bring fishing rods if you want. I don't think we'll be there long. Unless we can coax something out of KP on the 'new guy in town,' Mandy and I will not do much chit chatting."

"No," Zubinski said.

"Good thing, huh?" Weber said.

"Yes," Zubinski said.

"Since Mandy and I are supposed to meet KP at sixteen hundred on the second pathway that goes down to the river, Smoke and Vince, you can either go in on the first or the second and move about halfway down if that works. It's easy to hide in the thick foliage," I said.

"Right. Vince, I'll have someone drop us off and we'll get there by fifteen twenty. The only thing we know about KP is that he does not meet clients at his place. We don't know what else he does to cover his tracks. He may be smart, careful to scope out his surroundings. If there are other vehicles there, he might check around the park to see who the owners are. In case he needs to change his plans," Smoke said.

"I s'pose," Weber said.

"If KP happens to get there before we do, we'll take the first pathway, wind our way closer to the second and set up shop. After Corky and Mandy are safely back in their vehicle, we'll wait for KP to adios and then catch a ride back to the office," Smoke said.

"You'll get someone to follow KP?" I asked.

"Yep, I'll ask Mason. We'll get KP's info from his plate unless he's driving a buddy's car. In any event, not everyone updates the info on their licenses when they move," Smoke said.

"That happens with some of those guys. They move a lot," Weber said.

"Mason will be in one of impound's finest, parked along the road so he can keep an eye on the access. Corky, Mandy, I'll have binoculars to watch KP when he gets there and will call Mason with his vehicle description and plate. Any questions, team?" Smoke said.

"No questions, but I have a request. We'll need the drug money, a few hundred. According to Mac, we will be having a party and are in search of some good coke," I said.

Smoke nodded. "I'll take care of that."

"Thanks," I said.

"All right then, thank you, everyone," Smoke said.

Weber and Zubinski left, and I took a seat in the visitor chair. "Smoke, have you decided when to have that talk with Doctor Watts, about his wife?"

"My next order of business. I'll see if he can come in today. Although, I gotta admit the way Ms. Jessen fell apart unnerved me a bit. So given the possibility Watts might have a similar breakdown, if we need to wait until tomorrow to break the news about his wife's other secret, that would be okay by me."

"It will be a big blow. Probably worse than when he found out his wife had been using illegal drugs," I said.

"He didn't believe it then, and I have my doubts he ever came to terms with it. Really accepted it," he said.

"You could be right. I did notice he looked better than before, but this new info will not be good for his health."

I was in the small sergeant's office reviewing reports when Smoke phoned. "Doctor Watts said he'll be here after he finishes up with a call he's on. Be about thirty minutes."

"Anxious to hear what you need to tell him?"

"No doubt. I told him we have some new information about his wife."

"I wonder if he thinks we found out who sold her that deadly combo last year," I said.

"I'm afraid he might. As we said before, nothing about this will be easy."

"Got an interview room picked out yet?"

"They're all open at the moment. I'll go stick a note on the door to reserve B and let you know when Watts arrives," he said.

"Okie doke." I hung up and I felt for Dr. Watts. He was about to get a major gut punch, and from the reports of his behavior after his wife died, it was a valid concern. He was a strange man, and I worried he would get stranger still.

Smoke called twenty-four minutes later. "Watts is at the front counter. I'm on my way to meet him so go ahead and slip into the viewing room."

"Will do, and I'll say a prayer."

"Thanks."

When Dr. Watts walked into B, he looked like he had already gotten the report. His face was dark, more tanned than a few days ago. And flushed a deep red besides. He seemed to fall onto the chair. His hands were in fists when he plopped them on the table. Watts faced my direction, frowned, and pursed his lips like he was in pain.

"Did you find out who killed my wife?" Understandable why he phrased it that way. And maybe it was true. We knew with the current overdose cases someone had deliberately killed the dealers.

Smoke studied him a moment. "Unfortunately, no. The reason I needed to talk to you is, well, it concerns something we came across in a recent investigation." I felt sorry for Smoke.

Beads of sweat popped from pores on Watts's forehead and cheeks. His jaw was set, and he looked like a bundle of nerves. An involuntary response, a flashback to the time he sat across from the same detective who handled his wife's death investigation? The doctor lifted his arm and used his sleeve to wipe his forehead and cheeks. Smoke slid the tissue box kept on the table toward him.

"What is it then?" Watts managed in a voice so quiet I struggled to hear him.

"There is no easy way to tell you this. In the course of an investigation, we found some videos. Long story short, your wife was in a couple of them."

The flush left Watts's face and he went pale. "What are you talking about. What videos?" Again, just above a whisper.

"They were found among a decedent's possessions. Pornography." Smoke kept his voice steady.

Watts stared at Smoke for a moment then jumped up from his chair. Smoke did, too. Watts pointed his finger back and forth at Smoke. "What in the hell are you talking about? Did you see them?"

"A little. Enough to confirm it was your wife."

"You must mean a woman who looks like my wife," Watts said.

"She was identified as Eloise W. Your wife."

"That's impossible. I need to see the videos."

"They're in the evidence room." Smoke paused then said, "Doctor Watts, the only reason I'm telling you this is in case the videos are out in the cyber world. We didn't want you to get blindsided if someone you know happened to see them and felt they should tell you."

"No, no, no, no, *no!* Why would my wife do anything that crass? She is a beautiful, intelligent woman. We were never into *porn.* And now you tell me the whole world could find out about this. Who had these videos? What *decedent* are you talking about?"

"I guess you have the right to know. His name was Pearce Bennet from Little Mountain. He was going by Percy Bennet."

Watts sank back down on the chair like his legs had given out. He put his face in his hands and wept.

"Does that name mean anything to you?" Smoke asked in a lowered tone.

Watts shook his head back and forth. "No," he managed.

"All right. I've had tragic ordeals in my life, but not like this, and I can't know what you're going through. So, tell me, what can I do? Can I contact someone for you? Did you have a professional you talked to after your wife died?"

Watts nodded.

"Did it help?"

"A little." Watts stood again and clenched his jaws and fists. "Last year you told me my wife had been buying illegal drugs, yet you found nothing in her phone, or her computer. And now you say she was in *porn* movies. How can I believe that?"

"Because it's the truth. You asked why your wife would do what she did, and we don't have that answer. There is no one left to ask, as far as we know."

"If that Pearce was still alive, I would kill him with my bare hands," Watts spit out and punched a fist into his open hand.

"I would feel the same way if I were in your place. I would be tempted to do that very thing but would leave it up to the authorities to handle his punishment. If he were involved in anything illegal. Crass is one thing, but illegal is another," Smoke said.

"I have to leave; I think I might be sick."

"I'll walk you out, and if you need to stop at the restroom, there's one on the way."

27

Blake

Blake had high hopes when the day started out sunny with a clear sky. But by noon it had gone to hell, from bad to worse, from worse to worst. The worst he could have imagined. *Not* imagined. He was overwhelmed when the detective dropped the bombshell news that his beloved wife had cheated on him, engaged in illicit behavior. If that creepy dealer he knew as Percy Bennet had touched his wife, or if she had touched him . . . Blake could not even go there.

He had to believe there had been no physical contact between his wife and Bennet. Or with anyone else in the videos. A final nail in his coffin. *And then what?* He could not change a single moment of the past.

Blake tried to block mental images of his wife with next to nothing on in the videos, but they invaded his thoughts. It was difficult to comprehend that she bought illegal drugs, but the things she engaged in with a sleazy Pearce chipped away at his soul.

Had he known his wife was addicted to drugs, he would have gotten her into treatment. Minnesota has among the most successful programs in the country. He had kept nothing from his wife, yet the last year of her life revolved around a lie, a secret she kept so she could nurture her habit. Why had she chosen drug addiction over him?

Blake couldn't sit still so he grabbed a jacket and headed outside. The sun had set, and dusk settled in around him. Clouds hid the moon's light, but he had gotten comfortable navigating around in the dark. It gave him the necessary cover when he met with the two drug dealers that lived in neighborhoods where he might be spotted.

His mind would not shut off. Damn. His wife might be some kind of star in the sick porn world. The realization made him lightheaded and weak. Then a rush of heat blasted throughout his body, followed by cold sweats. Blake had to get back inside before something else happened. Like an actual heart attack. He patted his pocket to be sure his cell phone was there in case he needed to call 911.

Blake felt relieved he made it home and collapsed on the couch in the great room. He had to close the door in his mind where his wife's activities played again and again. He took one deep breath after another until his heart settled at a slower rate.

Then his thoughts traveled to earlier in the day when things first went south. He had finally set up a meeting with KP. Then who of all people but Corinne Aleckson was in Henry Olson County Park when he got there. And still there the next time he checked. When KP told him she had left, and Blake met him on the trail, KP turned out to be none other than Kelvin Dean. What were the odds, *what were the odds*?

Thank God Blake looked and sounded different enough to convince Kelvin he was not someone he knew. He hoped so. Or else he had lost his chance for a next and final meeting. It was the first time Blake had come up with an accent on the spot and sent a mental thank you to his old college buddy from Pakistan when he imitated him. He also thanked his lucky stars he had communicated via text messages with KP before that.

Blake once again wished he had someone to confide in, to ask what he should do about Kelvin Dean. He respected the Deans and loved their horses. But their son turned out to be one bad dude as far as Blake was concerned. Should he go through with it; give Kelvin the lethal drug combination, or not? He had five days to decide.

28

Smoke and I lay on our backs in bed, exhausted by the day's events, but too keyed up to rest. We needed to hash things out so we could relax and fall asleep.

"Way too many balls up in the air," I said.

"One way to put it. The Wausau police officer that checked on Ms. Jessen said she was okay. But I got the feeling I should go pick her up, bring her here, get her some help so she can take care of things. Her son's body, the other son's house, vehicle, possessions."

I rested my hand on his stomach. "I think you should. Maybe her friend can follow you here. Betty will have a lot to navigate and could use a friend's shoulder to cry on, help her make decisions. We can get folks from Human Services to lend a hand, too."

Smoke put his hand on mine and gave a squeeze. "We've got Bennet's garage to process tomorrow, and I'll call her after that, Thursday or Friday, see what we can work out."

"I hope she agrees to come. Maybe get a cleaning service in beforehand, make sure there are no drug remnants in the house."

"Sounds like a plan. I want the results on the partial fingerprint from the baggie we got at Bennet's. And identify that shoe brand from the hundreds out there."

"The sole doesn't look like any running shoes I've had," I said.

"No. If we had more than the top half of the sole, we might've gotten lucky and had the company's name stamped on it."

"I have pairs that do." I rubbed Smoke's fingers with my thumb. "I can't help thinking about Doctor Watts, how he reacted when you broke the news about his wife's secret acting career. When he jumped up like that, I was glad the table was between you."

"No doubt. It put me on instant high alert. In all my dealings with him last year, it was obvious how devastated he was, but he never lost it like that," he said.

"It's a lot different getting the news your wife died than your wife was in porn movies."

"You got that right. From what I gathered, self-blame and guilt compounded his grief last year was. Maybe this new twist will ease some guilt and shift the blame."

"Bad news to find out after her death and not be able to talk to her about it. Yell at her if it would make him feel better. Whatever her reasons—and we can guess—she could explain, ask for forgiveness, work it out with him," I said.

"All I can say is it's a good thing Watts didn't know Bennet, because if he had to imagine his wife close to him . . .

well, all I can say is I didn't even like you in the same room with him." He took my hand and kissed it.

"I didn't like me in the same room with him either."

Smoke chuckled, moved my arm, and rolled on top of me. "You've reminded me once again how downright blessed I am to have you."

"I won't argue with that."

He nibbled on my neck. "How about that?"

"Won't argue with that either."

I found his lips with mine and our kisses made me forget any cares I had.

Wednesday morning Smoke left for work at seven a.m. He and the crime lab team wanted to get an early start on Bennet's garage. It was also meet KP day and one I had semi-dreaded since we set it up. But it gave me the morning to do other things. I planned to take a long run and bring Queenie over to see Gramps.

It surprised me when Rebecca phoned at eight twenty a.m. "Hi, Sergeant Corky. You know how Justin drives us to school?"

"Sure."

"Well, he and Tina got out and I stayed in the car for a minute to finish reading something. When I got out, a car pulled up next to me. It was Kelvin and he smiled at me and said, 'Did you call the cops about the party at Catelyn's?' The way he smiled and looked at me kinda like scared me. I shook my head and said 'No.' He said, 'Well, you and your friend left early so I thought you might've.' So I said 'No' again. He smiled really big then and said, 'Good, 'cause I like you a lot.'

All I could think to say was, 'Bye, I gotta get to class,' and I sorta like hurried into the school."

Oh, dear Lord. Kelvin *likes* Rebecca. A lot. Pulses hammered against my temples from the second she said Kelvin's name through the whole story. *Take a deep breath to sound calm.* "Rebecca. Gosh, I can see why that scared you. What kind of car was he driving?"

"I don't know. It was blue."

"Two doors, four doors?"

"Oh, yeah, it was a two-door," she said.

"How about the size?"

"A smaller one that looked like it cost a lot of money."

BMW, Corvette, Mustang? "All right. Maybe we can look at photos later, see if we can figure that out." Unless I can view the footage. "Where'd Justin park?" I asked.

"In the back row, like over to the right, if you're looking at it from the school. I really gotta get to class, Sergeant Corky."

"We'll touch base later. Take care."

I felt my blood pressure rise. Did we need to hire a guard to protect Rebecca? Her parents could file a no contact order. If they knew Kelvin's last name. First order of business: call the school.

I looked through the contact list in my phone, selected Mrs. Goldin's number, and hit the talk button. "Good morning, Missus Goldin speaking."

"Missus Goldin, hi. Corky Aleckson with a request."

"Good to hear your voice, Sergeant. What is it?"

"Rebecca saw Kelvin in the student parking lot a few minutes ago. He stopped and talked to her."

"Oh, dear."

"Oh, dear is right. I'm wondering if I might have a look at the footage, see if I can get a plate number, figure out who this Kelvin is. He was driving a blue two-door car that Rebecca said looked expensive," I added.

"Of course. And that reminds me what I forgot to tell you. I could not recall a Kelvin in this school as long as I've been here, so I went back in the records and didn't find one here in the last twenty years."

"Hmm. It brings us back to the questions, is that his real name or is he new around here? We will keep working on that. Meanwhile, what's a good time to view the footage?"

"Whatever works for you. We're here all day," she said.

"A half hour?"

"See you then."

I dashed upstairs for a three-minute shower, brushed out my hair and let it hang loose then pulled on jeans, a light blue t-shirt, navy hoodie, and tennis shoes. I grabbed my purse and phone and was on the road in a flash. I watched for two-door blue cars all the way to the school.

The receptionist buzzed me into Goldin's office where she and Officer Casey Dey sat in front of her giant computer monitor. "Welcome," Goldin said.

"Thanks. Already at it, huh?" I said.

Dey smiled. "Oh, hi. I thought you were a student for a sec."

I laughed. "Dressed to fit in. Day off." Except for the drug deal later on, that is.

"It works. Yeah, we are just bringing up the parking lot footage. What was the approximate time?"

"Just before eight twenty. That's when Rebecca called me. When she ran me through their exchange, it was maybe a minute long. Said when she got out of the car Kelvin pulled up next to her, so we could start at eight fifteen, see if he knew she was in Justin's car and waited for her. Justin parked in the back row, on the west side."

Dey hit some buttons. "Camera A should give us a good view. It captures from north to south. Let me turn the monitor so we can all see it." It was on a swivel stand and moved with ease. I walked to the other side of the desk as Dey selected the time. Vehicles pulled into spaces and kids piled out. At eight sixteen, Justin's car parked then he and Tina climbed from the front seats and headed toward the school.

Less than a minute later a sleek blue car drove up from the east and stopped a few cars back from Justin's. When Rebecca got out, the car eased forward and stopped. Their exchange was thirty-two seconds long. Then Rebecca walked around the back of his car toward the school. The camera view ended at the doors.

"Looks like it was a Corvette, but from the side view it's hard to tell. And we can't see the plate or Kelvin," I said.

"I'll go to Camera B. It'll be the car's driver's side view." When the image came up, Dey froze the shot. Rebecca stood away from the window. It gave us a side view of Kelvin's face. He had his elbow on the open window, wore sunglasses and a stocking cap pulled down over his ears, hair hanging halfway to his shoulders.

"Is it just me, or does he look like a thug?" I said.

"Kelvin seems both smart and dumb at the same time. First off, why would he be in the school parking lot with all the cameras?" Dey asked.

"My guess is he wanted to talk to Rebecca and must have somehow known she rides to school with Justin. He prepared for it, covered his face well. But maybe not so smart if he didn't figure out that we can run his plates. Casey, what about cameras on the east and west side so we have a front view of his car," I said.

"Sure." Dey selected the one that faced east. "I'll go back to eight ten and take it from there." At eight thirteen the blue car drove in and Dey panned in and froze the shot. "Yep, it's a Corvette, like you thought."

"Let me jot the plate number down," I said, and Mrs. Goldin pushed a notepad and pen my way.

"There's a glare on the windshield so we really can't see inside," Dey said.

"No. But we should learn his identity soon enough." I pulled out my phone and called Communications. "Hi, Robin, Sergeant Aleckson. Wondering if you can run a plate for me?"

"Sure can."

"It's One David Two Oscar Henry David."

Robin repeated it, and within seconds told me, "Those plates come back as stolen."

"What?" I crosschecked the plate on the car with what I had written down. They matched.

"Stolen last week from a Ford Escort in Hennepin County."

"That's why the number seemed familiar; the report came across our mobile terminals at the time. You can let everyone know they are on a blue Corvette last seen at Oak Lea High School this morning. Thank you." I hung up and shook my head. "Good ole Kelvin stole those plates from a vehicle in Hennepin County last week."

"Serious? I guess that explains that. We don't want Kelvin within ten miles of here," Dey said.

"Make that a hundred," Goldin said.

"Yeah. He sells drugs to kids, hounds them, steals license plates, and is involved in who knows what else," Dey said.

"I swear his encounters with Rebecca in the last week have taken a year off my life," I said.

Goldin reached over and patted my arm.

"Thanks," I said.

"I heard you reported Kelvin was at a party in town where kids were vaping last Friday," Dey said.

"Keep the details quiet, but Rebecca and Tina were at their friend's house, and some kids were outside vaping. Rebecca spotted Kelvin outside there, too. She and Tina didn't want to be there, so they walked to Holiday and called me for a ride. We drove past their friend's house, and I saw kids outside vaping.

"Of course, I couldn't get a good look at Kelvin. Called your PD and they responded in minutes, but Kelvin was gone when they got there. Kelvin asked Rebecca this morning if she was the one who called the police. She told him no. Then on Sunday, we were at Parlor, and she spotted him looking in the window at us. I hurried outside to find him, but he vanished. Again."

"What a rat," Dey said.

"I have secretly given him two different names, Chameleon Kelvin and . . . well, the other one starts with an A, ends with an E, and rhymes with mole."

They both laughed.

"I know." I turned to Dey. "Casey, will you check the parking lot videos when school lets out? In case he comes back. And if your detective is available to keep watch in an unmarked, that would be great. Now that we have a legal reason to pull Kelvin over."

"Good plan. I'll check with the chief, ask the detective to show up twenty or so minutes before school lets out. Because ten to one, if Kelvin comes back, he will slip in early," he said.

"If a detective can't make it, give me a holler and I'll see if one of ours can," I said.

"Sure," he said.

"I plan to talk to the Brenners after school, make sure they know the latest. I want them to keep a watch out for Kelvin, too. It bothers me to no end he actually sought out Rebecca this morning," I said.

"Definitely. Rebecca is young and inexperienced so it's a relief she feels comfortable enough to call you, to tell you what's going on, not keeping it to herself." Goldin said.

I nodded. "It sure is."

I stewed about Kelvin all the way home. Then Queenie's sweet face cheered me up a bit. "Girl, Gramps would love to see you. Wanna go to Gramps' house?" She whined and moved her head back and forth. "I'll change, and we'll be on our way."

I put on my running clothes and clipped the Smith & Wesson on my belt. Queenie followed me to my car and navigated her way on to the back seat with little effort. Another sign she was on the mend. Gramps was over the moon to have Queenie spend some time with him. She sat by his chair with her head on his lap while he petted her and uttered words about what a good girl she was and how happy he was she was better. I left Queenie with him and jogged north on Brandt Avenue. I turned west at County 35 and fell into an eight-minute mile pace.

Most vehicles going either direction were not blue in color, so when I spotted one I paid close attention. No Corvettes. Not a surprise since they weren't common. A white Ford F-150 passed me, and I hoped it wasn't Dr. Watts. It was moving too fast for me to catch the plate, and it did not stop. Good thing. I had to face Watts in two days for Queenie's checkup. How should I act around him, what should I say? He must be distressed over what Smoke told him. Maybe he would call in sick and Queenie could see another vet instead.

I turned around at the three-and-a-half-mile mark. As I headed back to Gramps' house, my thoughts turned to Gram and how much we all missed her. Especially Gramps, of course. Like Grandma, she was a true partner to her husband farmer. Worked alongside him, tended to the house and garden. Canned and froze their produce. Knitted and crocheted and sewed. I loved to wrap myself in the afghan she made me. It was a surprise to us all when she got hooked on pain meds. Like Eloise Watts, she had a healthy lifestyle. Mrs. Watts had been injured in a car crash, and Gram suffered with arthritis. Different ailments, but each caused enough pain to seek a remedy that led to their addictions.

Dear Lord, help me think of something positive. I started to count my blessings and it helped. When I got back to Gramps' house, I grabbed a towel from my car, wiped the sweat off my face and neck, then let myself into the house. Gramps was asleep in his chair and Queenie slept at his feet. They both stirred when I stepped into the entry.

"There you are, Corky. Just resting my eyes a minute," Gramps said.

I smiled at the familiar line. "A good thing to do, too. Thanks for watching Queenie for me. She was really excited to come see you."

"I missed my girl, and it's good to have her here."

"Gramps, we'll need to leave in a minute. Is there anything I can get you before we go?"

"Your mother brought lunch over on her way to work, so I am all set."

I leaned over and gave him a kiss. "Gramps, is it okay to use your car this afternoon?"

"You know it is. I won't be needin' it."

"Thank you. Until next time. All right, Queenie, time to go."

She stood, and Gramps gave her head a parting scratch.

29

After I showered and dressed, I sent both Jean and Dale Brenner a text message, asking them to call me on their lunch break. Forty-eight minutes later my phone rang, and Jean's name popped up on my screen. "Hello, Jean."

"Hi, Corky. Dale's here, too. We're in the teachers' lounge on speaker phone."

"Okay, good. I wanted you to know what happened this morning between Rebecca and Kelvin."

"Rebecca and *Kelvin?* What was it?" Jean used her outside voice, and I pulled the phone away from my ear.

I went through the details, what Rebecca had told me, the captured video, Kelvin's car with stolen plates, and that a detective would watch for him after school.

"I feel like we're caught up in a nightmare," Jean said.

"It is. A criminal is targeting our daughter. We need to put a stop to it, like yesterday," Dale said.

"I agree with you, a hundred percent. We *will* find Kelvin and we will stop him. Arrest him and put him in jail. The charges against him are mounting."

"We feel so helpless," Jean said.

"You are not helpless. In fact, there are some practical things you can do. For one thing, I'd like you to ask Justin to walk Rebecca and Tina to his car after school dismisses for the day. The PD will be watching for Kelvin, but you know what a cluster it is—the afterschool mass exodus. There is a very slight possibility the PD won't spot Kelvin. I doubt that he'll return this afternoon, but we want to have all the bases covered."

"That's good," Dale said.

"Until we get Kelvin, make sure the girls don't go out on their own. And all the other safety tips you know, like keeping the doors locked. It doesn't hurt to have the blinds drawn, especially on the street side. Kelvin may contact Rebecca again, and you'll want to be prepared, in case," I said.

"Dale nodded, and we both agree you're right," Jean said.

"I'll send Justin a message about waiting for the girls after school," Dale said.

"Thanks. We'll be in touch," I said.

I would have been at Oak Lea High School when school dismissed if I hadn't had another assignment. Amanda Zubinski and I met in our drug-buying clothes at the impound lot at three p.m. I wanted to be a good sport and act like one, too. We both had human hair wigs that were as natural as our own hair. Zubinski's blonde one had a loose wave that touched her shoulders. It was a nice contrast to my dark brown layered wig that hung halfway to my waist.

I wore too much makeup, and she wore little. She had on a pair of skinny jeans with no slits in them, and I had my grunge-look ones with slits. Zubinski wore a long-sleeved dress, a sleeveless sweater over her jeans, and short brown boots. I had on my jean jacket and clodhopper boots.

"Well, let's party on, girlfriend," she said when we faced each other in the lot. "I almost forgot how different you look in that garb."

"Likewise. And I'm glad you are in a good mood, Mandy. You'll help raise my spirits."

"Not feelin' so good?" she asked.

"I'm okay. Things are going on with Rebecca. And I keep thinking about Bennet. I mean, Mac and I were there Saturday and his death kind of haunts me. Makes it harder to meet another drug dealer and act like nothing happened," I said.

"Oh, I get that for sure. I didn't sleep Monday night after finding Bennet like that. It seemed like it took an hour for Smoke to get there after I called."

"Takes forever when you're waiting like that. Well, let's find something semi-classy because we are a pair who has enough money to buy cocaine for twenty or so people."

We scanned over the list, and both pointed at a black Nissan Maxima at the same time. "I'll sign us out. Here are the keys if you want to drive," I said.

"Yes. Even nicer than my ride."

Zubinski pulled the vehicle up next to me a few minutes later and I climbed in. "It's even clean."

"Poor guy had his car all cleaned and gets it taken away for something he shouldn't have done," Zubinski said.

"We've got a whole lot full of confiscated vehicles for that very reason."

"It's about thirteen miles to the park from here so we'll get there plenty early," she said.

"Smoke and Vince took off a while ago to get there before KP," I said.

"In some ways, we got the easy part. We're with the drug dealer and can watch him, get a handle on what he's like, see if he starts to do something hinky."

"I agree, Mandy. I'm more tense when I'm on the other side, especially when there's silence, when nobody's talking. It hit me that I hold my breath until somebody talks again."

"I do the same thing. Like I said, it's easier being the one with the dealer," she said.

We didn't want to arrive too early, so Zubinski said, "Why don't we head south? A quarter mile down there's a field road we can take back to a clump of trees. It's a good spot to sit, work on reports, and keep an eye out for crazy drivers. I've done that a few times."

"Sure, I've parked there myself."

On the way, I got a call from Officer Dey. "Hey, Casey."

"Hey. Well, our detective sat in a stall on the east side of the parking lot, saw no sign of the blue Corvette after school today. With the usual long line of parents picking up kids, he paid close attention. I watched the videos, too. The 'Vette didn't appear in any of them."

"I guess that's both good and bad. I don't want Kelvin anywhere near Rebecca. I want his ass in jail."

"It'll happen. His behavior and actions are bound to catch up with him," he said.

"For sure, and thanks."

"You bet. Later then."

I told Zubinski the story and the concern for Rebecca I had alluded to earlier.

"You know how stunning she is, and she's not even fifteen yet. But she seems older. There's something otherworldly about her," she said.

"Otherworldly? How did you come up with that?"

"I don't know. Ethereal, maybe. She has sort of a mysterious spiritual presence about her."

"Gee, Mandy, you are right on. Rebecca has a special beauty," I said.

"After my near-death experience, I started paying closer attention to people. Not to sound too far out, but some people give off bad vibes, others comforting ones. You know that; you're pretty intuitive. All I can say is I notice it more now," she said.

"It's important to read people in this business, that's for darn sure. But a few people manage to fool us. I like that you've taken your observations to the next level."

"Thanks. Not to make you feel worse about Rebecca, but lots of guys will fall for her along the way. She could pass for nineteen now."

"I know, and that adds to the worry mix."

We made small talk and watched the world go by until three fifty, then drove to Henry Olson County Park. Not too early, not too late.

"It doesn't look like he's here," I said as we pulled into the park.

"And it's close to meeting time. He would've called, right?" She parked then looked at her watch.

"You'd think. I'll send Smoke a text." *Any sign of him?* I sent from my work phone.

No. A sedan was here, but the guy left 4 minutes ago. FYI, ran plate, wrong initials. He texted back.

Okay, I'll activate, and we'll head down the path.

10-4, got you covered.

I nudged Zubinski. "All right, we are going live so we will remain silent."

"That's our right, right?"

I laughed. "Right." I activated the device and we got out of the Nissan.

We made our way to the pathway and started the trek down. A tall man with a shaved head, presumed to be KP, stood by a tree about halfway to the river. It startled me and took a second to find my voice. "You KP?"

"Yeah, you girls look a little scared," he said.

"You kinda took us by surprise since there're no cars in the lot. Did you walk here?" I asked him.

"No."

I shrugged. "Okay, no big deal. It's just that I'd offer you a ride if you needed one."

"I got it covered, thanks." That meant either his vehicle was hidden somewhere not far away, or someone had dropped him off and would return for him. That alerted Smoke and Weber, sent them the message.

KP raised his hands chest high. "First things first. No weapons, right?"

"Right," I said, and we both lifted our arms and turned around to show him we knew the drill.

"Good. Figured you'd be clean, but in this crazy world, I need to check. So. I understand you girls are lookin' for some fine coke."

"We sure are," Zubinski said.

"We got a party next week," I said.

"Not this week?" he asked.

Did I say something wrong? "Next week works better for us," I said.

"Well, hell's bells, turns out that works better for me, too. I found a new supplier who has the best sniff I've had in a long time. I'll be getting more from him soon to get for my clients, like you girls." KP's smile revealed perfect teeth. Not always the case with users. It made me think he had parents with enough money to feed him well and pay for braces.

Did I dare? "Nice. One of our other dealers got a new supplier a couple weeks back, too. We saw the guy, in fact. Younger, wears his long hair in a ponytail?" A safe, vague description that fit a bunch of dealers I had known.

"Not him, but I think I know who you mean. My guy is older, short hair with a beard. Dark skin and talks with a different accent that made me think he might be from the Middle East. Wears dark glasses for some eye condition. Kind of a familiar look about him. Maybe reminds me of some actor or athlete I can't place."

I inwardly smiled at the picture his words had drawn. I could almost envision the supplier and wished I were a sketch artist.

Zubinski shook her head. "Nah, I don't know anybody like that."

"Nope," I confirmed.

He pulled four baggies from his pocket. "You will find out how good this stuff really is. I'll be out of town for a couple of days. So, you think this will hold you over for a few? I'll be back Sunday if that works."

Zubinski and I looked at each other and pretended to have a mental debate. I shrugged and she nodded. "Yeah. That'll be good. Where should we meet?" I asked.

"How about here? Not many people around. I like that," he said.

"Sure," I said.

Zubinski pointed at the baggies. "So how much coke have you got in the bags? An ounce?" she said.

"Right. Each one has an ounce, so you got five good lines per bag. Hey, you know what? I got a deal, so I'll pay that forward to you girls. Each bag will cost you a mere hundred."

I raised my eyebrows. "That is a super deal," I said with as much enthusiasm as I could muster.

"Wow, for sure." Zubinski turned to me. "Well, I guess you got the dough."

I withdrew a small stack of hundreds from my jacket pocket, counted out four, and handed them to KP.

"Thanks," He pocketed the bills in a practiced move.

"You have my number, so you'll call me with a time for Sunday?" I asked.

"Yeah. It'll be afternoon. I got appointments, people to connect with, so I'll let you know as soon as I do." He wiggled his eyebrows up and down in a teasing gesture that made me cringe. "Have fun, girls."

Zubinski put her hand on her pocket. "Lots of fun."

"Don't I know it," he said.

We followed the trail back to the Nissan. Zubinski climbed back in the driver's seat. I settled in the passenger's and turned off the Bluetooth. "Oh, my gosh, did that guy give a great description of his supplier, or what? It was worth putting up with his other comments," she said.

I nodded. "He is observant, I will give him that. And I'm sure it comes in handy in his line of work. Now the question is, who is his new supplier? Would he be the killer targeting dealers?"

She started the car. "You gotta wonder. We'll see KP again on Sunday. He'll get arrested and out of the killer's reach."

"True. The earlier in the afternoon, the better."

I got a text from Smoke. *You two rock.* I held it up for Zubinski to read, and she smiled.

"I'd love to see where he goes, where his car is, so we can catch his plate number. I'll text Smoke. They should be able to see which direction he takes," I said.

Smoke responded with, *Carlson is waiting in the wings, Mason is watching the exit.* I read that out loud. "Mandy, should we hole up somewhere, see if they get a bead on KP?"

She backed up to turn around then shifted into drive. "We could go south, back to where we waited before."

"Yeah, let's. I'll tell Smoke. We don't want to blow our cover, but if KP heads that direction, we can see what he drives and alert Mason if he somehow missed him."

"All righty." She returned to the spot where we waited. And waited. And waited. We figured KP must have had another meeting after ours.

Long minutes later I sent Smoke a text. *He still there?*

We think he ditched us. Weber's checking.

"I don't believe it," I said.

"What?"

"KP might have gotten away somehow."

"Serious? Like he followed the river west on foot?" she said.

"Or went east to the county road. I'd think the guys would have seen him, or at least heard him, but with the river sounds, maybe not."

"They were stationed halfway down the trail and it's another twenty, twenty-five feet to the river. I can see how he could've left without them seeing him," she said.

"Let's hang out a while longer, see if something happens," I said.

When Smoke called, I put my phone on speaker. "Weber took the second pathway to the river. No sign of KP. I got Mason and Carlson on their way to help do a quick search of the trails and grounds, but it appears he left the park," he said.

"He's young, struck me as clever and evasive. Mandy wondered if he followed the riverbank west, I wondered if he went east and had his vehicle somewhere off County Six," I said.

"Could be he lives around here and hiked over. It'd be an easier trek, but a longer distance if he came from the west. If he walked in from the east, he'd have to navigate the steep bank that drops down from the road. We'll see if we can figure out which way he traveled. The good news is you got another meeting on Sunday and we'll be better prepared next time," Smoke said.

"I guess there's no reason for Mandy and me to hang around. We'll go back to the office, get the drug evidence checked in, write our reports," I said.

"Sounds like a plan," Smoke said and disconnected.

"A bummer to lose him like that," Zubinski said.

"He is one careful dude. Doesn't meet anyone at his place, apparently doesn't want us to see what he drives. Unless like

Smoke said, he lives around here and it's just as easy to walk, cover his tracks that way," I said.

"I know deputies swing through our parks a lot, but it makes me think we should ramp that up even more. We know not everyone uses the parks for legal recreation," she said.

"That's for sure."

Smoke and Weber joined Zubinski and me in the squad room an hour later. We were about wrapped up with our written reports. We had returned the Nissan to the impound lot and entered the baggies of drugs into evidence, to have the contents tested and KP's fingerprints lifted for his identification.

"Well geez, who would've thunk this KP would turn out to be smarter than the average drug dealin' bear," Weber said.

"Yeah, who would've? Not me," Zubinski said.

"He must have a good reason he doesn't meet people at his place. We know that some desperate druggies are downright dangerous. Maybe KP doesn't want his buyers to know what he drives in case they see him somewhere and flag him down," I said.

"All the reasons you noted should warn 'em to pick a lawful career instead," Weber said.

"If only," Zubinski said.

30

I was in the squad room when Smoke phoned late Thursday morning. "We got the lab results back, confirms that Pearce Bennet died from a lethal combo of cocaine and carfentanil. And the hopeful part, the broken bag of powder on Bennet's floor?"

"Yeah?"

"High quality, pure cocaine. And from the same batch found in trace amounts on Bennet's body, and in what he ingested. The cocaine that had carfentanil mixed into it."

"Wow. So it's safe to say the dealer gave Bennet the lethal combo. The dealer also gave Bennet the pure coke baggie, or accidentally dropped it," I said.

"Safe to say. I think the dealer/killer dropped it, didn't realize it. Why leave it there on purpose? He had a lot going on what with Bennet sniffing the drug, keeling over, dying. No doubt that happened when the killer was there because the inside door was left unlocked. Bennet would have locked it after the dealer left if he was still alive," he said.

"Not to mention the shoe print. What about the alleged meth and cocaine we bought from Bennet, have they tested those?"

"Not yet. We sent the drugs you bought from both Kip Lewis and Pearce Bennet to the Regional Crime Lab on Monday, and the drugs from KP went to the lab today. I have my doubts they'll find any carfentanil in them. Of course, we'd like those test results, a-sap, but their priority case list is a mile long," he said.

"I agree. If it turns out carfentanil was present, I doubt either Lewis or Bennet knew about it. Same goes for KP. What about the partial print on the baggie, anything on that yet?"

"The lab is running it through AFIS as we speak." The Automated Fingerprint Identification System.

"We'll have the results soon enough then," I said.

"Within thirty minutes, give or take. If we get a hit, we won't have to track down the shoe brand from the print, where they are sold, who bought 'em. Would save us a whole lotta time," he said.

"For sure. Smoke, back to what you said about calling Betty Jessen."

"Yeah, I went back and forth between today and tomorrow, and decided today was better. After I take care of some things. We need to send her son's body to a mortuary, and I want to give her a day or so to mull over my proposal."

"I'd like to be there when you make the call. If I'm not tied up, that is," I said.

"Sure. It'll be an hour or so."

It was close to noon when Smoke got back to me. I was on patrol, a few miles from the office. "Be there shortly."

I stepped into Smoke's cubicle. His eyes were fixed on the computer screen. He swiveled his chair my direction and slid his readers to the top of his head. "No match on the fingerprint from the baggie at Bennet's. Damn. That means if the dealer is the 'new guy in town' he has managed to avoid arrest up to this point."

"If he's the same guy who sold KP that top grade cocaine, KP thought he might be from the Middle East with his dark skin and accent."

"That he did. And it's the first description we've gotten of the possible unknown dealer or supplier. Kip Lewis said he gets his stuff from a guy in the Twin Cities who has a runner from Mexico. Bennet said his stuff came from Colombia and he got it from his supplier who's based in Chicago. Colombia and Mexico are hot spots, Chicago's a hub," he said.

"Yep."

"I'll see if we can get a faster turnaround on the results. Since the cocaine and carfentanil that killed Griffen Houser and Tad Michels came from the same source, I believe it will match what killed Bennet, also. That should move the test to high priority in the drug chem lab."

"The lab was good to us when we had the ODs last year. Never found the source, but we had matched results. I hope to get more from KP on Sunday. Maybe I could tell him Mandy and I thought about doing a little selling on the side and we wondered how that would work," I said.

"Heaven help us. Doesn't hurt to ask, I suppose. He'll most likely offer to be the one who sells to you. But there is a slim chance he'll send you to his supplier. Depends on his business, how much he wants to grow. Does he want the hassle of having sellers under him, in the event they don't pay?" he said.

"The illegal drug world is full of problems, all those big decisions like that."

Smoke raised his eyebrows. "You think? Well, let's check to see how Betty Jessen is doing."

I counted the fact that Jessen answered Smoke's call a positive first step. "Ms. Jessen, Elton Dawes, Winnebago County. I wanted to touch base with you, see how you are."

"I should be mad at you," she said.

"Why's that?"

"You sent that police officer over to check on me, didn't you?" she said.

"I won't lie to you. After our conversation, I needed to be sure you were okay," he said.

"Well, it is nice to know you cared." Another female in the Smoke Dawes fan club.

"That I do. To cut to the chase, I would like to make a proposal."

"What kind of a proposal?" Not *that* kind.

"Your son Percy has a house here. Property. And we need to make the final arrangements for Pearce. I'd like to drive out to your place, bring you back here to Winnebago County. I'll have a female officer with me," he said.

"I don't understand, why would you do that?"

"Serve and protect. Truth be told, I like to offer a hand when I can. We have folks in the county that will help get the house ready to sell, tend to other details. You might ask the friend you mentioned to come here at her convenience, too," Smoke said.

"I don't know what to say. Is it all right if I call you back?"

"Of course. Understandable to take a little time, think it over. Let me give you my personal cell number. You can reach me on it, twenty-four seven." He recited it when she was ready.

"I don't know what to say," she repeated. "Thank you." And then her voice cracked, and she sniffed a few times. "Bye."

Smoke smiled as they disconnected.

"You have good instincts, Detective Dawes."

"From what Betty told us, she's been to hell and back who knows how many times. I wouldn't doubt Pearce caused the nerve problems that have debilitated her to some degree. After she gets here, when we get to that point, you could talk to her about getting some professional help."

"Me?"

He gave me a sweet smile. "You can be pretty convincing."

"I'll see what I can do. I certainly can share how my psychologist and minister helped me after bad incidents."

He reached across the desk and squeezed my hand. "Thank you, Sergeant. Hey, wanna take a drive out to Wausau, Wisconsin with me?"

I grinned. "If I'm not on duty I will be happy to go."

"Good. Change of subject, any word from Rebecca today?"

"No, and I know she would call or text if she spotted Kelvin somewhere. I'll check in with her later. She was freaked out yesterday."

"As well she should be. We need her far away from that criminal."

"Mandy talked about how beautiful Rebecca is, how she looks older than her age. I think it has a lot to do with her life with Alvie. She had to grow up faster than she should've. And then to find out Alvie had killed three people—"

"Four," Smoke corrected.

"Four, but she doesn't know about that one and deserves to, I guess. Someday. Rebecca thinks she is old enough to hear the truth, but I want to protect her from it. And you know about the letter Alvie wrote that supposedly spells everything out. What I struggle with is, is she old enough to learn the whole truth?"

"As they like to say, it's complicated."

"The strange thing in all this . . . actually it's two things. The first is that Rebecca has never said anything about her father, except that he died before she was born. She never mentioned that he was in prison when he died. I haven't brought up his suicide in case she doesn't know. And I don't have anything positive to say about him. He was my classmate and a troublemaker. A criminal as soon as he was old enough to be deemed one," I said.

"I wonder what Grandma Alvie had to say about her son in the letter. She loved him enough to kill for him, right? And kept baby Rebecca, raised her when her mother left her on Alvie's doorstep," Smoke said.

"That's the second thing. Why doesn't Rebecca ever ask about her mother? Where is she anyway and why did she leave her beautiful baby with strange Alvie of all people? Did she leave the state, start another family?" I said.

"You got her name from Rebecca's birth certificate."

"But I can't let myself track her down, not until Rebecca asks about her. When she's ready to find her."

"I'd be curious," he said.

"I am, too. We're cops and cops are curious. We have to be. I will confess when I found out her name, I did type it into a search engine. Only once. When nothing popped up in Minnesota, I decided I would wait on Rebecca, out of respect for her."

"Seems to me Rebecca has been more secure since she settled in with parents and siblings who love her. She never knew her father, or her mother, and might not feel the need to look for her," he said.

"Maybe. If Alvie didn't mention her in the letter, I was thinking when Rebecca turns eighteen, if she hasn't asked about her mother before then, I would think of a way to gingerly bring it up."

He raised his eyebrows and smiled. "Are you sure you can wait that long to *not* snoop around the search engines?"

"I will make myself."

"I'd be interested to find out what her mother looks like. Rebecca no doubt takes after her."

"Or someone on her mother's side."

"Yep."

31

Blake

Blake knew when he got up Thursday morning he had to go to work. There had been no way he could have faced another human being on Wednesday. Not after his meeting with Detective Dawes on Tuesday. His wife appeared in porn movies, and the videos had been found in drug dealer Bennet's possession. How could that be true? He was a scum bag if ever he met one.

God, if he had touched her in an intimate way . . . Blake felt sick to his stomach again and took slow, deep breaths to ease the churning. He was a person who rarely vomited, but after Dawes talked to him, he couldn't stop himself, and came close a few more times since.

When he thought nothing in the world could be worse than his wife's death, he learned there was. No matter how many times the detective's words repeated themselves in his brain, he felt like he was in purgatory and had to escape from it at some point. Or die. That might be the only way. Would he reunite with his wife in heaven, or in hell?

When it came down to it, Blake still loved his wife and had taken lives to avenge her death. But could he forgive her? Maybe after Kelvin Dean was dead like the others. And after he and Corinne Aleckson got to know each other better, developed a personal relationship. Married. He knew so little and yet so much about her. Like how she loved and cared for Queenie in a special way.

He would see her tomorrow when she brought Queenie into the clinic. That was enough to motivate Blake to shower, dress, and go to work.

32

The big plan to take Smoke to Queenie's veterinarian appointment fell through after Smoke told Dr. Watts about his wife and her activities with Pearce Bennet. So I lost my doggie's checkup escort. If I brought Smoke with me, Dr. Watts would have taken one look at him and left the room, no question. On the drive there, the conversation between Smoke and the doctor played through my mind like a bad movie.

When I got the reminder call for the appointment, I wondered how Dr. Watts was coping. The fact that he was able to work and tend to his patients was a positive sign. He had been in adamant denial when Smoke told him about the porn videos. It had been over a year since her death, a year to work through the things he needed to come to terms with. And then he got news that must have shocked him to the core. Maybe he was able to move it to the recesses of his mind.

I felt for Dr. Watts, but if he asked me if I knew anything about his wife's case, it would be uncomfortable for me to admit it, and unethical to discuss it. I couldn't imagine him doing so, but needed to be prepared, in case. I would tell him to talk to the investigating detective. The new twist added to the emotional mix, and I had to hide my increased discomfort being around him.

The receptionist called Queenie's name and we followed her to an exam room. Dr. Watts did a double take when he came in and saw my uniform. "Oh. Hello. I, um see you're working. Or are you finished for the day?"

I shook my head. "On a lunch break."

"Ah. Well." He smiled. "I have to tell you that your Queenie is one of my favorites. How is she doing?" He took a short glance at my dog then studied my face until his eyes landed on my lips with a gaze that felt personal. I was tempted to wisecrack, "Do I have a coffee latte mustache, or what?"

I leaned over and scratched Queenie's head in lieu of the comment. "She is way better than I expected her to be this soon."

Dr. Watts took Queenie's head in his hands and moved it from side to side. "Good. That is very good. Let's get the recovery suit off and look at the stitches." He gently removed it. "Oh yes, the stitches are healthy looking. Her skin is pulled together well, no gaps, good pinkish color. The stitches should be ready to come out next week." He looked at his watch. "Thursday will be two weeks post-op so you can schedule her next appointment for Wednesday, Thursday, or Friday. Any of those days will be fine. Whatever works best for you."

What? I thought today would be remove-the-stitches day. "Oh, all right then, I will do that." And still would not have Smoke as my escort.

Watts sat down at his desk, jotted a note, and then looked at me. "How are you, um, doing, Corinne? Feeling better now that Queenie is? Better, I mean."

Corinne. Back to me to answer a personal question. "I am, thank you."

He crossed his legs, and I noticed the tread pattern on the soles of his athletic shoes. It looked a lot like the print left in the powder on the floor at Pearce Bennet's death scene. I didn't recognize the brand. They were different from any running shoes I had owned.

"Do you mind if I ask what shoe brand you're wearing? I guess you know that I'm a runner. I'm due for another pair and those look nice. Stable. And comfortable, too."

Watts glanced down. "Oh. Um, yes. They're Giesswein. Giesswein is a Swiss company, and to affirm your comment, they are very comfortable. I don't, ah, run very often, but I'm on my feet much of the time. And, um, walk quite a bit."

"Giesswein. Gosh, I'm not familiar with them," I said.

"My wife bought them for me. She was big into physical fitness. They must have been for my birthday because I found them in the box in her closet after . . ." He stopped mid-sentence and a pained look crossed his face. His wife. Her death. Her sinful ventures?

To distract him I said, "The uppers of the shoes look like they're made from wool."

It took him a second to respond. "Um. They are, yes. Merino wool. They keep your feet warm in the winter and cool in the summer."

"I know what you mean. I have merino wool socks and love them for that very reason. Thanks for the info. I'll have to check them out." Dr. Watts smiled and for some reason it relaxed me, lifted my angst about his reaction when he told me about his wife's gift. He'd gotten emotional, couldn't finish his sentence. It was evident he still loved her, no matter what Smoke had told him. Maybe the two days since had allowed him to process it, come to grips with it. Maybe he had consulted his counselor. I allowed myself a moment to study him and noticed he had a fresh haircut. And a darker tan that made him look healthier.

"I see you've taken advantage of the sunny days we've had." Before the appointment, I vowed not to say anything he might interpret as personal but did it anyway. After his shoe question response, I wanted to lighten the conversation for a minute, hoped it lifted his spirit a bit.

His eyebrows rose then he looked down at his arms. "Oh. Um, yes. I have been outside more than normal."

"Sorry for being snoopy," I said.

He waved his hand. "No, um, no. Not at all." But his jaw muscles tightened, and I wondered why.

"Well, I need to get back to work. Things have been hopping in the county," I said.

"Busier than usual?"

"It's always busy, but we've got some bigger cases that take time to investigate."

"Oh. Um, I guess we don't always hear about them."

Queenie pulled on her leash. "My girl is ready. I guess she senses my need to get moving. Thank you and enjoy the weekend."

"Um, yes. And you, too. See you next week then, Corinne." *Corinne again. Yes, I will see you one last time, Lord willing and the creek don't rise, to use Smoke's recent expression.*

I delivered Queenie to the comfort of her kennel and was back on duty when I heard Smoke tell Communications he was 10-19. Back at the office. I had a lead to share with him. When I was 10-19 myself, I wound my way to Smoke's cubicle. He was in the middle of a phone conversation and held up his pointer finger. I sat down and waited until he finished. "You look like you have good news, Sergeant. About Queenie, huh? I was a little surprised when you got the appointment reminder with Watts."

"I know, but he seemed surprisingly like his regular self today. A little strange to me, but normal for him."

"I'm relieved to hear that. I thought of checking in with him, make sure he wasn't contemplating self-harm."

I shook my head. "After the way he acted in the interview room, the same thing crossed my mind. But I didn't get that impression today. At all."

"Good. So, tell me about Queenie. The good news."

I nodded. "That's part of it. The doctor was pleased with her progress. I thought her stitches would come out today, but it'll be another week." I snapped my fingers and moved my elbow in a "darn it" gesture. "What I wanted to tell you is I got a lead on a shoe brand to check out. Doctor Watts was wearing a pair with a sole that looked a lot like the shoe print at Bennet's, so I asked him the brand. They're Swiss, called Giesswein. Not sure of the spelling."

His eyebrows rose. "How did you happen to see the bottom of his shoes?"

"When he sat down, he rested his foot on his knee."

"Hmm. Let's check it out." His search engine found the company in seconds. "They have slippers, sneakers, runners, hiking boots. Nice looking. The uppers are different, made from merino wool," he said.

"We love our merino wool socks."

"That we do." He grinned, pulled out his phone, and checked the photo taken at the scene. "I agree. The Giesswein soles are very similar, if not identical, to the shoe print."

I went to his side of the desk and glanced from the sole view on his screen to the print on his phone. "I guess."

He raised his hand in a high five and we tapped palms. "Great observation skills, Sergeant. Gives our team a lead to follow. Carlson and Weber have been working in the sole search amongst their other duties with no luck so far. I believe they've focused on U.S. companies." Smoke shifted his attention back to the monitor. "I see the company has online stores, including one in the U.S. Where did Doctor Watts say he got them, somewhere local or online?"

"He didn't say, and I don't know that he knows. They were from his wife. He found them in her closet after she died. It should be easy enough to locate the closest retailer if it turns out they are Giesswein. I am intrigued by the shoes, how they feel, and plan to check them out myself."

He smiled. "We can put you on the shoe assignment."

"You mean try to track down a known drug dealer that bought the shoes?"

"Something like that. A lot of shoe stores have customer records. And credit card sales records," he said.

"When we figure out the likely shoe size, that will help narrow down the pool of potentials. If we find a familiar name who bought a pair with his credit card, that would be the icing on the cake," I said.

"You know well the thing I both love and hate about computers. When people purchase things with credit cards, it makes it much easier to obtain data and information nowadays."

"The reason you use cash most of the time."

"Like the guy said, 'just because you're paranoid doesn't mean they aren't after you.' And of course, we are the good guys after the bad guys every day. I just don't want to make it too easy for any bad guys who might be interested in what I eat or brand of beer I buy," he said.

"As if you have anything to hide."

"Call me private. Protective of my privacy. Our privacy."

"We've had this discussion before, and I see your point. You'll have our major crimes team look into Giesswein?" I asked.

"First we'll have the Regional Crime Lab check whether the shoe print matches the sole. They can nail down the size, and then we'll get our team back on the search."

"Sure." I looked at my watch. "One o'clock on a Friday afternoon. What are the chances they will get at it today?"

"Slim to none. But I'll grovel and see if that persuades 'em," he said.

Back on the road, I pondered things as I drove along. It was clear Dr. Watts still loved his wife. He was in disbelief about the videos, and when it sunk in—unless it already had— he would either forgive her, or not. He wore the shoes his wife had bought for him, that he found after her death. If I were him, would I have kept the shoes? After I felt betrayed by a loved one?

Watts was focused when he attended to Queenie. He looked better, seemed better. But I had to wonder about his overall emotional wellbeing and prayed he was on a good path. And would find another woman to love someday. Even if I wasn't engaged and madly in love with Elton Dawes, there was no earthly way I could get involved with Watts. Perhaps what I knew about Eloise Watts played into how I felt, but the bottom line was he wasn't my type. I needed someone who would notice if my behavior changed. If I needed professional help or treatment.

Someone without darkness around him.

After the porn videos news, it would be natural if Watts felt humiliated. And worried one of his colleagues, or someone who knew him, would come across them. Once released into cyber space, nothing a person did could call them back. The whole Eloise porn star reveal left me more conflicted about what to tell him if he ever did ask me out. I needed a spiel that was honest yet didn't further damage his ego. It made me wish I had chosen another vet clinic in the first place.

I got a call from Smoke and pulled over to answer it. "I talked to the crime lab director himself. They know about the three ODs, of course. When we discussed how they had all occurred on Sundays, three in a row no less, he decided to give top priority to the shoe print and Giesswein sole, see if they match."

"That is awesome, and you didn't have to grovel?"

"I did not, so we can call that a win-win," he said.

My head was halfway inside the refrigerator freezer when Smoke and Rex came into the kitchen. "Cooling off?" Smoke said.

"Ha. Looking for something to feed you."

He held up a bag and tempting aromas woke up my olfactory. "Look no further. I figured it was my turn to cook so I ordered some Mexican takeout. Shrimp fajitas for you and beef fajitas for me."

I closed the door and gave him a kiss. "Yum."

"You and Sara haven't had your girls' Friday night get together with takeout and a movie for a while, so I thought I'd fill in the gap."

"Very thoughtful, my dear. Thank you. After we got engaged, and Sara and John Carl got together, our tradition sorta got detoured. But we'll do it again one of these weeks. You got the food; I got the beer." I pulled Stellas from the refrigerator, popped off the tops with an opener, and carried them to the dining table.

We sat down with our furry companions on the floor by our feet. Smoke reached in the bag for the containers, napkins, and utensils. After he slid my dinner to me, we said our prayer of thanks, and dug in.

"You'll be as happy as I am the crime lab was able to match the picture of the print to the Giesswein sole."

I reached over and squeezed his hand. "Why didn't you call me or tell me that the second you walked in the door?"

"You looked so darn cute when you pulled your head out of the freezer with a forlorn look on your face, I got kinda distracted."

I shook my head. "Seriously? Tell me more about the match."

"They looked at the soles of the company's footwear and found the runners were a match. The soles are different on their sneakers and hikers and slippers. Each one is unique. With their computer program, it didn't take the lab techs long to superimpose the print photo on the image of the sole.

"They determined that given the width of the print, the shoe would be either a men's size eleven or twelve. They calculated that because shoes get a little wider each size up. It's a graduated increase. They wanted to call the company and ask them to give them an exact measurement, but sixteen hundred our time is twenty-three hundred in Switzerland," he said.

"Of course. Different time zone, and it is way past business hours. What about local retailers? I did a quick search myself, but when I looked at the official site, I didn't find a list of local retailers. Maybe the list would be too long, I don't know. I looked at Schubert's Shoes and found they had Giesswein in five stores, but only carry a few styles of slippers, not other styles. They don't have runners," I said.

"Sheriff authorized overtime for our major crimes team, Mason and Carlson, to track down stores in the Twin Cities and Saint Cloud areas, see what they come up with. But if Schubert's doesn't have them, you gotta wonder what stores would."

"I know. Schubert's has a huge line of shoe brands. And the tried-and-true running and athletic shoes they're known for. Some smaller shoe stores, or athletic gear stores, might specialize in shoes their customers wear. Like Giesswein. If Mason and Carlson come up dry after a search, I'll phone

Doctor Watts, see if he knows where his wife got them. There must be a sales receipt, or bank or credit card entry."

"Should be," he said.

"Two more days until Sunday. I hope we can get a lead from shoe store sales, but forty-some hours is a tight time frame."

"Tight is right. Say we find a few retailers, are able to get a list of size eleven and twelve shoe buyers, and don't need warrants for the info, it will still take time."

I nodded. "Another thought. We have a lot of known and suspected dealers in the county, and the sheriff could assign deputies to keep an eye on as many as possible on Sunday."

"That might be tough to coordinate at this point," he said.

"I know we have limited resources, but at the least the drug task force guys can watch dealers they've been working with."

"We've talked about that. It's feasible."

"I have a doom and gloom feeling we'll have another cocaine carfentanil victim on Sunday. Unless it was three strikes for the killer and he's out," I said.

"We have tomorrow and hopefully part of Sunday to get a lead on the Giesswein wearer." Smoke held up his bottle. "Here's hoping that comes to fruition."

"Hoping and praying," I said.

"You got that right."

33

Blake

Blake barely made it through the day after his short time with Corinne Aleckson. Being near her. In touching distance. Despite his reticence and innate fear of guns, the one strapped to her duty belt made him feel secure. Protected. Because he trusted her more than any woman besides his mother and one grandmother. But they had passed. His views were no doubt clouded by what he learned about his wife after her death. In retrospect, he realized he had worshipped her even more than he loved her.

When it came to light she wasn't a saint, that she was human like the rest of the world's population, Blake fell deep into an abyss for months and months. He was a good enough looking guy, but his wife had told him he was the most handsome man in the world. He didn't know if she really thought that. He was too grateful she had married him to quibble over details. Now he wondered.

Corinne showed she cared about him at Queenie's appointment. Her face took on a sad look when he told her the shoes were from his wife and that she died before she could give them to him. Corinne was interested in the brand so she could get a pair for herself. She even complimented him on his appearance, his darker skin tone. If she preferred him that way, he would continue tanning.

The immediate problem was he had to keep distance between them until he finished his mission. In two days, he would be free to look ahead to the first day of the rest of his life. Blake had pulled back his pursuit efforts as he sensed he should. And then Corinne opened up to him, was more receptive. If he moved too fast it might scare her away. They could have decades together where he would shower her with love and anything else she wanted.

34

The four meetings—three down and one to go—with the drug dealers altered my work schedule, so I had Saturday off.

Smoke was up and out the door long before I was able to coax my own body from the bed. He left a note on the kitchen counter to tell me he was at the office and both dogs had been out and done their business. I gave Queenie and Rex a little attention, then added a pod to the single cup coffee machine and watched the brew drip into my mug. I was impatient for answers that had so far alluded us.

Who was Kelvin, and where was he from? We were not able to obtain driver license records on a man with that first or last name in his approximate age group and race in Minnesota. Was Kelvin his real name, I wondered for the hundredth time. Was he a recent transplant from another state and hadn't yet applied for a license here, or was he driving without license? He had stolen plates from a Hennepin County vehicle on his car. Did he live there, or was he based there, and had a multi-county operation that brought him into Winnebago County?

A positive thing was there had been no sign that Kelvin had entered Oak Lea High School since last Tuesday, and no evidence found he had been in the school prior to that. I was angry he had crashed the young teens' party the week before and livid he had confronted Rebecca in the school parking lot. Three days had passed with no word from, or about, Kelvin so I prayed he had moved on, gone away for good.

The more critical issue was the dealer killing other dealers with a deadly combo of cocaine and carfentanil. I knew it wasn't feasible to assign a deputy to every suspected dealer in the county on Sunday given the resources we had, but in addition to the ones the drug task force would monitor, I'd request a deputy to watch Kip Lewis, the one Mac and I had bought drugs from before we headed over to Bennet's house.

I carried my coffee to the living room and sat on the couch with the dogs at my feet. I took a moment to view the great outdoors. Smaller branches of trees on the back line swayed gently in the breeze as their colored leaves released and spiraled to the ground where they swirled some more. That was how I felt as my thoughts swirled and spiraled from one subject to the next.

Perhaps Sara had planted a worry seed that brought on my ominous feeling. It started after she told me she and the other probation officers were worried there might be another victim and who it would be. And how much she hated that I was undercover, meeting with drug dealers as an unarmed prospective buyer. She knew danger often presented itself when I was on duty, so what caused her increased apprehension? I had to believe it came down to the same thing that distressed us all. The elusive killer had not yet been identified.

I did some chores then phoned Smoke just before noon.

"Mornin', Sunshine."

The sound of his voice brightened my mood. "You were up and at 'em early this morning," I said.

"Got called to a burglary complaint, happened overnight. Met with the unhappy owner who forgot to set the security system when he locked up last night. Burglar jimmied the back door lock. I got the list and photos of the stolen items and sent that off to pawn shops, so we'll see what turns up.

Our major crimes team, Brian Carlson and Todd Mason, are there processing the scene now, collecting whatever forensics they can. Anyway, that was a long way of telling you that when they are done processing, they'll be looking into area shoe stores for the Giesswein runners," he said.

"Good."

"I tried to contact the Giesswein company earlier for information on local stores and should have known their office wouldn't be open on Saturday."

"Not everyone in the world is open twenty-four seven like we are," I said.

"No. It's possible Eloise Watts ordered from their online store like a lotta folks do."

"True. Smoke, I think I'll get on some social media sites and post the question, 'I want a pair of Giesswein runners and am wondering where to buy them.'"

"Sure, why not? It's a generic question. Or get on a runners' group page and ask their members," he said.

"That's a better idea. Thanks."

"Also, Pearce Bennet's phone records were on my desk when I got here. I asked our guys to go back fifteen months, just before the last string of overdoses occurred. I've been looking through them, cross-referencing them with Griffen Houser's and Tad Michels' records, checking for shared numbers. I started with their most recent calls and am working my way backward. In the week before each of their deaths, they didn't make a call to, or receive a call from, the same number."

"That doesn't make sense," I said.

"No. We know the killer had to have been in phone contact with each one. You don't just show up at a dealer's place unannounced. Damn burner phones. Maybe the killer had forethought, figured we would check phone records, so he used a different phone with each dealer. That involves detailed planning."

"I feel your pain. It's been an exercise in futility so far."

"Yeah, that's what it feels like, all right. There are some shared numbers, but they're on random days. No pattern. I'm going to fast forward to the weeks from the last ODs. See what turns up—hold on, I got Communications calling my work cell." When he came back, he said, "Gotta head to Oak Lea Hospital. Stabbing victim, female, just showed up in the ER," he said.

"Oh, no. Maybe you should call in another detective."

"I'll see how it goes and will do so if need be. Later, then," he said.

We disconnected and I sent up a prayer for the victim. And for Smoke who was on overload. Then headed to the den office and turned on the computer. I found a local runners' group on Facebook. Some members trained together and posted tips and exercises. It was a good page to check back to at some point. I wasn't a competitive runner, although I had done several 5k runs over the years. I posted my question, and in short order had fifteen responses. All of them were familiar with Giesswein and one had bought a pair at a store in Minnetonka that specialized in natural fiber products, like cotton and wool. A lead to follow.

I "liked" their responses then opened a new tab and found the store's website. They had an eclectic array of organic products, from clothing to shoes to bedding to bath products. The store carried other wool shoe brands besides Giesswein, but they were the only brand with running shoes. Bingo. I hoped.

Then it hit me, how many people in the drug world were drawn to natural products? Besides Eloise Watts, that is. On the other hand, the dealer had used high grade cocaine to kill his victims. His higher-class tastes likely spilled into other areas of his life I surmised. The "new guy in town." The killer.

I couldn't make an official call as a sheriff's office deputy and request the store's sales records because I wasn't on duty. I'd pass the information to Smoke when he cleared from his interview at the hospital. Or to Mason and Carlson when they finished with the burglary, whoever wrapped up first.

It was after noon, long past time to get dressed, and I opted for exercise gear, motivated by the runners' group page. A long run would elevate my spirits, give me some energy. I donned the Smith & Wesson, stuck my phone in a jacket pocket, and trusted Queenie and Rex would be good when I was gone. The gentler breeze in the morning had shifted to a brisker one. When I reached the county road, I turned west toward the wind's direction so it would be at my back when I headed home.

At the three-mile mark, I turned east for the return trip. I was surprised, yet not shocked when Dr. Watts's truck passed me, then slowed and pulled onto the shoulder. He climbed out and waited for me to reach him.

"Hello," I said. I wanted to ask, "Why do you feel the need to stop when you see me out on a run?" But did not.

He smiled, then his eyebrows drew together. "Hello, Corinne. Um, it's not very nice out and rain is moving in. So, I, ah, wondered if you need a ride."

"Thanks for the offer, but I should be home before it gets here," I said.

"I hope so. In the event, um, there's lightning, too."

Should I ask him about the Giesswein purchase? What was there to lose? "I hope this question doesn't upset you, but do you know where your wife bought your Giesswein shoes? I'm not sure where to look."

He frowned and cast his eyes downward. "Oh. Um, well, I guess I don't know. I never thought about it with everything, um, at the time. I know the receipt wasn't in the box. There may be a record on a bank statement. Oh, unless she paid with cash." The muscles in his face tightened. He was stressed.

"Not a big deal and no worries. I thought maybe you knew where she liked to shop," I said.

"Oh, um, she and her friends shopped different places, I guess."

I waved my hand. "As I said, no worries at all."

"Um, if I find out, I'll let you know," he said.

"Appreciate it. Well, I better shove off in case the rain comes earlier than predicted."

"Yes, well, I'll see you and Queenie next week then."

I nodded. "See you then." Without further ado, I took off. What was it with Dr. Watts? I spotted people I knew walking and running and biking all the time when I was behind the wheel. Unless it was Smoke, or someone else I needed to talk to, I didn't interrupt them in the middle of their exercise routine. What continued to trouble me most was that something about Watts and his behavior I still could not put my finger on.

I was convinced it had to do with his wife. Like when I asked where she shopped, and he indicated he didn't know. Like he didn't know she was addicted first to opioids, and then to illegal drugs. And likely other things. Was it the guilt he felt as an absent husband that caused his peculiar behavior around me, maybe other women, too?

Smoke knew all the important and most insignificant things about me. Where I went, what I did, where I shopped. Maybe Eloise Watts didn't disclose her shopping locations for a reason. Maybe the explanation was as simple as she didn't think it was important enough to talk about, and her husband never asked. Perhaps the descriptive words "odd duck" applied to both Dr. and Mrs. Watts.

I was a few feet from my driveway when my phone buzzed. Rebecca. "Hey. How are you?" I asked.

"Hey. Well, I'm a little scared."

My heart picked up speed. "Where are you and what happened?"

"I'm home. Alone. And I saw Kelvin a little while ago."

Dear God. Could my heart beat any faster? I tried to keep my voice even. "You saw him where?"

"He was sitting in his car on our street. I was in the driveway shooting baskets and he must have pulled up when I wasn't looking. He like honked and I turned around and saw him with his window open. And he waved at me. I waved back then went in the house."

Yes, my heart could beat faster. "Did you lock the door?"

"I can do that now."

My heartbeats got more erratic. "Is he still there?"

"I don't think so. I'll look."

Palpitations took control of my heart rate as I reached the door. "Wait. If he's there, I don't want him to see you. Stand to the side of the window and lean only as much as you need to, to get a glimpse. All right?"

"I know what to do. I can see where he was parked, but he's not there now," she said

"Okay." I wished he was still there, so when I called Oak Lea PD, they could catch him. I let myself in the house, grabbed my purse and water bottle as I talked. "I'm coming to pick you up. Don't open the door for anyone until I get there but call me immediately if you see Kelvin again."

It took her a moment to answer. "Oh. Okay."

"I'll be there in eight minutes. Or less. Hold tight." I phoned the PD and asked them to have a car drive around the Brenners' neighborhood, to be on the lookout for a blue Corvette, and gave them the stolen license plate number.

I slid behind the wheel of my car and backed out when the overhead garage door opened. I was protective of Rebecca, but the whole Kelvin thing had turned me into a helicopter parent like my mother. Maybe worse. Of all the things in the world, it was something I did not think possible.

And why was Rebecca alone outside? I thought her parents would keep watch on her until Kelvin was caught. As the garage door closed, I took a moment to get my heart rate under control before I drove. *Breathe in slowly through your nose, out slowly through your mouth.* I did that a few times as I assured myself, *Rebecca is safe, and we will track down that rogue, Kelvin.* The palpitations dissipated and my heart rate returned to a near normal pace as I reached County 35 and turned east.

I watched for the blue Corvette as I had on a continual basis after Kelvin confronted Rebecca in the Oak Lea High School parking lot. I was mystified why he hadn't been caught since law enforcement agencies had the make and model and stolen plate number on his vehicle.

Kelvin was clever. He wasn't on social media sites, had not been arrested. At least not as Kelvin. Yet he was bold. His actions flew in the face of laws and authorities. That would be his downfall, and I prayed it would be sooner rather than later. He provided kids with drugs and popped up here and there. Like today. The thing that alarmed me most was that Kelvin was tuned into Rebecca, was interested in her, knew where she lived.

I pulled the GTO into the Brenners' driveway and wished I had taken the extra minutes to get Gramps' Buick instead. In case Kelvin drove by and spotted my car and saw Rebecca getting into it. I was the only one with a 1967 red GTO in the area.

I phoned Rebecca and she was out the door seconds later. I met her halfway for a quick hug. "Let's go." We climbed into the car then I asked her, "Where's the rest of your family?"

"Justin's baseball game. I just wanted a little time alone if you know what I mean."

"I do."

"You won't like this, but Kelvin called me a few minutes ago," she said.

"*What?* How did he get your number? What did he say?"

"Um, I don't know how he got it. He like told me he loved basketball, too. Then he asked if I could meet him some time and keep it our little secret."

"I can*not* believe the hoodlum's audacity. Does he know how old you are? He's an adult, as far as we know. And involved in criminal activities. How stupid is he? Keep it as your 'little secret.' That's what an abuser would say," I said.

Rebecca started crying. "I'm sorry."

I reached my hand around her back and drew her as close as the bucket seats would allow. "I'm the one who's sorry for getting so upset. You have no reason to apologize. I didn't even wait for you to tell me how you answered him."

She sniffed and brushed at the tears with the backs of her hands. "I was like surprised he called and all I could say was, 'I'm not allowed to go on dates or meet boys at places yet.' And then I said, 'bye' and hung up."

I gave her an extra squeeze. "Perfect response. You are wise beyond your years, you know that?"

"Thanks," she said.

"You have his number, right?"

She looked at her phone, gave it to me, and I added it to my contacts. Grateful for that. A way to track him down at last.

"You let your parents know I picked you up?"

"I texted Mom, and she texted back 'Okay.'"

35

Blake

Blake had vowed to stay away from Corinne but couldn't resist when he saw her running at about the same spot as the last time he stopped. It was a fair distance from her house and proved she was fit. In her line of work, she had to be. Blake would get into better shape himself, try running. He had the right pair of shoes. It threw him off for a minute when Corinne asked where his wife had gotten them. It was unexpected and he didn't know how to answer.

Not because he had to admit he didn't know which store it was. Rather, it stirred up guilt feelings because of what he had planned that afternoon. He needed to see if his wife's videos were posted somewhere on porn sites. Blake decided to use his wife's laptop for the searches. When he was done, he would run over it with her vehicle, along with her prepaid cell phone, and the ones he no longer needed. Then dispose of them in various places.

After tomorrow he would be released from his mission and ready to move on to the next chapter, a positive new life that didn't involve illegal drugs, dealers, or pornography. And the best person he knew to be his life partner was someone who respected the law and enforced it. Sergeant Corinne Aleckson.

He plugged in his wife's computer and set to work. In short order he entered a world he had never been tempted to dabble in. Like the illegal drug world. The only thing he had to go on when he started that project were the contacts in his wife's phone. He experienced actual fear when he called a couple, ones his wife had not communicated with in some time, to find out where to get good cocaine. One who didn't deal much in cocaine was helpful and gave Blake the contact information of a seller in California.

He had read news reports about people who had died from carfentanil mixed with another drug and knew how dangerous it was. He didn't use it often in his practice, but it was an effective drug to sedate large animals. It was 100 times more potent than fentanyl, 4,000 times more potent than heroin, and 10,000 times more potent than morphine. Blake took great care and followed protocol when he mixed it into the cocaine.

He wore protective clothing, gloves, and a face shield, as he did when he administered it to animals. He did not want to get it on his skin or accidentally inhale it. Drug users and dealers added it to other drugs because it was cheaper and gave a more potent high. If they knew what they were doing and didn't kill themselves, or someone else, in the process. Or knew what they were doing, with the intent to kill a targeted victim. The minute amount he added to the cocaine had caused instant death to the dealers.

Blake was in the middle of a search, trying to find a porn video of his wife when her prepaid phone rang. It startled him half to death. Who would have the number over a year later, not know she was dead? He decided to answer it and find out. "Hello?"

"Oh. I was wondering if El is available?" A youngish man asked.

"No, she's not. Can I take a message?"

"No. I had done some business with her a while back, and thought I'd reach out, in case she needed any products."

"She's set." Blake hung up. Sweat spilled from his pores and he started to shake. El, huh? Had she done any favors for him as well? Yet it took him over a year to get back to her? He looked through her phone contacts list and didn't find one with that number. He didn't know who it might be, but he knew it was not one who had sold his wife drugs the day she died.

After he drank some water and composed himself, Blake went back to his search for another ten minutes until his wife's phone rang again. It unnerved him to the max. Why would she get a second call on the same day? Minutes apart. He looked at the number, but of course didn't recognize it. No need to answer it. He carried the phone to the garage, found a hammer in his tool chest, and pounded it to death. He had gotten all he needed from it and would dump it somewhere on his travels.

Blake decided to call the video search quits for the night. He didn't find his wife in any of the videos, and he could stomach only so many repugnant sights and sounds. Tomorrow was the big day, and although he didn't want to bring pain and suffering to Kelvin's family, Kelvin had sold his wife drugs. One of four dealers had killed her, a twenty-five percent chance it was Kelvin. Same as with the other three. What was fair for one was fair for all.

Blake couldn't spend the night alone in his house. Memories of his wife washed over him no matter which room he wandered into. She was everywhere. He packed what he needed the next day. The drugs were already in baggies, so it didn't take long. Over a year later, he still tried to grasp how his wife allowed unscrupulous people to capitalize on her addiction. They didn't know what they were selling half the time, nor did he believe they cared, from what he observed over the last months.

The porn video news had crushed him. He would work his way through it with some support, mostly from a special young woman he looked forward to knowing better. No matter what his wife had done, the Eloise he fell in love with, had spent over a decade devoted to, would always hold a special place in his heart.

He had to forgive her to get on with his new life. But it would take time. At thirty-eight years old, Blake needed to appreciate all the good in his life, all he had taken for granted for too long. His career, the animals he loved caring for. He had been too focused on building his practice to enjoy what he should have.

But that would change. He would make it happen. After one last task in the drug world, he would be a free man again, and not look back. When his mission ended, that would be that. He would discard all things connected to it. In fact, he decided to talk to his partners, tell them he didn't want to use carfentanil on animals any longer. He'd present a strong case. It held its dangers and other drugs were nearly as effective.

36

Queenie and Rex were happy to see Rebecca and she entertained them as I slipped away, first to down a quart of water and then to send a text to Smoke. It was two twenty-one p.m. and I figured I would have heard from him or the major crimes team before then.

I got Kelvin's phone number.

Smoke sent back, *Still tied up. Have Communications track the number and let me know.*

10-4, I responded.

I reached Randy in Communications, gave him the Brenners' address, the scoop on Kelvin, and his number. "It should've pinged off the tower nearest the Brenners about thirty minutes ago.

"I'll check it out," he said.

"Thanks, Randy."

After a needed shower, I joined Rebecca in the living room where she sat on the floor with the dogs.

"Hey, how about a game of Scrabble? We haven't played that in a long time," I said.

"Sure." She was a better player than me.

We set it up and talked as we played.

"Rebecca, you gave a fair description of Kelvin, but close your eyes a moment and tell me how old you think he is. You thought he might be eighteen the first time you met him. You've seen him a few times since. Do you still think so?"

She shrugged. "Maybe. Or maybe like twenty. It's hard to tell. He has a sorta young-looking face but seems older."

"The young face must be how he gets into places he shouldn't be."

"I guess."

"I know how much you love to shoot hoops, but will you do me a favor and have someone with you when you leave the house, even if it's in your own yard? Until Kelvin is caught. I need you to be safe and I do not trust him one bit," I said.

"I guess so."

"Kelvin scares you, and I have to tell you he scares me a little, too."

Communications Officer Randy phoned a little after three p.m. "Sergeant, no pings on that phone anywhere in the county. Sorry."

"You're sure?"

"I'm sure." He repeated the number again and we confirmed it was the correct one.

"Okay. Thanks for your help, Randy. Until next time."

"You bet."

I sent Smoke another text, *Call me.* It took him about a second. "Detective," I said then mouthed, "Back in a few," to Rebecca and headed to the den office.

"Just got back to my desk. Long story short, the assailant was the victim's husband. I tracked him down at their home, and it wasn't too difficult to coax a confession from him. He had sobered up and I pointed out the cuts on his hands, in addition to the wound he inflicted in the left side of his wife's belly. She will recover, thankfully. He's getting booked into jail as we speak," he said.

"Poor thing."

"So tell me how you got Kelvin's number." After I explained, he said, "That weasel."

"But no luck tracking his phone. Not a ping from a single tower in the county," I said.

"He most likely disabled it so it can't be tracked. I'm surprised he's smart enough to think of that given all the dumb things he does."

"No kidding. Maybe he thinks he's safe if law enforcement can't pinpoint his location. I am beyond disappointed. I want him found before he contacts Rebecca again, and he always manages to show up when we aren't around," I said.

"Or puts stolen plates on his car when he knows there are cameras around. He must always be looking over his shoulder. My gut tells me time is running short for Kelvin."

"I have that same feeling, so let's count on the fact we must be right. On to the other investigation. Ready for a Giesswein update?"

"What've you got?"

I relayed what a member of the runners' group had to say, and the natural products shop in Minnetonka. "Then I ran into Doctor Watts. Actually, he pulled over on County Thirty-five when he saw me on a run."

"That guy is starting to get on my nerves."

"Likewise. But Queenie's next appointment will be her last with him, so the end is near. Anyway, I asked if he knew where his wife got his shoes, and he had no clue where she shopped. See what I mean? One example of how he is."

"No doubt. I'll tell Mason and Carlson about that shop, see what they can find out about their customers, who bought size eleven or twelve runners."

"Thank you. I bet you're worn out, huh?" I asked.

"Probably am. If I had time to think about it."

Rebecca's mother Jean came to pick her up after they returned from the out-of-town baseball game, a little before five. We sat in the kitchen where Rebecca filled her in on Kelvin's visit and his phone call. Jean put her hand on Rebecca's. "We all need to keep an eye out for him and call the police if he shows up again."

"Rebecca agreed to have a buddy with her when she goes out, even in your yard, until we catch Kelvin," I said.

"That was our agreement," Jean said.

Rebecca looked down at their hands. "Sorry, Mom. I thought it would be okay."

"We'll get through this. We best leave Sergeant Corky to get on with her evening." Jean stood and turned to me. "Thanks much for all you do for us."

I gave them both a hug. "No thanks necessary. I love being part of your family, and I'm happy to pitch in."

It was about dinner time. Smoke had phoned to say he would be home by six p.m. and my guy deserved a good meal after his long day. But what to fix? My culinary skills would not win an award anywhere, but I had learned some go-to recipes the last couple years. I opened the refrigerator freezer and pulled out a bag of large raw shrimp for the fastest, easiest, and one of the most delicious meals I knew. And frozen cauliflower for a side.

I dug out a large pan from the cupboard, set it on a burner, and turned the heat to medium. I stirred in olive oil, butter, lime juice, lemon juice, minced garlic, and Cajun spices. I rinsed the shrimp then added them to the pan when the other ingredients were warm and blended. As they sauteed, I put potatoes in the microwave and the cauliflower in a pan with a little water to steam. When the shrimp were pink and the cauliflower started to boil, I turned the burners to low.

The microwave beeped, but I left the potatoes in it while I opened and tossed together a bagged salad kit we liked, even though it had kale in it. Go figure. I set the table, then gathered serving dishes to make the dinner feel more special.

The overhead garage door opened and alerted the dogs that Smoke was home. I cracked open two beers, then stood there with one in each hand and a silly grin on my face when Smoke came in. He gave the dogs their awaited head scratches, then slipped his arms around me and nibbled on my mouth. "Darlin', you smell even better than the aromas of some mighty tasty food."

"You do, too."

"I showered and changed before I left work. Left behind whatever I may have picked up at the places I was at today." Smoke kept a change of clothes in the sheriff's office locker room. As most of us did.

My elbows rested on his with the beers against his biceps. "Are you feeling a chill?" I cracked.

"Now that you mention it. But other parts of my body are warming right up." We exchanged a sound kiss then stepped apart and I handed him a bottle. He clinked it against mine. "Here's to a better day tomorrow."

"I'll drink to that." We took sips of our brews. "Have a seat at the table and I'll dish up the bowls."

He lifted his eyebrows and smiled. "I feel like I'm at a restaurant. Only better."

"Good." It took a few minutes to get the food on the table, and when I sat down, we gave thanks and dished up.

Smoke scooped up a generous serving of shrimp. "You will never guess who called me about an hour ago."

"Betty Jessen?"

He chuckled. "Let me rephrase that question. And, yes, you are correct."

"Smoke, you have a way with people, women in particular," I said.

"Ha."

"What'd she say?"

"That she would like to come to Winnebago County any time I can arrange it. Said her friend will follow in a week or two. That way Betty can get started going through her sons' things, figure out what to do with all their stuff," he said.

"Wow, she certainly did a one-eighty. A good thing, huh?"

"She told me it was for Percy. After she thought about it, she knew she needed to take care of their belongings. And hoped Pearce didn't throw Percy's things away. There might be photos, other treasures. I told her tubs on garage shelves probably held Percy's personal effects, from what I gathered on our search."

"Percy died a while back. She's finally ready to start the healing process?"

He swallowed a bite of salad. "I think so. Regarding Kelvin, I'm sorry you didn't get a hit on his phone, Corinne."

"Can you believe it? As mad as I was that he called Rebecca—after he stopped by her house for heaven's sake—a big part of me was excited we'd be able to track him. Or not. Chameleon Kelvin."

"Good name for him. That was pretty much how it was with the natural store in Minnetonka. Mason got nowhere with the clerk. Flustered the guy is about it. Told Mason he'd have to meet with the owner on Monday when he's back at work because he wasn't authorized to give out customers' information, even if he knew it. Like the ones he knows personally, or others who made credit card purchases. He did tell him they sold a lot of the Giesswein house shoes and slippers and a fair number of the runners. They are catching on, more and more."

"How about other stores?" I asked.

"They searched the Twin Cities and Saint Cloud areas. It was after five by the time they located four stores, tried to contact 'em, but they were all closed. One is open Sundays and is the Minnetonka store. I'll give them a ring tomorrow." He took a sip of beer. "I wrote a warrant to get access to the natural store's records, and Judge Adams agreed to sign it. Carlson was on his way to his house when I left. We'll deliver it tomorrow, see what turns up."

"Good. What do you think the chances are that a drug dealer we're familiar with bought a pair of Giesswein with a credit card in the last however many months?" I asked.

He raised his eyebrows. "What do I think? Slim to none, but it's worth a shot."

"What time does the natural store open tomorrow?"

"Noon."

"Sounds like the better chance is after we catch our bad guy, his shoes will prove he was with Bennet at the time of his death. Or arrived after the fact. Maybe the one who reported it," I said.

"That reminds me, we found out the person who called in Bennet's welfare check, the same phone number, also called Bennet's phone. Twice. Ten days before he died, then again two days before. I tried to call it and it's dead, so no help there. Add to that, that number wasn't in the other victims' phone records," Smoke said.

"But others were."

"Yep. They were drug users, for the most part, and small-scale dealers. Nobody that stuck out. Mason is cross-checking phone numbers from last year's ODs," he said.

"Good."

We enjoyed our meal in mutual silence until Smoke's phone rang. "Speak of the devil. Mason." He pushed the talk button. "Todd, I'm with Corky and will put you on speaker."

"Sure. Hey, Corky."

"Hey, Todd. What's up?"

"I think we're onto something. Back to the last string of overdoses, Pearce Bennet, Griffen Houser, and Tad Michels all had the same number in their call list on a particular day. Not necessarily a surprise there. However, Bennet was the only one with a name attached to that number. And come to find out, all three had gotten a call from that number the day Eloise Watts ODd," Mason said.

"No way," I said.

"Way. So I called the number listed as 'El' in Bennet's phone," he said.

"Who we figured was Eloise Watts," Smoke said.

"Correct. Since no unknown or suspicious contacts were in her personal cell phone, we know she must've had a burner. I called the number, figured it wouldn't go through. But, lo and behold, a man answered. And I asked for El."

"*What*?" I said.

Smoke leaned forward. "What did he say?"

"Said *she* was not available."

"Not available, huh?" Smoke said.

"Yeah, I acted like I was a dealer, said I had done business with El in the past and wondered if she needed anything. The guy said no. I had Communications check to see if the number pinged in our county but no such luck," Mason said.

"Like with Kelvin's phone. I want to call that number, listen to the man's voice," I said.

"What are you thinking?" Smoke said.

"There are two possibilities. Either Eloise Watts lost, or threw away, her burner phone and someone found it. Or, she hadn't destroyed it and her husband found it among her things," I said.

Smoke stood and slammed his fist into his other palm a few times. "Damn. I can't believe it didn't cross my mind Watts might be involved in this round of overdose deaths. I have been too deep in the forest to see the trees. I believed him when he said he didn't know Bennet. I guess because of who he is, how he acted, I didn't figure him for this."

"I get that," Mason said.

"I was right there with you," I said.

Smoke scratched at the back of his neck. "Time to regroup. You're right, Corky. Say Watts found a phone his wife had hidden and saw who she contacted the day she died. Someone has the phone, and it's got to be Watts himself. My question, and a major concern, were there any other dealers she called that day, or even a day or two before?" Smoke said.

"Let's hope not," Mason said.

I got up and laid my hand on Smoke's arm. "If Watts turns out to be the killer, that's going to shock a lot of people. He's a successful veterinarian, a trusted community member."

"No doubt," he said.

"To build on what you said, he fell hard when his wife died, maybe it warped his mind in the process. He gives me weird vibes that make me wonder if he is hiding something. Could be a big something," I said.

Smoke nodded. "Get your undercover phone so you can make that call to El's phone. Mason, what's the number?" Smoke was jotting the number on his memo pad when I ran upstairs, retrieved the phone from the charger, and rejoined him. He recited the numbers and I punched them into my phone. It rang, but no one answered.

I shook my head and hung up. "If it was Doctor Watts that picked up for Mason, maybe he got freaked that someone, and then another one, called his wife's number after all this time."

"Probably did. We know that phone wasn't used in recent calls to the dealers. Like I said, our three victims didn't receive calls from the same phone number in the ten days prior to their deaths.

"Last year, when I met with Doctor Watts, one thing I asked about was the carfentanil. If his wife had access to the drug cabinet at the vet clinic. He said she didn't. But he obviously does," Smoke said.

"And wears Giesswein runners," I said.

"That, too. I need to take him into custody, bring him in for questioning. Todd, can you meet me at the doctor's house? I'll need backup. I've seen what angry looks like on him."

"Sure. I know where he lives. Ten, fifteen minutes?" Mason said.

"I'll be there in twelve. Park away from view of the house," Smoke said.

"Ten-four."

I tensed up the moment we surmised Dr. Watts was the likely suspect. After Smoke left, I paced around the house in loop after loop from room to room. It kept the poor dogs on alert. Time seemed to creep by as I waited for word on Watts.

Smoke phoned about twenty minutes later. "Watts didn't answer the door, appears to be out. It's dark inside his house, except for a single light in what I figure is the kitchen."

"He could be out on a sick animal house call," I said.

"Could be. I have Communications trying to track his cell number. I also asked the sheriff to spare an on-duty deputy to watch for Watts and I'll wait till the deputy gets here. No reason for Mason to hang around. When Watts makes an appearance, I'll return here and we'll surprise him with a knock on his door."

"See you soon." I sank down on a chair with Queenie and Rex at my feet. "Sorry I make you nervous when I get keyed up. Queenie, you would not believe the secrets Doctor Watts has been keeping, the awful things he's done."

She whined as if she understood.

When Smoke returned, I snaked an arm around his waist. "Try to rest a bit while we wait."

"Think I can sleep?" he said.

"Probably not. I stuck our supper dishes in the fridge. How about I reheat some food for you?" I suggested.

"Thanks. As fine a meal as it was, I kinda lost my appetite."

"Me, too. Plus, I know how it is when you catch a break, or a probable one. Like a dog after a bone, everything else takes a back seat."

"Yep."

A half hour later Randy called to report they hadn't been able to track Dr. Watts's cell phone but would continue to try throughout the evening and overnight.

"Seems that Watts either left the reach of towers in the county, or he disabled the location app in his phone," Smoke said.

"Smoke, we know he'll turn up. Maybe he went to the Twin Cities to meet a friend. You need sleep. Go to bed. The deputy will call you if Watts shows up. And if Communications calls with his location, I promise to wake you."

He nodded then took me in his arms for a sweet kiss. "Good night, darlin'. And try to let it go, about Watts I mean."

I lifted my shoulders in a half-shrug. "I knew something was off with him, but he's a good vet, took great care of Queenie."

"Like a lotta people who do bad things, they do good things, too."

"Good night, dear Elton. Sleep tight."

37

Sunday morning rolled in without a word during the night from Communications on Dr. Watts's cell phone pings. Or from the stationed deputy. I slept in the guest bedroom with our dogs on their rugs, so Smoke had a quiet room to slumber in.

He stretched as he entered the kitchen. "I can't believe I slept ten hours. No idea the last time I got eight."

"Your body and brain were in desperate need." I set down my mug. "Still no word on Doctor Watts."

"Damn. I'll swing by his house on my way to the office, check in with the posted deputy. When I woke up, I called the sheriff, got a meeting approved for this afternoon with the drug task force, and those assigned to the ad hoc undercover drug team," he said.

"What time?"

"Fourteen hundred. Everyone in the department knows we're on higher alert today, given what happened the last three Sundays. I also sent a message to Luke Andrews on the drug task force, asked him to assemble a list of known dealers within a ten-mile radius of Oak Lea."

"Good."

I heard my undercover cell phone ring from the living room and ran to answer it. KP.

"Hello?"

"Ms. Corky?"

"Hello, KP. Hey, I need to tell you that was some fine stuff you gave us." I walked back to the kitchen.

I heard him chuckle. "Told you so. You and your friend up for a meet this afternoon for some more good stuff?"

"Sure thing. What time?"

"Does four o'clock work again?" KP asked.

"Four it is. Same spot?" I nodded at Smoke.

"Yep. See you there." He disconnected.

"Glad we have a time nailed down, and fourteen hundred should work for the meet. Gives us two hours until KP time," Smoke said.

"It should."

Smoke's phone dinged. He pulled it from his back pocket and read the message. "That was fast. Andrews named seven. Sheriff said when I had the list, Chief Deputy would call in extra bodies to surveil them. We have two from the task force, so I'll let the chief know we need five more." He typed a short text and hit the send button.

Smoke scratched his chin. "Anyhow, the deputies will meet with our group, and then head to their stations for an eight-hour shift. We know we've got some wild cards out there like KP who are operating within the area. And like in his case, we don't know where they hang their hats. Guys like him have slipped through the cracks, but we'll do our best."

"When we meet with KP this afternoon, after you and Weber surprise and arrest him, he will be taken into the protective custody of the Winnebago County Jail. One known dealer off the streets," I said.

"Music to my ears, Sergeant."

The group gathered in a sheriff's meeting room to confer about the dealers the deputies would be assigned to watch, the three dealers' death investigations, and to find out who our number one suspect was. The big reveal.

The five road deputies, two from the drug task force, Smoke, Weber, Mason, and Carlson were in casual clothes, with their sidearms and badges concealed under jackets. They had picked up impound vehicles as directed. Zubinski and I were in our drug-buyers garb. She wore ripped jeans and a long sweater. I wore leggings, a casual knee-length dress, and a jean jacket. We were all ready for duty. Smoke gave a summary of the overdose investigations.

After a pause, he said, "A couple of you know this, but it seems Doctor Blake Watts is likely the one who killed the three dealers." Smoke filled in the details.

"Ah geez, not the doc. He was a wreck back when his wife ODd. A lost sheep. I know he's gotta be smart, but I never figured him for cunning. I almost can't believe he put this whole scheme together, killed people," Weber said.

"Yeah, what Vince said. Really hard to wrap my head around it," Zubinski said.

Smoke huffed out a breath. "Right now, the worst thing is we don't know where Watts is. Communications has been trying to track his cell to no avail in this county. Did he take off for parts unknown? One possibility we considered: he has another victim in mind who is outside of Winnebago County. We have other counties checking, too. So far, no pings in Hennepin, Carver, Sherburne, Stearns, or Meeker."

"He could be anywhere. I saw him early afternoon yesterday and for all we know, he could be in Switzerland by now," I said.

"Buyin' those Giessweins?" Weber said.

I raised my eyebrows. "You never know."

"Could be he turned off his phone, left it at home, is out there with a burner. Especially if he's calling dealers," Zubinski said.

"Likely scenario. Corky and Mandy got a description from a dealer who has a new supplier that has top grade coke. Said the guy was older, but that was in response to Corky mentioning a young dealer. KP said the guy has short hair, beard, dark skin, wears dark glasses. We believe it's Blake Watts," Smoke said.

I picked up a photo and held it for everyone to see. "Doctor Watts is very tan now, dark skinned. Has short hair, might have a fake beard. We had his photo doctored. No pun intended."

Weber nodded his approval. "The doctored doctor."

A few muttered comments under their breaths.

"There is a copy of the 'doctored' photo for you. Be on the lookout for Watts, or another guy who fits the description. Now that we've identified our prime suspect, know who we're looking for, it's a given we will find him." Smoke paused then said, "Okay, we have a dealer's name, last known address, and phone number for each of you on surveillance duty."

I handed them out.

Smoke continued, "These guys move around, as you well know. They may be home, they may not. If need be, have Communications track their phones. If they aren't blocked, that is. Hopefully you won't have to chase them around too much. Anybody got a final question?" he asked.

Deputies shook their heads.

"All right, then, go ahead and take off. Reminder that if you have something we all need to hear, use our radio Channel Two. Otherwise send me a text. Thanks again for your help this Sunday afternoon. Corky, Vince, Mandy, Todd, Brian, hang tight for a few," Smoke said.

The deputies picked up Watts's photo on the way out, then the six of us gathered in a loose circle. "We're back for round two at Henry Olson County Park with KP. This time to arrest him," Smoke said.

"It feels like déjà vu all over again," Weber said.

"Thanks, Yogi," Zubinski said.

"KP wants to meet Mandy and me at four," I said.

"It's two forty-three now," Mason said.

"You want Todd and me where?" Carlson said.

"You two you can ride in one vehicle, hang in the park as backup in case something goes south with KP. Go ahead and take off so we don't all show up at the same time," Smoke said, and they headed out.

Weber's shoulders bounced up and down a few times. "We should get out there ourselves, boss."

"Yep. Doesn't hurt to get there early. We'll find us a good spot, wait for Corky and Mandy."

"Before we leave, I should try Doctor Watts's cell. I've been thinking about this, and there's a good chance he'll take my call. If he answers, and he's back in range, we can take it from there," I said.

Smoke nodded. "Sure, go ahead. I'll let Communications know."

I waited on Smoke then dialed Watts's number. He answered after the first ring. "Corinne?" I nodded at the team.

"Oh, Doctor *Watts*? I'm sorry. I meant to call a friend and guess I accidentally selected your name instead."

"Oh, um, that's okay. Not a problem. It's good to hear from you, anyway," he said.

"Thanks. You, too." Smoke gave me a thumbs up sign, and then a cut it off signal. "Well, I won't keep you. Have a good one." Or not.

"You as well."

When we disconnected Smoke reported, "Watts is in Henry Olson Park."

"*What*?" We all said together.

"I'm prayin' it's a coincidence," Weber said.

"Move team, we're eleven or so minutes away," Smoke said.

We ran to our vehicles in the lot outside the sheriff's office. I jumped in the Nissan's driver's seat and Zubinski rode shotgun. I saw Smoke climb in the passenger side of his unmarked squad car with Weber behind the wheel.

Smoke's voice came over the radio. "Three forty, Winnebago County, on two."

"Three forty, go ahead on two," Communications Officer Robin replied.

"Six oh eight, Seven fourteen, Seven twenty-eight, and myself are clear ten-nineteen, en route to Henry Olson County Park on a suspect check."

"Copy that."

"Is there another car in that area?" Smoke said.

"Negative. Aside from Seven ten and Seven twenty-three also en route there."

"Ten-four. Seven ten, seven twenty-three, copy that?"

"Copy," Mason said.

Weber and Smoke were in the lead car, and when they left city limits on County Road 35 their speed increased to seventy miles an hour. So did ours.

Smoke sent a text to our group. Zubinski read it out loud, "Suspect in park is Watts. He just took a call from Corky, for what it's worth. Todd, Brian, when you get there, pull into the far south end of the lot by the big trees and check out the trail that goes into the woods. Weber will park my unmarked in the trees off the park's entrance. Corky, Mandy, park in the main lot, as you would to meet KP. He'll be on the second pathway at four. Could be KP is with Watts now. Weber and I will take that path. Corky, head to the first one, Mandy to the third, listen for movement, voices." Zubinski paused then said, "I replied with 'copy.'"

"Thanks."

"You think KP is Watts's next victim?" Zubinski said.

"I don't know. Must be. But why would he answer the phone if he were about to kill KP? Or has he already done that?"

She sucked in a loud breath. "What a deal. At least we're armed this time, prepared for whatever goes down."

"Radios would be good, but we got our phones, I guess. This whole day went sideways."

"Big time."

It took forever to get to Henry Olson. Weber pulled to the right into the foliage that hid Smoke's unmarked squad. I drove in at what felt like a snail's pace and parked. A gray Kia SUV was parked higher up on the hill. I couldn't see the plate, but the belief I had seen the same vehicle in the park before made prickles dance all over my skin.

"I wonder if that is Watts's Kia up there." I turned off the engine then sent Smoke and the other deputies a message, *Todd, Brian, check the plate on the gray Kia and the other vehicle. Watts might be on the trail.*

Mason got back with, *Copy, calling them in.*

"If Watts is up there, Todd and Brian will track him down. And the other one might be KP's," I said.

"Let's hope. Instead of some innocent fisher or hiker," she said.

Smoke sent another message, *Communicate via text, call if you need to.*

I handed Zubinski the car keys. "You have jeans on. Can you put them in your pocket?"

"Sure."

"Here we go. Act casual. Be safe," I said.

"You, too."

We got out and headed to our assigned pathways. My sidearm was in its holster, strapped to my thigh, and Zubinski's laid across her chest. I sent up a prayer, asked for protection for everyone in the park. Before I got to the first pathway, I saw Smoke and Vince with fishing poles and a tackle box headed to the second.

I was about six feet down the path with thick brush on either side when I heard someone move beside me. Before I could turn, strong arms went around me from behind and pinned my arms against my sides. An adrenalin jolt shot through every inch of my body. My captor remained silent. *Stay calm. If I scream, it could make it worse.* "KP, you checked me last time for weapons."

"Corinne?"

Dr. Watts. Oh, dear God. What should I say? "Oh, thank God it's you, Doctor Watts."

He did not release me. "Why are you here in that get-up? Who is KP, how do you know him?"

"People might recognize me otherwise. We have private business together," I said.

He stepped back, turned me around, maintained a firm grip on my arms. "My God, you made yourself look like a tramp on purpose? By private business, you mean something illegal. I find that hard to believe. Is KP the one you were calling when you called me instead?"

Dr. Watts seemed like a different person. Firm, articulate, focused. And he didn't look like himself with the beard and dark glasses. I cast my eyes at the ground to appear guilty. "I can't talk about it."

He gave my arms a shake. "Tell me."

"KP has something for me," I said.

"Drugs?"

I shrugged. "Let me go, and I'll leave. I won't meet with KP. You can watch me drive away. We can pretend our meeting here never happened." He likely had the lethal drug combo on his person. I was unsure about his mental state, didn't know if he was armed, didn't know what he would do if I drew my weapon and trained it on him. If I could reach it in time. I needed to put distance between us, needed backup so we could take him into custody. Or we both might end up dead.

Watts shook his head. "No. You're a witness."

"To what? I haven't seen anything or anyone here," I said.

"You've seen me." He lurched forward to grab me, but I ducked and rolled away. I yelled, "Help!" as loud as possible before Watts threw his body on mine and it pushed the air from my lungs.

My arms were trapped under me. I pushed my hands into the ground and worked my knees toward my middle and lifted my butt in a quick move. It was enough momentum to buck Watts off, but he was faster to get to his feet than I was. "Help!" *Where were Smoke and Weber, couldn't they hear me?*

Watts put one arm around my waist and clamped the other over my mouth. He carried me down the path toward the river and I used both hands to try to pry his hand from my face. When that didn't work, I started to wiggle and kick. We were on the riverbank when he dropped me and grabbed my arms again. Damn, he was strong. I yelled again, "Trail one, at the river!"

"There's no one here to save you. The last thing in the world I wanted was that anything bad ever happen to you. Sad thing is you were in the wrong place at the wrong time. You have to die because you would have figured everything out after today, and then my mission would have counted for nothing."

That made no sense. He was more irrational by the minute. "Whatever it is you think I might figure out will not take anything away from your mission, whatever that is." I lifted my foot and dug the inside edge of my boot into his shin, slid it down to his ankle, then stomped my heel into the top of his foot as hard as I could.

"Owww!" he shouted.

I lifted my knee to his groin with enough force to double him over. Watts let out a loud, long moan. But before I could escape, he stuck out his foot and tripped me. I landed face first into some brush, and as I scrambled to my knees, he pulled me to my feet and against his body. My arms were pinned again.

38

"It's time to say goodbye. I'll see you on the other side." Watts backed me up until we stood at the riverbank's edge.

He plans to kill me! And himself. Where is my backup?
Watts leaned forward and fell into the river with my body pinned beneath his. The water was frigid, and I sucked in a mouthful. We sank beneath the surface and Watts's grip eased enough for me to push him away. I surfaced and coughed out some water. I was a good swimmer, but my clothes weighed me down. At least the current was slow, the one positive thing. I held my breath, dropped down in the water, slid off my boots, and struggled to pull off the jean jacket that clung to me like a second skin.

When my air was depleted, I surfaced and spotted Watts a foot away. He grabbed my arm and pulled me under the water with him. I drew my legs up and slammed them into his chest. He lost his grip. That bought me a few seconds. I swam as far underwater as I could manage before I needed to come up for air. Watts was a few feet away and reached for me but missed. I swam west toward the other pathways and yelled,

"I'm in the river," as loud as was possible with my lowered lung capacity.

Weber broke out from the brush near the second path, and Smoke appeared at the river's edge on the first.

"Corky, swim to Vince. I'll call for backup." Smoke called out the location on his radio to Mason and Carlson, then phoned Zubinski.

When I reached Weber, he bent over and gave me a hand up. "Geez, Sergeant, you okay?"

"Didn't drown."

"Geez Louise, didn't even lose your wig. I woulda flipped mine."

I spotted Watts thrashing around in the water. Maybe he had second thoughts, decided not to die after all. I started to shiver. "Go help Dawes," I told Weber.

It was a rough area for him to navigate to the next path, through vegetation and over rocks. I ran up the second path and down the first to the river. Weber was there beside Smoke at the river's edge. Would I help or hinder their attempt to coax Watts from the river?

Smoke took a quick look at me, his face flushed. "Dear God," he muttered. I moved off to the side and doubted that Watts noticed me. He went underwater then bobbed up again. "Doctor Watts, we need you to swim to shore," Smoke said.

Watts didn't answer, nor did he drop beneath the surface. Zubinski joined us, her inhales and exhales fast and loud. She looked at me, took off her sweater and handed it over. "Thanks," I said then stepped behind a tree, slipped off my dress, put on the sweater, and pulled off the wig. My upper body warmed up a bit.

Carlson and Mason arrived seconds later. Smoke turned to them so Watts wouldn't overhear. "He's trying to summon the courage to drown himself."

"Brian and I can go in and grab him," Mason said.

Carlson nodded. They were experienced swimmers and divers.

"Go for it," Smoke said.

They slipped off their shoes, jackets, and belts then took off their holsters and handed them, along with their badges, phones, keys, belts, and wallets to Zubinski and Weber.

Carlson pointed. "I'll go right, you go left. I'll go under, turn him around, and get my arm around his neck. Get your arm around the other side of him if you can."

"Ten-four," Mason said.

The two deputies jumped into the river, and I caught the surprised look on Watts's face when they did. Watts went under; Carlson followed suit. Mason watched from above the surface. A moment later, Carlson came up with Watts, his arm around his neck in a classic lifesaver's maneuver. Watts twisted and kicked. Water splashed around them. Mason got into position on Watts's other side and helped Carlson. Two against one did the trick.

They swam to the bank with their captive. Smoke and Weber grabbed Watts's arms and pulled him up. The fight had left him. Weber held onto him then Smoke stepped behind him and cuffed his hands. Weber pat searched Watts then unzipped his windbreaker pockets and pulled baggies filled with powder that appeared dry. A nice, tight seal had preserved the evidence.

Smoke pulled his radio from its holder on his belt. "Three forty, Winnebago County."

"Three forty?" Communications Officer Robin answered.

"I need a deputy at our location to transport one adult male to our jail."

"Ten-four."

"Seven eighteen, Winnebago County, I'm near the park and will respond there," Deputy Levasseur said.

"Copy, Seven eighteen. Copy, Three forty?" Robin said.

"Ten-four." Smoke released his radio button. "Mason, Carlson, if you'll walk the doctor to the parking lot."

Zubinski and Weber gave their gear back to Mason and Carlson. They donned their sidearms and held the rest of the items. It was then Watts spotted me. "You tricked me. Pretended to be someone you're not." His words and cold stare made me think he was talking to his wife. Another shiver ran through me.

"Let's go," Mason said. He and Carlson guided Watts up the pathway and the rest of us trailed behind. Deputy Levasseur pulled in as we reached the open area. Smoke talked to him a minute, then Levasseur assisted Watts into the backseat of his squad car, got in himself, and drove away.

"Todd, Brian, you need to shed those wet clothes with the chill in the air. I'll take Corky home so she can do the same," Smoke said.

"Boss, you want Mandy and me to meet up with KP, finish that job?" Weber said.

Smoke frowned. "That's right. KP. Mandy, you okay meeting KP without Corky?"

Zubinski nodded. "No problem." She caught my eyes. "I'll tell him you got sick."

"That works. You got the drug money on you," I said. "I do. How are you holding up?" she said.

"I'm okay." I looked at Smoke. "What time is it now?"

Smoke glanced at his watch. "Three twelve."

"We could get back here before the meet with KP."

He shook his head. "Not a good idea given what you just went through."

"How about I get cleaned up and take it from there?" I offered.

"We need to get going. Don't want you getting hypothermia," Smoke said.

I waved to Zubinski and Weber, then Smoke cupped his hand on my elbow and guided me to the car. He opened the trunk, pulled out a wool blanket, and wrapped it around me. We were in the car and on the road in a flash.

"I'm cold and numb at the same time, and it's not because I'm wet," I said.

Smoke turned the car's heater on then reached over and squeezed my hand. "Of course. I can only imagine. We figured out Watts was the killer about twenty hours ago, but the last thing I expected was that he'd go after you. He is unbalanced, no question. Did he say anything before he pushed you in the river?"

"That it was time to say goodbye, that he'd see me on the other side." Saying the words out loud made me gulp.

Smoke bopped his fist on the steering wheel. "I can't interview the guy, not after this. I obviously need to recuse myself, stay far away from him. Carlson is the named arresting officer, was the first to put hands on Watts. Levasseur will sit in jail booking with Watts until Carlson is clear to sign the intake form with charges a mile long."

"Smoke, this may sound messed up, but I don't think I can hate Watts, even now. After the shock wears off, we'll see.

I know it will be some time before I'll feel brave enough to face him in court," I said.

"You know how long it takes to bring a case of this magnitude to trial. If Watts pleads, you won't ever have to face him again."

"When he looked at me, said those words before he was led away, I'm convinced he thought he was talking to his wife."

"He's delusional." Smoke let out a "hrrff" then went quiet. He was angry, but I knew he also felt conflicted about Watts's mental health status. As I did.

We pulled into my driveway. I jumped out and headed straight to the laundry room to shed my wet things. I left the holstered gun on the dryer to attend to later. The dogs barked from the kennel. We'd take care of them later.

All I could think about was my need to finish the job with KP. After I was clean and dry, I pulled out my other druggie outfit and a pair of shoes. Good riddance to the boots, jacket, and druggie phone in its pocket, now somewhere in the river. I used the hair dryer on the wig then pulled it on, applied makeup in record time, and found a sweater to give Zubinski.

Smoke raised his eyebrows when I joined him in the kitchen. "You were serious?"

"I am. I need to be there with Mandy."

He drew me into his arms for a bear hug. "What you need is a debrief."

"We'll do that later. Right now, we have unfinished business with KP. I would feel way more jittery if I weren't there for the buy."

"All right, I do understand," he said.

"I lost my phone in the river, the Bluetooth is likely toast. And the Glock seventeen got wet."

"Use your service weapon and work cell. I have a spare Bluetooth."

I retrieved the phone and weapon, and he pulled a Bluetooth from his pocket. I attached it inside the wig and clipped the gun on the back of my waistband.

"The dogs are back in the kennel. We better hustle, the meet up is in twenty minutes. Send Vince and Mandy a text. Tell them I will park in the same spot as before. You can meet Mandy at her vehicle, and I'll join Vince on the first pathway," he said.

"Ten-four." We got into the unmarked, and I sent the text.

Eight minutes later, I jogged up the hill and climbed into the Nissan. Zubinski gave me a broad smile. "You didn't have to do this you know. But I'm glad you're here."

I gave her the sweater. "I did have to do this, maybe to put off processing what happened with Watts. And I want to see KP's face lose that arrogant look when he gets arrested. He will not be happy but will eventually find out we saved his life."

She wiggled into the sweater. "Yeah. I'm glad the park is dead, makes it easier for us. Ready?"

"Or not, here we come." I turned on the Bluetooth and we headed down the pathway.

KP wore that same smart aleck grin when we reached him. We figured he wouldn't frisk us again, and he didn't. "Hey girls, I got some good smack, but my new supplier never showed, so it might not be as much as you wanted. But I can get more in a day or two."

"So KP, how much have you got with you?" I asked.

"Three ounces."

Zubinski and I looked at each other, then she said, "That should do us for today."

KP pulled the bags from his pocket and waited until Zubinski handed him the cash. Then she took the baggies from him.

"I appreciate doing business with you girls again," KP said.

Smoke and Weber appeared with their weapons drawn, in the ready position. Each had his badge attached to a front pocket. "Detective Dawes and Deputy Weber from the Winnebago County Sheriff's Office. Put your hands on your heads." And we all did.

"What's goin' on?" KP asked.

"We've been alerted to drug activity here and just happened to overhear your transaction," Smoke said.

"*What?*" KP said.

Smoke looked at Zubinski and me. "You ladies take three steps back." We did as we were told.

Weber nodded at KP. "Turn around." KP complied without argument. Weber moved KP's hands from his head to behind his back, one at a time, and applied the handcuffs. "Have you got a weapon on you, anything sharp in your pockets?" Weber asked.

"No."

"Just drugs and money?" Weber asked as he pat searched him.

"Keys, wallet."

"What's your name?"

"KP."

Weber gave KP's hands a little shake. "Ain't got time for no games."

"Kelvin Dean."

Did I imagine what he said? Kelvin, as in *the* Kelvin. Chameleon Kelvin? And Dean. As in his father was Kendrick Dean? I leaned into Zubinski for support. Weber stood behind KP and turned his head our direction. His eyebrows shot up, and his mouth formed a "wooh." Smoke faced KP and maintained a poker face. Zubinski and I turned to each other. Her eyebrows were raised, and her mouth was open. I think mine were, too.

There had been no way to predict or anticipate a second big reveal that day. Kelvin had gone from longish hair to a shaved head and back to longish hair in the span of a week. A wig was an effective way to change one's appearance.

It took everything I had not to grab Kelvin, scream at him.

Weber pulled out a couple bundles of bills, a few baggies with weed and powdered substance in them, and other things from Kelvin's pockets. He handed the wallet to Smoke who opened it and looked at his ID. "He is who he says he is. Kelvin Phineas Dean, age twenty-two." *Twenty-two.* "You live in Connecticut?"

"I went to school there. Boarding school, then college for a few years," Kelvin said.

"Your permanent residence is in Minnesota?"

"Yeah."

"How long have you been back here?" Smoke asked. "A while now."

"Your Connecticut license expired a year ago."

"Yeah?" Kelvin said, knowing it had.

"Where's your vehicle?" Weber asked.

He leaned his head to the left. "My motorcycle's over there, close to the river, down the hill from the county road."

"Okay. Time to head out. Your ride is on the way," Smoke told him.

KP strained his neck to look at Zubinski and me. "What about them?"

"They gotta wait their turn. Don't worry about it," Weber said.

When the two were out of earshot, Smoke said, "Levasseur is making a return visit here to pick up Mister Dean."

I shook my hands and rocked back and forth on my feet to release the tension. "I can't believe it. I cannot believe it. Can *not*. Shouldn't I have somehow known KP was Kelvin? But I guess I only got a poor view of him on camera those times. Then from a distance at that party. Wore a stocking cap with hair hanging a couple inches below it. He's had a shaved head the two times we've met him, so it didn't trigger suspicion in me."

"They have caps with fake hair, for women and men." Zubinski pulled out her phone, found a picture, and held it up.

I nodded and so did Smoke. "Yep. I gotta say, when KP said he was Kelvin Dean it blew us all away. We'll add this turn of events to the debrief."

Tears formed in my eyes. I blinked them away but more came with force. "It's been a rough afternoon."

"Mostly for you. Hence the need to debrief. On a positive note, we finally got an ID on Kelvin. He will be on his way to jail momentarily and booked charged with supplying drugs to underage kids, crashing at least one of their parties, harassing and stalking a fourteen-year-old."

I swiped the tears from my cheeks. "You're right. Kelvin locked up in jail is what I've hoped would happen for nearly two weeks. It almost makes up for what Watts tried to do to me. Maybe not." I shrugged.

Smoke squeezed my arm again. "Not by a long shot, in my book. When Weber hands Kelvin over to Levasseur, we'll find the motorcycle, call for a tow. Then Weber and I will head back to the office, check paperwork, write reports."

"We need to write ours, too," I said.

"Tomorrow is soon enough. You two can go off duty, have an adult beverage together. Unwind. Celebrate catching the dealer killer and putting another drug dealer out of commission for a while. After we saved his life," he said.

"That's a good idea, Corky. I'll take you home, return the impound car, change and then join you for a glass," Zubinski said.

"Okay."

39

I got cleaned up, changed into sweats, then sat in the living room with my back yard view, but didn't zero in on anything special. Queenie and Rex lay at my feet, offering support the way they knew best. It would be some time before I processed everything that had transpired that afternoon. Would I ever be able to fully comprehend, believe, that Dr. Blake Watts had tried to kill me? And himself? I knew it was a spur-of-the-moment action driven by panic. His attorney could argue it was not a premeditated act.

However, he had taken three men's lives and planned to take a fourth. That required careful planning and deliberate actions, likely over the course of months. I was curious what Watts had to say, what a detective could wheedle out of him in the interviews. What a search of his property would uncover? His wife's missing phone, his own burner phones, his drug stash?

I fretted over the accusation Watts spit out at me before Mason and Carlson led him away. Was he talking to his dead wife, as I supposed? Or was it to me, or to both of us? I bore some resemblance to her, and that might have sent him into a fantasy land, of sorts. I knew from the way he sought me out, looked at me, talked to me, he found me attractive. When Watts put me in that death grip, my face was pressed into his chest so I couldn't see his face. I wondered what his expression revealed, what he looked like in those last seconds before he dropped into the river with my body pinned under his. Anger, acceptance, fear?

In those seconds, I'd sent up a fervent prayer, then focused on survival. When I was rescued, I thanked God for protection and for another day on earth.

I had planned to cut ties with Watts, but in a far less drastic way.

Kelvin Dean, with his long list of charges, would spend years in jail. I hoped. His parents were good people. Did they have a clue what he was up to these days? My guess was he had gotten into trouble as a youth, and that's why they sent him to school in Connecticut.

Another thing: how many vehicles did Kelvin have access to, anyway? I knew of three, with the motorcycle. The fact that he had the motorcycle hidden off the beaten path explained how he had left the park without getting spotted. He hiked to his bike and took off.

Smoke said we should celebrate. Blake Watts and Kelvin Dean were the identified criminals we had searched for and were incarcerated at last. I wholeheartedly agreed.

Zubinski returned and it stopped my musings. When I let her in the front door, she threw her arms around me in a tight grip. "I was so scared for you." She eased her hold, stepped back, and looked at me. "You doing okay?"

"I am, pretty much. It will take time to believe what happened really did. And then more time to heal from it."

"I still can't wrap my mind around the way Doctor Watts must have changed after his wife died, that he actually killed those guys."

"It's a tough thing to grasp, all right." I headed into the kitchen with Mandy in tow. "I've got a buttery chardonnay, or a red blend."

"The red blend sounds good on a cool fall almost evening. Let me get the glasses."

She pulled them from the cupboard, and I opened the wine. I poured, and red wine splashed into the glasses. I handed one to her and held up the other. "Smoke told us to celebrate Watt's and Kelvin's captures, right?"

"A good thing to toast," she said.

We raised our glasses then took a sip.

"Nice," she said.

"Let's go relax in the living room." Mandy settled in an armchair, and I took my usual spot on the couch. "I should let Rebecca know about Kelvin before it gets any later since it's a school night."

"For sure."

I had Rebecca on the phone in short order. "Sergeant Corky, hi."

"Are you feeling better after yesterday?" I asked.

"Yeah, I was like freaked, but kinda got over it," she said.

"Good to hear. And I have some news that will make you feel even better. It sure did me."

"Like what?"

"Kelvin was arrested this afternoon for selling drugs to undercover Winnebago County deputies," I said.

"Fer real?"

"For very real."

"Undercover. That's cool," she said.

Someday I may tell her I was one of the deputies. "Turns out Kelvin's last name is Dean, he lives east of Oak Lea. And he's twenty-two."

"Twenty-*two*? That's kinda creepy and gross."

"I agree. His age along with the fact that he was supplying minors with drugs and doing other bad things will not help him when he stands before a judge," I said.

"Oh."

"I'll keep you posted. A detective will most likely want to talk to you at some point about your encounters with Kelvin, so they can pass that on to the county attorney's office for the case against him."

"Oh, like wow."

"With your parents' permission. I can be there, too. If you want," I said.

"Okay, like sure."

"Tell your family about Kelvin, all right? And I haven't forgotten about your grandma's letter. Maybe your parents will think it'll be okay for you to read it when you turn fifteen."

"I'll ask them," she said.

"Have a good night, dear one. You will be able to sleep tight, right?"

"Yeah." We said our goodbyes.

"What'd she say about talking to a detective?" Mandy said.

"'Oh, like wow.'"

She laughed.

"Which means she's fine with it. Her statement will be damning for Kelvin. When I told her Kelvin was twenty-two, she said that was 'kinda creepy and gross.'"

Mandy laughed again. "Good way to put it."

We sat and chatted about the cases and how relieved and happy we were the bad guys were in custody, and we could go off the undercover drug assignment.

Mason and Carlson stopped over, followed by Weber, and finally Smoke. Each one hugged me and said things that made me feel better.

"Help yourselves to a beer," I said. When they all had one in hand, we celebrated that both Blake Watts and Kelvin Dean were in custody. Watts was fingered as the killer of three men, and KP was identified as Kelvin, the thorn in my side for too long. Watts would never breathe air as a free man again, and Dean would end up with a lengthy sentence himself.

The six of us had an informal debriefing session, and hashed over the day, play by play. And that might be all we needed to help us cope, to move us to acceptance. My moments of terror when Watts tried to kill me eased as the afternoon turned into evening. He was incarcerated. I was home safe and sound with friends and loved ones.

When I woke up Monday morning, it took a while to get oriented. Sunday afternoon Dr. Watts had the villain role in a nightmare I got caught up in. It was unreal how the efforts and resources the sheriff's office had flushed out the "new guy in town," the supplier, the drug dealer killer. Officials should never rule out those deemed as unlikely suspects until they're investigated and cleared of any involvement in a crime. Our bad. In Watts's case, he wasn't even on the sheriff's office radar, unlikely or not. The way the events unfolded from the time Watts answered my phone call and we pinned down his location to the time he was in custody was filled with heart-stopping moments.

I wasn't a psychologist but had dealt with many people who had mental health disorders in my years with the sheriff's office. I believed the stress following Eloise Watts's death had caused her husband's grip on reality to spiral downward until he convinced himself his deadly actions were justified. Did he lose his final hold on what was moral and right when he discovered me on the pathway in Henry Olson Park, and made a snap decision about how to handle that? Unpredictable actions that people committed under duress alarmed me more than just about anything because they were . . . well, unpredictable.

I stared at the ceiling and pondered life in general and my career in particular. When Watts dropped us into the river, I wasn't filled with the same level of terror as in past critical incidents. I was panic-stricken and frightened, sure. But I also had hope and a means to escape. Help arrived in short order.

I sat on the side of the bed, stretched, stood, and stretched some more. Smoke had gotten up and left early for the office. I wasn't on the work schedule but had been authorized overtime to write my reports so the Winnebago County Attorney's Office would get them in short order. Time to get a move on.

Smoke sat on the edge of his chair and I stood. We were in a room that adjoined Interview Room A and watched the proceedings through a two-way mirror. Dr. Watts's non-interview was first, followed by Kelvin Dean's. Before questioning them, Detective Harrison read the Miranda Warning, and each one declined to talk to him without a lawyer present.

It was early afternoon when we got word Dean's attorney had arrived, and as expected, Harrison did not get him to admit guilt. The same held true for Watts when his attorney showed up around an hour later. No confession. No admission. No surprise.

Both would make their first appearances before a judge on Tuesday, and I anticipated a hefty bail for Kelvin Dean, and expected that Blake Watts would be held without the option to bail out. Or the judge would set it so high, he would have to be a billionaire to pay it.

I imagined what Kelvin Dean would say when he was shown Dr. Watts's photo. Asked if he was his new drug supplier, the one who was a no-show on Sunday. Did he know Watts? He may have treated the horses on their farm. Would Kelvin consider it ironic that the undercover deputies instrumental in his arrest were also the ones who saved his life? Oh, the times I wished I were a fly on a wall when people saw the light, so I could catch the expressions on their faces. The "aha" moments.

I would be called to testify at both trials, unless one or both took a plea deal instead. I hoped Watts would. If he stood trial, it would be nothing short of ugly. The press would have a field day. Everyone had the right to a trial and was presumed innocent until proven guilty. But evidence showed Watts planned at least four murders and committed three of them. And his attack against me was witnessed by law enforcement. If he admitted guilt, it would save sheriff's personnel and the attorneys hundreds of preparation hours, and taxpayers a ton of money in the process.

Amanda Zubinski came into the squad room as I worked on my reports. She looked at me and frowned. "Hey."

I smiled. "Hey, cheer up. Not only did we survive, we're off the ad hoc drug task force."

Her face brightened. "Amen. And Watts and Dean are in jail."

"We all need to write detailed reports so they will remain there for a long, long time. Or in Watts's case, forever."

"Yep."

Mid-afternoon, the sheriff called together all those involved in the Sunday afternoon incidents for a debriefing session. He was trained and skilled in the process. Smoke, Weber, Zubinski, Mason, Carlson, and I sat around the table in a conference room. The sheriff led off with, "As each one of you has learned, after a traumatic event, your minds keep running the events that happened over and over. We need to stop that process for our own peace of mind. Right?"

We knew we did, and after an hour of hashing and re-hashing, my own spirits lifted. Not only were all of us safe, but my attacker was incarcerated and would be behind bars forever.

"Hey, Vince, good news," I said.

He raised his eyebrows. "What's that?"

"You didn't have to wear that stupid undercover wig after all."

"Ah geez, how lucky can a guy get?"

I looked around the room at my friends and colleagues and sent up a thank you that each one was in my life.

40

Smoke arrived at my home Tuesday afternoon filled with news of the day.

"Kelvin Dean made his first appearance before Judge Adams this morning, as scheduled. Dean shuffled in, hands cuffed, feet shackled, head down. His parents were there."

I had decided not to be in attendance. "How did they look?"

"Not happy."

"I guess not. When Mister Dean showed me around their farm back when, I thought he was a decent guy. I don't know that we've ever had a complaint call there," I said.

"Not that I recall. Back to the appearance. The judge provided Dean with the criminal complaint that cited his long list of charges, and the maximum penalties possible if he was convicted. Dean's attorney spoke for him and entered a plea of not guilty, as expected. Judge set his bail at five hundred thousand."

I smiled. "Yes!"

"Blake Watts was called up for court at one thirty. He was hampered by his shackles and cuffs, but his spine was straight. He held his head high but had a blank look. It took Judge Adams some time to read the lengthy criminal complaint and then apprised him of the maximum penalty. His attorney also entered a plea of, 'Not guilty, Your Honor.' It didn't take long for Judge Adams to respond. He said, 'Doctor Watts, based on the charges against you, it is evident you are a danger to society. Bail is denied.' And then he struck his gavel."

"Thank God for that. He will never be free again."

"No, he will not. I hope Watts tells us how he got the names and numbers of the dealers. If not, at least we have evidence the same person called the three deceased dealers the morning Eloise Watts died. We also obtained Kelvin Dean's phone records this afternoon, and lo and behold, the same person had called him that morning, too," Smoke said.

"Wowser."

"So, the evidence locks up that part of the case. We've surmised whoever gave Missus Watts the lethal mix didn't do it on purpose. The old 'don't bite the hand that feeds you.' Watts had to have found his wife's phone, saw who she had called, who she talked to that day," he said.

"A safe presumption."

"The problem Watts must have faced is he didn't know which one sold her the drugs. Instead of coming to the sheriff's office, he went off on a vigilante justice rage."

"I know. Way scary. Animal doctor by day. People killer by night," I said.

Smoke shook his head then blew out a short breath. "Change of subject. I talked to Betty Jessen earlier, let her know we arrested the man who killed her son Pearce. She admitted she felt bad he died like he did. The mother in her still loved him. But her human side will probably always hate him."

"Heavy stuff."

"We chatted for a while, and she told me she was ready for a ride to Winnebago County whenever. I said, 'How about tomorrow?' since we have a little lull in the action."

I raised my eyebrows. "Tomorrow? Are you afraid you might be forced to take a day off, or something?"

He smiled. "Watts and Dean both made their first appearance today. We had a good debrief with the sheriff yesterday, were able to let a lot of our anxieties go. Let's just say it will feel good to tie up this one loose end. You have the day off, so it works out. How about taking that road trip with me?"

I gathered his hands in mine. "It will be good to bring Betty here, and I will be happy to go with you, Detective. To Wausau or anywhere else in the world."

He captured my body against his and held me tight. "I love you more than I can ever show you."

"That's not true. You more than show me all the time."

His kisses filled me with fervor, and I held on for dear life.

Winnebago County Mysteries

Murder in Winnebago County follows an unlikely serial killer plaguing a rural Minnesota county. The clever murderer leaves a growing chain of apparent suicides among criminal justice professionals. As her intuition helps her draw the cases together, Winnebago County Sergeant Corinne Aleckson enlists help from Detective Elton Dawes. What Aleckson doesn't know is that the killer is keeping a close watch on her. Will she be the next target?

Buried in Wolf Lake When a family's golden retriever brings home the dismembered leg of a young woman, the Winnebago County Sheriff's Department launches an investigation unlike any other. Who does the leg belong to, and where is the rest of her body? Sergeant Corinne Aleckson and Detective Elton Dawes soon discover they are up against an unidentified psychopath who targets women with specific physical features. Are there other victims, and will they learn the killer's identity in time to prevent another brutal murder?

An Altar by the River A man phones the Winnebago County Sheriff's Department, frantically reporting his brother is armed with a large dagger and on his way to the county to sacrifice himself. Sergeant Corinne Aleckson takes the call, learning the alarming reasons behind the young man's death wish. When the department investigates, they plunge into the alleged criminal activities of a hidden cult and the disturbing cover-up of an old closed-case shooting death. The cult members have everything to lose and will do whatever it takes to prevent the truth coming to light. But will they find an altar by the river in time to save the young man's life?

The Noding Field Mystery When a man's naked body is found staked out in a farmer's soybean field, Sergeant Corinne Aleckson and Detective Elton Dawes are called to the scene. The cause of death is not apparent, and the significance of why he was placed there is a mystery. As Aleckson, Dawes, and the rest of their Winnebago Sheriff's Department team gather evidence, and look for suspects and motive, they hit one dead end after another. Then an old nemesis escapes from jail and plays in the shocking end.

A Death In Lionel's Woods When a woman's emaciated body is found in a hunter's woods Sergeant Corinne Aleckson is coaxed back into the field to assist Detective Smoke Dawes on the case. It seems the only hope for identifying the woman lies in a photo that was buried with bags of money under her body. Aleckson and Dawes plunge into the investigation that takes them into the world of human smugglers and traffickers, unexpectedly close to home. All the while, they are working to uncover the identity of someone who is leaving Corky anonymous messages and pulling pranks at her house. An unpredictable roller coaster ride to the electrifying end.

Secret In Whitetail Lake The discovery of an old Dodge Charger on the bottom of a Winnebago County lake turns into a homicide investigation when human remains are found in the car. To make matters worse, Sheriff Twardy disappears that same day, leaving everyone to wonder where he went. Sergeant Corinne Aleckson and Detective Elton Dawes probe into both mysteries, searching for answers. Little do they know they're being closely watched by the keeper of the Secret in Whitetail Lake.

Firesetter In Blackwood Township Barns are burning in Blackwood Township, and the Winnebago County Sheriff's Office realizes they have a firesetter to flush out. The investigation ramps up when a body is found in one of the barns. Meanwhile, deputies are getting disturbing deliveries. Why are they being targeted? It leaves Sergeant Corinne Aleckson and Detective Elton Dawes to wonder, what is the firesetter's message and motive?

Remains In Coyote Bog Bodies marked with religious symbols are recovered from Coyote Bog and send Sergeant Corinne Aleckson and Detective Smoke Dawes on a quest. Who buried them in the bog? They pore through missing persons' files, consult an FBI profiler, and are soon in pursuit of an angel of death. Their investigation leads them into unchartered and dangerous territory, but they'll stop at nothing to end the death angel's reign.

Made in the USA
Monee, IL
15 August 2023

41054736R00184